PENGUIN BOOKS

FRAUD

Anita Brookner was born in London in 1928 and, apart from three postgraduate years in Paris, has lived there all her life. She trained as an art historian and taught at the Courtauld Institute of Art until 1988, when she abandoned her title of Reader in the History of Art at the University of London for the anonymity of a small flat in Chelsea and the cultivation of certain fictional characters who may one day appear in future novels.

Also published or forthcoming in Penguin are the novels *A Closed Eye*, *Lewis Percy*, *A Start in Life*, *Brief Lives*, *Providence*, *Look At Me*, *Family and Friends* and *Hotel du Lac*.

ANITA BROOKNER

FRAUD

PENGUIN BOOKS

PENGUIN BOOKS

Published by the Penguin Group
Penguin Books Ltd, 27 Wrights Lane, London W8 5TZ, England
Penguin Books USA Inc., 375 Hudson Street, New York, New York 10014, USA
Penguin Books Australia Ltd, Ringwood, Victoria, Australia
Penguin Books Canada Ltd, 10 Alcorn Avenue, Toronto, Ontario, Canada M4V 3B2
Penguin Books (NZ) Ltd, 182–190 Wairau Road, Auckland 10, New Zealand

Penguin Books Ltd, Registered Offices: Harmondsworth, Middlesex, England

First published by Jonathan Cape 1992
Published in Penguin Books 1993
1 3 5 7 9 10 8 6 4 2

Printed in England by Clays Ltd, St Ives plc

I

The facts, as far as they could be ascertained, were as follows. Miss Durrant, a woman in middle years, living alone in apparently comfortable circumstances, had been missing for some four months, although no one had seen her leave her flat in South Kensington, and her cleaner, who had a key, and who was used to finding the flat empty, thought little about the matter until the money, which was usually left on the kitchen table, was not replaced. The police, who were eventually contacted by Miss Durrant's doctor after she had missed several appointments, visited the flat with a spare key obtained from a neighbour on the same landing, but found nothing out of the ordinary. The flat was clean, quiet, very tidy. Nor could they judge whether any of the cupboards had been emptied, as if in the act of packing for a journey: there seemed to be an abundance of clothes still hanging, still folded away. This was the first sight of anything unusual, the lavishness of the materials – the fine tweed, the cashmere, the silk – and the brilliance of the colours, surely a little exorbitant for a woman of Miss Durrant's presumed age. The bedroom of the little flat contained a long looking-glass on a stand, and a faint odour of gardenias issued from the opened door of the built-in wardrobe. In the bathroom they found several bottles of expensive scent, some of them still sealed and in their original packages.

The second unusual circumstance was that the neighbour

from whom they had obtained the spare key was unable to tell them anything about Miss Durrant's presumed disappearance because he was recovering from a stroke, and tended to muddle his words and also to mispronounce or forget them. So strenuously did he attempt to answer their questions that they were bound to him in pity and discomfort for far longer than was necessary, for they had seen at a glance that he could tell them nothing, yet, being young and kindly, they could find no formula with which to compensate him for his efforts. 'That's all right, Sir,' said one of them eventually. 'I expect she'll turn up. Must have gone on holiday.' The man, Eric Harvey, a retired solicitor, shook his head, advanced a mottled hand, touched a sleeve. 'No. Would have heard. No door.' From which they deduced that if Miss Durrant had been going away on holiday, or for any other purpose, she would have rung his doorbell to let him know. In addition to which she would surely have offered to help him with shopping and possibly cooking, if she knew him well enough to entrust him with her spare key.

After this they went back to the doctor who had alerted them in the first place. 'Well, Sir, there's no body, no sign of a struggle or a break-in. What exactly were you worried about?' The doctor, Lawrence Halliday, was tall, with receding fair hair, attractive in a Tell England fashion, as if he were an officer returning on leave from the trenches in the First World War. He looked uncomfortable, passed a hand over his hair before replying.

'She's missed several appointments, something she would never dream of doing. She was a regular patient, a private patient. My secretary telephoned more than once and got no reply. I began to feel a little uneasy – that's why I contacted you.'

A notebook was produced. 'You say she was a regular patient. Was she ill, Sir?'

'Not really. She was mildly anorexic, perhaps getting slightly more so. Women of her age are always at risk, although she was asymptomatic. I thought it sensible to

6

keep a regular check on her, preventively, you understand. I believe in preventive medicine. She didn't complain of anything, but then she was a stoical kind of woman.'

'You say you felt uneasy, Sir. Why, exactly? She might have gone on holiday.'

'A rather long holiday, surely? Three and a half months? More? I last saw her just before the summer. It's now the beginning of October.'

'Has anybody seen her?'

'That's the thing,' said the doctor explosively. 'She didn't seem to have any friends. Her mother, whom I attended, died a year ago, and she moved shortly afterwards. I don't know anyone who knows her, with the possible exception of Mrs Marsh. Another patient,' he added. 'Though one whom I rarely see. Anyway, that's hardly my business. What is my business is that she seemed to have no other contacts.'

'Was she very dependent on you, Sir?'

He shrugged. 'She may have been.'

'In love, perhaps?'

'I wouldn't know.'

'And you, Sir. Were you attracted to her?'

'Good God, Inspector! She was a woman of fifty! Anyway, I'm happily married. She's met my wife. We asked her to dinner, earlier this year. Some months ago, now. Before she disappeared.'

The younger of the two policemen noticed that he still looked uneasy, and a little flushed, since mentioning his wife, but could not at the moment think why this should be so. Any irregularity would be so easy to check that there was hardly any point in concealing it. Besides, he put the doctor's age at about forty-six or -seven, and could not conceive why anyone would fall in love with a woman of fifty. He was twenty-nine and married to a girl five years younger than himself.

'We found these pills,' he said. 'In the bathroom.'

'Oh, a mild hypnotic. They wouldn't have done her any harm. Anyway, as you can see, the bottle's nearly full.'

'Could you describe her, Sir?'

'Well,' he sighed. 'She was thin, slight, about five foot three. An ordinary sort of face, quite a good colour. Poor skin, some slight trace of adolescent acne. Rather fine dark red hair, a lot of it. She wore it long, coiled up, somehow.' He described a vague circle round the back of his head.

'Normal, would you say?'

'Oh, well, normal. Nobody's normal.'

'Could you be more precise, Sir?'

'She was mildly eccentric, perhaps, but no more so than any other woman of her age, living alone. No family – I think I said that.'

'Whom did she know? Did she have friends?'

'My wife thought not. But she wasn't depressed, far from it. Good-tempered. She was a good woman.'

'Was?'

'I'm sorry. I believe she was friendly with one or two of our old people. Mrs Marsh – I think I mentioned her. I think she took her to church. Very kind like that.'

'And you can tell us nothing else? You see, we've nothing to go on.'

'Well, that's your affair. I've notified you. And now, if you'll excuse me, I really am very busy.'

'Thank you for your time, Sir.'

'You'll let me know . . . ?'

'I doubt if there'll be anything to tell you. Women disappear all the time, sometimes because they want to. She might have gone on a cruise, or something. If you could give us this Mrs Marsh's address?'

'Might as well walk,' said the elder of the two policemen, glancing at the paper in his hand. 'I could do with a breath of air.' He regretted, as ever, his Suffolk boyhood, for which this mean dirty London failed to compensate him. In Cheltenham Terrace, outside the surgery, the early October air was mild, damp. From the barracks came a faint sound of marching: as they walked towards the King's Road iron heels thudded to a halt somewhere out of sight. The light was fading, yet in the dusk they could make out a tree, still with its leaves, which a dry summer and a beneficent autumn had turned to gold, like a tree in Paradise. Leaves, those which remained, floated silently down on mysterious currents of air. There was no wind: it was almost warm. The solemnity of the early evening, and the touching sight of two elderly men, each with a stick, each with a dog, but deep in conversation, reduced them both to silence. They got on well together. Neither was given to excessive spirits.

They walked across the King's Road, down a side street, referring once again to the paper which the doctor's receptionist had given them, until they came to a looming block of flats.

'This is it,' said the sergeant.

They took the lift to the first floor, and rang the bell. The door opened on to the urgent music which heralded the news programme. Lights blazed from the hallway lantern, as advised by the local security officer. The elder of the two men showed his warrant card to Mrs Marsh, a tall grey-haired woman, whose look of violent annoyance seemed habitual. She examined the card closely, then scrutinized their faces. They noted that she was not in the least intimidated.

'Inspector Maigret! Well, well. What can I do for you?'

'Butterworth, Madam. This is my colleague, Barry Talbot. A few questions, if you don't mind. We shan't keep you long.'

'It's not my daughter, is it? Or my son? Nothing's happened to Nick, has it?'

'Nothing like that, Madam. May we come in?'

In contrast to the brilliant hall the sitting-room was dim, lit only by wall lights and a lamp near the armchair in which Mrs Marsh had been sitting, preparing to listen to the news. A copy of *The Times* was draped over the arm of her chair. A half-empty teacup and a spectacle case were on the table beside her.

'Now what is all this? I was just settling in for the evening. I don't like to be disturbed when it's dark, and as

9

far as I can see there's no reason why I should be. One or two of these flats have been burgled: one hears such stories. Are you sure you're policemen?' She looked at them through narrowed eyes, her lips slightly drawn back from her teeth.

'Quite sure, Madam. We wondered if you might know the whereabouts of a Miss Durrant. A friend of yours, I believe.'

'Who told you that?'

'Dr Halliday. He reported the fact that she hadn't been seen recently and had missed several appointments.'

'Halliday is too soft. Oh, quite a good doctor, I suppose, but under the thumb of that wife of his. Attractive to women, which I dare say hasn't made his life any easier.'

'Miss Durrant, Madam.'

'Anna. You'd better sit down.'

She sat down herself, slowly. When she hoisted her feet on to a small stool which someone had recently covered with *gros point*, they could see that she was old, about eighty or thereabouts, perhaps more. Yet she was strong, a vigorous woman, only slightly impeded by age.

'What's this about Anna?'

'She seems to have disappeared. We wondered how recently you'd seen her.'

Mrs Marsh rubbed the cheeks over which age had laid a network of minute red veins.

'I haven't seen her recently. I assumed she'd gone on holiday. I thought she'd telephone when she came back.'

'Were you surprised not to hear from her?'

'Not really. To tell you the truth I thought she was offended with me. I may have been a bit sharp with her. I tend to lose my temper so easily these days.' She smiled wistfully. 'Don't get old, Inspector.'

'She was a friend of yours, Madam?'

'No. I used to visit her mother, when she was alive. She was frail, housebound. I doubt there was anything really wrong with her. But she died, so there must have been, mustn't there? Ten years younger than me.'

'And her daughter? She lived with her?'

'Indeed she did. She was devoted, too devoted, sacrificed her life. And yet she seemed to want to. There was something odd about that household, the mother so frail, so delicate, and the daughter so cheerful. Marvellous, really. And yet she was too good, too filial. Like a daughter in a Victorian novel. Little Dorrit. Tried to be daughterly towards me, called me Aunt Vera. I tried to put a stop to that, but she didn't take any notice.'

She took a last draught from her almost empty cup of cold tea. Her hands shook very slightly, as if with anger at Miss Durrant's remembered quaintness.

'I inherited Anna from her mother. I dare say she was terrified of being alone, although she gave no sign of it. She called here once or twice, on a Sunday, sometimes on the pretext of taking me to church, as if she thought I was too feeble to get there on my own. I hadn't the heart to put her off, although she rather got on my nerves, to tell you the truth. She came here once when I was ill,' she added remotely. 'Kind-hearted, you see. Twice,' she amended.

'Did she go to church with you? In which case we might ask the vicar . . . '

'No, she never would. "That's not what I'm looking for," she would say, with that everlasting smile of hers. "I'll have my walk round the park, and look in on Miss Carter, and then I'll collect you and walk you home." So naturally I had to ask her to lunch. Not too often – perhaps it was only once or twice. Once,' she added scrupulously. 'I was exasperated with her: she obviously thought me senile. I'm quite capable of getting to the Oratory on my own. I was a magistrate for twenty years. To tell you the truth I was quite relieved not to see her for a bit. She had an unsettling effect on one. I thought she'd taken my advice and gone on holiday. Poor Anna.' She brooded for a moment. 'But she can't be missing! That's ridiculous. She was very level-headed. She must be away. She had a friend in Paris, I believe. That's where she is, I dare say.'

'When did you last see her?'

'Well, I was away for most of the summer. Before that I told her I shouldn't see her until the autumn. This is the autumn, I suppose. It would be three months or more.'

'You didn't think to telephone?'

'Of course I did. There was no reply. I assumed she'd gone away. I wasn't *worried*. I knew I'd see her again. I was relieved, if anything, thinking she was enjoying herself somewhere. Oh, Anna.'

She got up and poured herself a small whisky. She held up the bottle enquiringly. 'You won't?' They shook their heads.

'I doubt if there was any reason why I should see her, or she me. We got on each other's nerves, although neither of us could bring ourselves to say so. She was far too good, of course, ever to think uncharitably of anyone. But she annoyed me, poor woman. She was too kind, made too much of an effort, fussed round me as she used to fuss round her mother. I wouldn't have it, and I told her so. I didn't want her for a daughter, poor Anna. I've got a perfectly good daughter of my own. And yet she was so well-meaning, so kind, but tactless, you know. Helping me up from my chair, taking my arm. I may be eighty-one but I'm not defunct.'

And indeed Mrs Marsh was built on an heroic scale, and dressed as if for some healthy outdoor pursuit, in a flannel blouse and a tweed skirt, her long feet encased in brown lace-up shoes.

'If you're sure you won't drink,' she said repressively, gesturing briefly with the whisky bottle. She poured herself another glass.

'A good woman. Unselfish. Probably missed her mother. But no *backbone*. I asked her to lunch when my daughter was here from Norwich, and the contrast! Anna was younger, of course.'

'What age would that be, Madam?'

'Forty-five? Fifty? Nearer fifty. Philippa is fifty-five.

But Philippa lives in the real world. She has to: she's a widow, with grown-up children, *and* a mature student.' Thus she referred to her daughter's weekly classes in art appreciation. ' "Why don't you do something like that?" I asked Anna. She gave me that smile of hers. "It's not what I'm looking for," she said. I even introduced her to my son,' she added angrily. 'Well, I was sorry for her. And my son's a very attractive man. Divorced, no children. I wouldn't have minded if he'd taken her out. But she was hopeless around a man.'

'How was that?'

'She seemed alarmed, dashed about washing up cups and glasses. I told her to sit still, but she merely gave me that smile of hers and told me to rest. My son hardly noticed her, I'm glad to say. Although she was always beautifully turned out. Made all her own clothes, beautiful little tweed suits and so on. And that remarkable hair. Quite a presentable woman, although one thinks of her as a girl.' She sighed. 'She was too good a daughter, I suppose.'

They stood up. 'Thank you for your help, Madam. You wouldn't happen to have the name of her friend in Paris?'

'No, I haven't. Marie something. Marie-France, I believe. My daughter might know. Anna spoke of her that day when they were both here. She spoke about her *most* affectionately, although I don't think she saw her all that often. She wrote, I know. That's what she sometimes did on a Sunday afternoon. Marie-France, I'm sure that was her name. That's where she'll be. With Marie-France.'

She saw them to the door. 'I'd be grateful if you'd let me know about her. There's not much point in my going round to Cranley Gardens if she's not there. I don't know whom else to ask.'

The elder of the two policemen, Butterworth, noticed that she had said 'whom' and decided that she was a reliable witness. Which was useful, for there were apparently no others.

Outside, on the pavement – and no trees visible now

in the mist and dark of the evening – Butterworth said, 'That appears to be that. No close friends. No relations. You might go back to that neighbour of hers tomorrow, try him again. Try to get the name of the cleaning woman. They usually know something.'

'Sounds a funny type. Old fashioned. Looking after the mother, and so on. Unmarried. Typical spinster, I suppose.'

'Except that there aren't any spinsters any more, Barry. They're all up there at the cutting edge. I blame Joan Collins.'

'Any chance of finding her, do you think? What if she doesn't turn up?'

Butterworth shrugged. 'Oh, she'll turn up all right. Somewhere or other. Trouble is, we won't know where to look.'

2

Mrs Marsh, perturbed in spite of the irrational anger which Anna Durrant always aroused in her, resolved to telephone her daughter in Norwich, although it was not Friday, the day on which she usually called. It was Wednesday, the dead centre of the week, and she was suddenly chilled and lonely. She saw no reason to upset herself on Anna's account, and yet Anna, she had to acknowledge, was an upsetting person. All that forbearance! Such saintliness would have been admirable had it not been administered with that smile, a smile that signalled merriment yet was underlined by something desperate. And who would not be desperate, thought Mrs Marsh, living through her youth and middle age with poor Amy Durrant in that terrible flat in Albert Hall Mansions. Mrs Marsh sighed. Poor silly Amy, who had felt faint at the hairdresser's one day and had been driven home in Mrs Marsh's car. She had been alarmed at the woman's pallor and her apparent frailty, and was relieved to see her regain her colour as soon as she sank into what was evidently her habitual chair, one of two placed on either side of the fire in that muted faded rose-coloured room. It was the room of an intensely feminine woman, with no sign of a masculine presence. A sofa under a window with leaded panes which made the room seem dark, a piano with some sheet music on the stand, the two armchairs covered with brown and pink chintz, and on either side of the door jardinières filled with evil-looking green plants, darkened from their original freshness by too little air and too much water. The only item of note in the room was a fine imitation Savonnerie carpet in blue and pink, the effect of which was marred by the addition of a white sheepskin rug before the hearth. The gas fire, ineptly disguised as a real fire, was accompanied by a set of superfluous fire tongs in the bleak blackish grate.

The air felt heavy, sweetish, as if the rooms were permanently inhabited by genteel women, and the windows never opened. And Mrs Durrant herself gave the same impression, of exhausted but cherished womanhood. Instinctively Mrs Marsh, who had had a vigorous marriage, looked around for signs, even relics, of a man, but found none. Her eye met only a rack containing fashion magazines, and library books, which, from their covers, looked as if they had been written by women. Yet Mrs Durrant was still attractive and must once have been a beauty. She had an intimate way of talking, was fulsome in her gratitude, was, in fact, pleasing, even intriguing. She had a soft voice, beautifully tended hands, with rosy polished nails. One of those hands had been laid upon Mrs Marsh's much larger rougher one, with its plain gold band. 'Don't go,' said Mrs Durrant. 'My daughter will make us some tea.' She padded over the pink and blue carpet to the door. 'Anna! Anna darling! Will you make us some tea, dear? I want you to meet Mrs Marsh.' The sound of a sewing machine, so faint that it hardly registered as such, stopped abruptly. Ten minutes later Anna Durrant had come in with tea things on a black japanned tray. Mrs Marsh noted her kingfisher-blue suit, in fine tweed, which she admired. 'Anna makes all her own clothes,' said Mrs Durrant proudly. Then the two women fell greedily into exchanging the stories of their lives, for such an encounter was not to be wasted. In fact Mrs Marsh was adept at dealing out the few facts she was willing to make public – the dead husband, one daughter, one son – knowing that this was the appropriate currency for a person of her age and type, but actually too curious about this affecting woman with her old-fashioned flowery elegance and her general air of bewilderment to waste time on herself.

Poor silly Amy Durrant! Visited many times, though not regularly, when Amy became too frail to leave the flat. A heart complaint, she gathered, one that made her gasp from time to time and lay a hand to the base of her throat, as if her heart had risen up and were choking her. But always glad to see a friend, particularly one as rough-hewn and sensible as Mrs Marsh, who in her turn was fascinated, almost against her better judgement, by the flower-like Amy Durrant, with her pleading periwinkle-blue eyes. Her story was charmingly and easily told, not without a certain narrative talent: in any event it beguiled Mrs Marsh. She had married beneath her, Amy laughed, or so her parents had told her. She had fallen in love with someone unsuitable and had simply gone ahead and married him. He was a violinist in the pit at Drury Lane, and they had met at a wedding. Mrs Marsh, who privately thought her hostess rather common, thought this a most sensible arrangement, and saw no trace of a *mésalliance*, although she had been invited to think along these lines. What money there was – and there appeared to be no shortage – had come from Mrs Durrant's parents, who had provided the flat in Albert Hall Mansions, together with the piano, the carpet, the brass jardinières, and a small but comfortable portfolio of stocks and shares. 'Anna will be well provided for, when I go,' said Mrs Durrant. 'But, my dear, I never thought I'd be left on my own like this! My husband worshipped me! I thought he'd always be there to look after me. And yet he died when Anna was only five – a heart attack. He'd just got home from the theatre one night. He collapsed without a murmur. But then he never complained.' Her eyes moistened; a small white handkerchief was produced from her sleeve. 'I did love him,' she said, this time without affectation. 'He was my first love. Dear David. We were so happy.'

And since then, Mrs Marsh had wondered, would you not have liked to be happy again? Widowhood had made her sturdy, self-reliant, but she could see that this woman was a romantic, not the sort of woman to be left on her own while still attractive and relatively young. 'You have Anna,' she said, almost briskly, as if to break the spell, as if to vanquish her own suspicion that this story was a little too pathetic. 'Indeed I have,' Amy Durrant had said. 'Anna is my life.' And there was the same authentic note in her voice as when she had said how much she loved her husband. 'What will you do when she marries?' Mrs Marsh queried, although she felt the question was rather mean. 'Oh, she won't leave me yet awhile,' was the answer. 'Of course, I long for it for her. I'm not a possessive mother. I urge her to go out, meet people, enjoy herself. "It's not what I'm looking for," she says.'

'What is she looking for?' asked Mrs Marsh bluntly.

'Her destiny, she says. Her fate.' Mrs Durrant suddenly looked tired, old. 'I don't always understand her. But she is so happy, so cheerful. And if the worst comes to the worst, well, she'll have all this. She'll be comfortable. And of course it's wonderful for me to have her with me all the time.'

'I wonder she doesn't want a career,' said Mrs Marsh, struck by the idleness of these two women, the anachronism of their existence in the felt-lined quiet and obscurity of Albert Hall Mansions. Apart from herself she knew almost no one with independent means; at the same time she was struck by Amy Durrant's lack of curiosity, which she supposed she had handed on to her daughter.

'I wanted her to go into the fashion business,' said Mrs Durrant, who clearly thought in terms of the dress shops of the 1950s, if not of the 1930s. 'But she said no. She went to university, and then she had a year abroad and she's been working on her research on and off ever since. It's convenient, really. We're so near the V. and A., and she can work in the library there.'

'What is she working on?'

'Something to do with the Paris salons of the nineteenth century.'

'Fascinating,' said Mrs Marsh, who had read her Proust.

'Yes, isn't it? You must get her to tell you all about it.'

But Anna, who appeared regularly with the tea-tray at 4.30, sometimes in her kingfisher-blue suit, sometimes in one of the same pattern in dark ruby red, simply laughed away the suggestion that she was any kind of intellectual and went on laughing as she handed Mrs Marsh her cup. Mrs Marsh, watching her keenly, could not decide whether she was very stupid or rather clever. She had patience, that was clear, and fortitude: she would need both if she was to waste her life in her mother's company, however good the mother (and there was nothing to indicate that she was anything else), and, yes, she had something more, she had a plain girl's faith in a happy ending, and Mrs Marsh saw that this was both her salvation and her undoing.

No man in either of their lives, she had thought impatiently, for she had had two proposals herself since being widowed. But what man would venture in here, into this faded and claustrophobic bower? Gone were the days when men preferred women to be compliant and passive, born to flatter and to praise. At least they might still want these rewards, but they were being trained not to expect them. And these two women – Mrs Durrant and her unfortunate daughter – were too hopelessly old-fashioned to compete in the market-place with other more hard-headed and enlightened members of their sex. They were handicapped, and although this might not matter for Amy Durrant it mattered terribly for the daughter, who had, past infancy, never known a father, and was thus eternally unprepared for the rules of engagement between the sexes in the least predictable and sentimental of games.

'I suppose you have to go abroad sometimes, for your research,' she said.

'I manage to do most of it here,' said Anna calmly, as if rebuking her for an untoward curiosity. She usually left them after tea, but reappeared when Mrs Marsh made her way to the front door. She kissed her goodbye, as if to obliterate the

19

impression given by what she wrongly perceived as her own taciturnity. This was not a good tactic, for Mrs Marsh prized taciturnity as a virtue and thought too few women possessed it. The girl's soft lips, and flat, almost unseeing eyes struck her as unnatural. At the same time she forced herself not to be brusque. There was something eerily emollient about this household. Outside, in the air, she was amazed to see normal rush-hour traffic, for inside the flat she had had no impression of real time, or of real time passing. She was aware of a faint antagonism towards Anna, for which she had the grace to feel ashamed.

On one visit she was surprised to see the tea-tray already in place, although it was only half-past three, and a casual-looking arrangement of biscuits on a plate instead of the elegant knives and forks and napkins which she had come to expect. 'Anna is not here,' explained her hostess. 'She has gone to visit her friend in Paris. I urged her to go, although to tell you the truth I hate being left alone now. But it's good for her to get away. I can't do much for her here – my silly heart. But she never complains. She's such a good girl.' Mrs Marsh, who was greedy, and who always enjoyed Anna's scones and teacakes, felt disappointed. Apart from her own pity for Amy Durrant, so obviously full of fear at being left alone, so tiresomely brave at trying to conceal it, she saw little advantage in Anna's going to Paris at this stage, for she was not of a nature to enjoy the city – too girlish, too spinsterish, too trusting – and in any event judged it too late for Anna to have made a bid for freedom, if that was indeed what she was doing. Like all of Anna's actions it was some-how mismanaged, mistimed, for Mrs Marsh could see that Amy Durrant's colour was bad and her breath occasionally caught in her throat, like those shuddering gasps with which one sometimes awakens from a dream. How tiresome of the girl – woman – to go and visit a friend at this stage, when her mother was so obviously in decline! 'She goes once a year,' explained Mrs Durrant. 'She didn't want to leave me, but I made her go. To tell you the truth I wanted to see you on my own.' Mrs Marsh felt unwanted responsibilities being marshalled in her direction. 'I wanted you to have this,' she murmured, with obvious pain in her voice. She handed over a tooled red leather box, of the kind sold in Florence, to hold jewellery or sewing silk. 'You have been so kind. And I feel I have imposed on you.'

'But, my dear . . . ' said Mrs Marsh.

'And I want you to take this,' said Amy Durrant, now in some distress, holding out a manila envelope stiff with paper. 'If anything happens to me – and it will shortly – I want you to keep this for Anna. It's a kind of letter I have written her.'

'But why don't you give it to her yourself?' protested Mrs Marsh, who had sensed obscurely that Amy Durrant had brought this odd friendship to the stage at which she wished to leave it.

Mrs Durrant smiled sadly. 'The minute I go she will throw everything away. I know her, you see. She loves me, but I've taken away her life. She will want to put me behind her, as I should have let her do years ago. But I clung to her, I admit. She was so strong, so good, just when . . . ' She paused. 'I have ruined her life,' she said. 'I want her to know how much I have loved her. Although she may not want to know that. She may even hate me for it.'

'Surely not,' Mrs Marsh had said, alarmed at this nakedness of feeling. She had always observed an amicable distance from her own daughter, whom she felt had inherited all her own stalwartness. She had never felt this visceral tenderness for Philippa once the girl was past babyhood. Her son . . . Her son was a different matter. She thought with shame of the relief she had felt when he had announced that he was seeking a divorce, as if at last she would have him to herself again. It had not been so, but she saw him more frequently these days, sometimes for lunch on a Sunday. She dressed up for him on these occasions, rubbed a little powder into her worn red cheeks, pressed both lips together over a thread of lipstick. He never noticed, of course, although he ate up his meal, over which she had taken so much trouble. For Philippa she bothered less, served up a small roast, omitted the powder and lipstick. But even with Nick she observed a certain reticence, would never have dreamed of leaving him posthumous messages, particularly of a sentimental nature.

'My dear,' she said, as gently as she could. 'Do you think it is wise? Anna is a grown woman, after all.'

Indeed she was, reflected Mrs Marsh. Anna must be fifty or more, old enough to know that she would never have children, old enough to reflect bitterly that nature had no further use for her. But in fact she had no reason to doubt Anna's good faith. All she had to go on was Anna's eye sliding past her vacantly as she bestowed her apparently affectionate valedictory kiss. For all she knew, Mrs Marsh reflected uneasily, Anna was as good as she seemed to be, a devoted daughter, in the manner of those daughters of a bygone age who sacrificed their lives unthinkingly, the way their brothers had done in the trenches. It was only because such sacrifice was now irrelevant, even faintly repellent, that one looked askance at it, knowing oneself to be unworthy by comparison. Mrs Marsh felt a sudden sharp unhappiness as she sought inspiration from the darkening sky beyond the diamond panes of the window and found none. It had been a November day, mild but overcast, never really getting light. Yellow leaves had floated down on the windless air. Two more weeks – less, perhaps – and the trees will be bare, she thought. She took the envelope and stowed it away in her bag. She had not meant to keep in close touch with Anna after what she now perceived as Amy Durrant's inevitable death. She sensed a coolness there. But in fact the handing over of the letter – that last missive – might be a way of putting an end to a relationship which she had not chosen. A telephone call or two throughout the period of mourning, and then a good wish at Christmas. For her part she would be quite glad to put the oddly disquieting couple out of her mind.

She had called once more in Amy Durrant's lifetime.

Anna had opened the door, dressed this time in forest green, the same suit fashioned endlessly from the same pattern.

'She'll be so glad to see you,' she said affectionately, and with no apparent loss of cheerfulness. Mrs Marsh grieved for her then, and for the hope that kept her in such good spirits. The flat had seemed to her darker and more muted than she remembered it, and she had a sudden pang of longing for her own faded blue sitting-room and for the chair in which Nick sometimes sat. She followed Anna into the bedroom, where Mrs Durrant, in a pink brushed nylon nightdress, was sitting up in bed.

'How lovely to see you!' she said, in her normal voice, but Mrs Marsh saw the effort behind it. 'Anna, darling, will you make tea?'

Mrs Marsh lowered her grey head to the head which remained obstinately blonde – or did Anna see to that?

'How are you?'

'Better,' said Mrs Durrant. 'Don't worry about us. We shall manage.' Mrs Marsh had felt dismissed, as if what was to come was too important to be shared with outsiders, as if the love of the two women could only feed now on itself. She had felt oddly excluded; she had also felt something like respect. When she got up to leave Amy Durrant had pressed her hand. 'You've been so good,' she said, which added to the impression of finality. 'You won't forget?' 'No, no,' Mrs Marsh had replied. But in fact she had forgotten, a fact which she attributed to old age and to the wholly irrational grief she had felt when Anna telephoned the following week to say that her mother had died in her sleep. Reaching into her bag for her handkerchief Mrs Marsh encountered the manila envelope. It was with something like anger that she thrust it into the drawer of the tallboy that stood against the far wall of her sitting-room. From her chair she could see this tallboy; it was in her direct line of vision. Therefore there was no danger of her overlooking the manila envelope.

At some point, she remembered, all this story of Anna

had become obscured. She had forgotten about Anna, or would have liked to. She would have liked to have put her entirely out of her mind. She had found her burdensome, and saw no reason why she should admit her to her life, which was, she reckoned, circumscribed, if only by her own wish. But then Anna had been kind, more than kind, useful, offering help on more than one occasion. Even so, even in moments of weakness, she had not really taken to her. The selfishness of age had met some resistance in Anna, which had left a discomfort in her memory. Quite simply she had not wished to see her again, and had been reluctant to contact her. She was aware that she had been remiss, had deliberately kept her memory short, had been ungracious. She had never been a convivial woman, even when she was much younger, and eventually had realized with something like relief that it was too late for her to change. But there had been dereliction, if only of duty. At the same time she recognized that it was not a duty she could ever, with any degree of sympathy, have discharged.

3

After Amy Durrant's death Mrs Marsh had relegated the matter to some forgotten corner. This she found easy to do. There were patches of loss in her memory, which she accepted uncomplainingly as part of the process of growing old. Although the past was startlingly vivid, recent events tended to get mislaid, or worse, misplaced. She had forgotten about Anna Durrant until she received a telephone call from her. There was a strenuous gaiety in Anna's voice. Apparently she was in the best of spirits.

'Aunt Vera! How are you?'

Mrs Marsh had no nieces. After an infinitesimal pause she said, 'I do wish you'd call me Vera, Anna.'

'Oh, I couldn't do that,' said Anna readily, as if prepared for a rebuff. Still maddening, thought Mrs Marsh, but said, 'How are *you*, my dear?'

'Oh, I'm perfectly fine. I was wondering if there was anything I could do for you. You were so kind to Mother, to both of us, really. I feel I should have been in touch much sooner. Could I come round and see you?'

'I am rather busy in the evenings,' said Mrs Marsh, aware of her churlishness, even as she spoke. She was not a sentimental woman and not even very interested in the young; above all she had neither the capacity nor the desire to penetrate what she divined as Anna's carapace of artifice. She was aware of a complicated existence behind the sunny face which Anna so determinedly prepared to meet the world, aware of enormous frustration, possibly of anger, certainly of resentment. She did not want the task of dismantling this structure which, after all, must have been built up consciously and with some care. Mrs Marsh had no patience with the attempts, often made by complete strangers, to understand those who, although possibly impaired, even faulty, were making valiant and even successful efforts to run their own lives. She was equally hard on herself, which, she felt obscurely, justified her in her occasional harshness towards others. 'Get on with it, Vera Marsh,' she would say, as she hoisted her stiffening limbs out of bed in the morning, looking forward at that early hour to the prospect of the next night's sleep. She lived alone, bleakly, but with a certain grim pride, cooked proper meals, at least at the weekends, went to the Oratory most Sundays, although she was not a Catholic, and was on the whole glad that there was no one at home to witness her inevitable decline. The prospect of having this painful and ultimately serious process interrupted by the visits of such a one as Anna Durrant was not to her liking. One of the weaknesses she permitted herself was the luxury of bad temper, and even of a certain generalized intolerance. The ardour of Anna, the near saintliness of Anna, which she sensed were based on a false premise, made her scowl. Above all she felt an old woman's repugnance for Anna's wasted girlhood, despised her obvious virginity, thinking it now mere folly, although she herself had been a virgin when she married (and had much regretted the fact in the course of her honeymoon), saw Anna's good humour as misplaced, rooted only in inexperience. At this stage of her life Mrs Marsh favoured only completeness, satisfaction, fulfilment, had trained herself to see these in another's smile, in another's calm, and tended to turn away if she did not find them. If she was lonely, if life was a burden to her, she said nothing, never complained, although the effort of not doing so gave her a grim expression, and to some she was

26

a forbidding old woman. She was aware that she had been chosen to be the recipient of Anna's beneficence, whatever form this might take. She was aware that Anna's beneficence would be unwearying. But above all she was aware of Anna's fear, of her desire to place herself under another's protection. She was even aware that this fear of Anna's might not be entirely rational, that it might in fact border on panic. She wished to have no part in Anna's deliverance, in the enormous rescue operation that must take place before Anna could be transformed into a sane, realistic, and no doubt drastically saddened human being.

'What about the weekend?' the voice went on.

'Well, I usually rest on Saturday afternoon, and then on Sunday I go to church.' She deliberately did not say whether she went in the morning or the evening, nor did she go into the complicated details of why she went to the Oratory when she was not a Catholic. She went because of the intensity of the ritual, which she hoped would fan the weak flames of her faltering belief (which she would need, she reasoned, at the end), and because the Oratory was a conveniently short distance from her flat.

'*I* know,' said the voice in her ear. 'I'll call on Sunday morning and walk you to church, shall I? I've got so much to tell you. I've moved, you know. I sold the flat a month after Mother died. I've got a dear little place in Cranley Gardens. You've probably not been able to get in touch with me. That's why I worried; I thought you might be needing a little help. I'd hate to think you couldn't call on me if you wanted anything.'

Mrs Marsh ignored the offers of help, which she thought were spurious, but felt surprise that Anna had been decisive enough to move, and so soon after her mother's death. This indicated a sense of purpose of which she had previously given no sign. She had thought of Anna growing peacefully old, amid the brown and pink roses of Albert Hall Mansions, and had even hoped it might be so, thinking an untroubled decline appropriate to one of Anna's age, temperament, and notional usefulness. Yet here was a manifestation of energy, of ruthlessness. What had Anna done with the furniture, with all those genteel appointments? Why had she disposed of her mother so efficiently, and with such apparent lack of senti-ment? Mrs Marsh was intrigued in spite of herself. Anna, she reflected, was not without power, even if that power were confined to the mystery which she both contained and partly concealed. The power was there, although latent: it had failed to come to the surface of her life, and was therefore not a subject for discussion.

'You had better come to lunch on Sunday,' she heard herself say. 'My daughter will be here.'

'Oh, but I'll call for you first, shall I?'

'As you wish, my dear,' sighed Mrs Marsh, and prepared to have her Sunday morning, and her grim attempt to retain contact with an Almighty in whom she no longer believed, disrupted. The casserole would have to go in on a lower gas than usual, she reflected, if they were to get anything to eat. Anna could talk to Philippa while she was in the kitchen preparing the vegetables. The prospect was annoying. But then she remembered the envelope and resigned herself to doing her duty, as she had done so many times in the course of her long life.

Her first thought, when she opened the door to Anna, was that the girl was beginning to resemble her mother, for a certain degree of embellishment had taken place, and Anna now wore the rosy make-up which had so enhanced Amy Durrant's faded pretty face. The result was pleasing, even surprising, as was the waft of gardenia scent as Anna leaned forward to kiss Mrs Marsh on both cheeks. Her sempiternal suit was of rust-coloured wool, which matched her abundant and cunningly contrived hair, beneath which her open childish-looking face beamed with joy. She would never be a pretty woman, thought Mrs Marsh, interested in spite of herself: her face was too broad, her eyes too flat, her mouth too wide for anything like beauty. The general effect was almost Dutch, Christmassy, maniacally merry: honest good cheer was conveyed, and a certain innocence, as if sex and all that pertained to it were confined to a distant civilization, a civilization in which marriage and giving in marriage were prevalent, such customs being unknown in the territory in which Anna had grown up. She is like a nun, thought Mrs Marsh, or a saint; she is determined to do me good. Of Anna's suspected rage there was no trace. Maybe it had been transmuted into this sudden taste for personal adornment, for she looked extremely smart, wore narrow shoes, flat gold ear-rings, and had an expensive suede bag hanging from her shoulder. The general effect, thought Mrs Marsh, is striking. If one were to see her a long way off one would think her an attractive woman. But as soon as one saw the face one would know that this attractive woman was merely a girl, plucky and good and desperate, and if one were a man one would move on. How unfortunate it all is, this business of sex, thought Mrs Marsh, adjusting her navy felt trilby in the hall mirror; if Anna met a man similarly deprived she could probably make him quite comfortable. But that is most unlikely to happen. Few men think of themselves as impotent or unattractive, yet so many of them are.

'Well, Anna, you're looking very smart, my dear.'

'And so are you, Aunt . . . I'm sorry. You look *lovely*.'

Mrs Marsh sighed and let her arm be taken.

'You're quite comfortable walking? You're sure it's not too far?'

'I usually walk,' said Mrs Marsh, as mildly as possible. 'We get so few quiet days. The traffic is not so bad on a Sunday, even in the Brompton Road. You will stay to lunch, won't you? It will be more interesting for you to talk to Philippa, much more so than talking to me.'

'But I love talking to you . . .'

'I'm an old woman, my dear, and I'm very selfish. I like my privacy, my silence. You will too when you get to my age.'

They crossed the road to the Oratory.

'Won't you come in?' asked Mrs Marsh with a smile that was almost kindly.

'Oh, no.' The answer was flatly given. 'I believe, in my own way. At least I did once. I tried to go on with it, but it wasn't easy. I'll walk round the park and collect you later, shall I?'

Since what Anna had said was almost interesting and might prove food for conversation on the way home Mrs Marsh acquiesced. I must do this with a good grace, she thought. It is practically an act of charity, might even be thought of as a spiritual exercise. I must give her a good lunch, hand over Amy's envelope, let her stay for the afternoon, if she shows signs of wanting to, and send her off cheerfully, having somehow conveyed that this is not to be a regular occurrence. Make sure that she is taking care of herself – she is very thin, surely thinner than she was. But the shock of her mother's death, and then the exertion of moving (that telephone number to be written down) probably account for that. Nevertheless she is too thin for a woman of her age: one tends to get heavier in the middle years, which are of course problematic in other ways. Her hips are scarcely wider than her waist, she thought, watching Anna's retreating back. Again there was a suggestion of uncharacteristic vigour in the way her heels clipped the pavement.

A profound smell of cooked meat pervaded the flat as they reached it after the service. Unpleasant, thought Mrs Marsh, removing her hat. Had she been on her own she would have had cheese on toast.

'I usually have a glass of sherry before lunch,' she said. 'Will you join me? Philippa should be here shortly, then I can leave you two together while I do the sprouts.'

'Shall I help?'

'No, no, my dear; let's sit and drink our sherry, shall we?'

Anna drank quickly, leaving a smudge of pink on the rim of her glass.

'Another?' enquired Mrs Marsh. At the back of her mind she could hear her father saying, 'Another? Sounds as if you're counting.'

'Good heavens, no, Aunt Vera. One is quite enough.'

She gazed about her expectantly. 'It's so pretty here,' she said.

Fortunately there is Philippa, thought Mrs Marsh, as the doorbell rang. It seems as if I am to be Aunt Vera after all. She went to open the door, although she had given both her daughter and her son a key. Philippa must have forgotten again. Mrs Marsh was forced to reflect that her daughter would not be much good in an emergency. Anna, on the other hand, would be assiduous. She must remember to take her telephone number.

Philippa Barnard was a big woman, as big as her mother, with the same reddened cheeks and wiry hair, which on her produced a not unpleasing effect. She offered a large hand and a welcoming smile, accepted a glass of sherry, and lit up the first of many cigarettes. Mrs Marsh left for the kitchen. 'What a pretty suit,' she heard Philippa say before she closed the door. She smiled. Philippa might look hearty, she might be unreliable, but she was matchless at putting the nervous at their ease. 'Don't mind me,' she would say. 'I've had a difficult morning (or afternoon). Do you mind if I tell you about it?' She had been a good daughter, Mrs Marsh reflected, brave and kind. No second marriage in the offing, unfortunately. But Philippa did not seem unhappy, certainly not discontented. Maybe she had even found a man, thought Mrs Marsh, in which case he was almost certainly married. She did not much mind. If he made Philippa happy she was grateful to him. So few things mattered as they once had. Immorality, she reflected, seemed less important. You got too old for sex, and that was that. Being young enough was a different matter. Live all you can, she thought. Dear Henry James.

Another of Philippa's virtues was her enormous appetite, which had overlooked her mother's indifferent cooking throughout the various stages of her life and was even now equal to the task of absorbing two-thirds of Mrs Marsh's casserole. Anna ate nothing, daintily manoeuvring morsels round her plate while laughing enthusiastically at most of

31

Philippa's remarks. She is such an obvious guest, thought Mrs Marsh; she is quite out of practice. Does anyone ask her out? 'There's only cheese and fruit,' she observed. 'But the cheese is rather good. And the pears are wonderful this year.'

'Nothing more for me,' smiled Anna.

'But you've eaten nothing,' exclaimed Philippa. 'Are you feeling all right?'

'Yes, Anna. You are most frightfully thin, you know.'

'I suppose it's the novelty of being here,' said Anna.

'Novelty?' Mrs Marsh's voice held a note of distaste. 'I don't see that this is very novel.'

'I'm sorry,' said Anna, her own voice dropping to normal. 'It's been quite a tiring year so far. I dare say I'm not as calm as I should be.'

'Perhaps you should have a check-up,' said Mrs Marsh. 'Yes, I think you should certainly do that. I wonder Halliday hasn't suggested it.'

'She probably needs a holiday,' observed Philippa, blowing smoke. 'Have you got friends you could stay with?'

'Oh, yes,' said Anna, brightening again. 'I have a very dear friend in Paris. Marie-France Forestier. I've known her for years. In fact she was an *assistante* at my school. She gave up her work when her mother died. She's been looking after her father since then. He's a writer, Bertrand Forestier. You might have heard of him.'

They shook their heads.

'He writes popular history books, lives of Napoleon's sisters, that sort of thing.'

'And what does she do, your friend?'

'She looks after him, and the flat, and so on. And they have a little house in the country, near Meaux.'

Another one who will be well provided for, thought Mrs Marsh. Another martyr. What profound emotional disposition made these women give up so early, yield to a sickly selfish parent, or perhaps, to be fair, to a protective and unthinking one, and spend the rest of their lives living so modestly, so incuriously? Did they perceive the world as threatening, or cruel, or simply so obscure that they could not hope to decipher it? Had they been infantilized at some point in their adolescence, when, with a different throw of the dice, they might have matured into some semblance of normality? Of course, I cannot speak for this Marie-France, she thought: she may be a perfectly capable middle-aged Frenchwoman, with that air of authority the French seem to have, as though they have been better fed, better nourished all their lives, and have grown stronger, harder on this adult diet. Whereas Anna, who could not tackle my admittedly not very appetizing casserole, seems to have grown up on pale sweet foods, as if her life were a more or less eternal teatime, and all her hopes vested in nothing more exciting than a festive tea party.

'You could go to Paris,' said Philippa. 'What fun. How I envy you.'

'Well, I could, of course,' said Anna. 'I usually go every year anyway. But there's the flat to get straight. I've only just moved in. There's quite a lot to do.'

She was pleading with them to let her be. In her extreme state she feared encroachments. Anna, thought Mrs Marsh, would be unexpectedly difficult to dislodge. Either that, or she would protect her own territory, just as she would protect her secrets, if she had any.

'Tell us about the flat, Anna. I must say I was surprised to hear that you had moved so quickly. Although I can see that Albert Hall Mansions might have been too big for you.'

Anna flashed her a determined smile. 'I don't believe in living in the past,' she said, thinking back briefly to the holocaust of her mother's clothes and possessions that had taken place in a single day of furious energy, of bags taken down to the Oxfam shop, of shoes dumped unceremoniously in the dustbin. 'Mother wanted me to be happy.'

'Indeed she did. We all want our children to be happy. As if life were that simple.'

'So I went to the estate agent the day after the funeral,'

said Anna, taking no notice, 'and found this straight away. It's a dear little flat, Aunt Vera – you must come round and see it. Just three rooms and a nice kitchen and bathroom. On the third floor. I can see the trees from my bedroom window.'

'I don't promise, Anna. I don't go out much these days. But leave me your telephone number.'

Mrs Marsh felt that she should offer them coffee, but was too tired to make the effort. Perhaps when Anna had gone, and she and Philippa were left alone. But Anna showed no signs of leaving. Mrs Marsh was aware of the Sunday papers, unopened, in the sitting-room. She had planned to get through them in time to watch *Songs of Praise*. She liked to watch the faces, so serious and trusting, on a day which was somehow always a slight disappointment. Now, if she were to have any time with Philippa and to watch *Songs of Praise* she would have to put off the papers until Monday, which meant that she wouldn't be able to read Monday's *Times* until the evening. She sighed. I must be getting senile at last, she thought, worrying over these details. But no, I do not care to have my Sundays interrupted.

'Such bad news,' she said to Philippa. 'My good lady is leaving me. Her varicose veins are too bad, she says. I was very attached to Mrs Wright. Twelve years she's been with me. Quite serious, at my age, to be without. You don't know anyone, do you, Anna? Two or three mornings a week are all I need.'

'I could ask Mrs Duncan,' said Anna doubtfully. 'But it might be too far for her to come. She lives in Paddington.'

'If she comes to you she could surely come to me. She could take a bus down the King's Road. I pay very well. Top dollar,' she added, a phrase she had picked up from her son.

'I'll ask her,' said Anna, picking up her bag, as if the request had driven her to make her escape. 'In any case I'll call for you next week, shall I? It's been lovely. And lovely to meet you too, Philippa.'

34

She kissed them both. Again Mrs Marsh was aware of the soft lips, of the flat eyes sliding past, contemplating some distant fulfilment. She could hear Anna saying, 'That's not what I'm after,' and applied it to herself. And yet she is assiduous, she thought. Maybe she is mad. Maybe her years of reclusion had driven her mad.

'Let me telephone if I need you, Anna,' she said. 'I may be out next week. Of course, you are always welcome.'

Philippa, who was more generous as well as less suspicious, returned Anna's kiss. 'Goodbye,' she said, 'and mind you book that holiday.'

'Wait a minute, Anna,' Mrs Marsh called after the retreating back. 'Your mother gave me this letter for you when I last saw her. I expect you'll want to read it in peace.'

Thank goodness I remembered that, she thought, closing the door at last. Otherwise I'd have had to invite her again.

They sat in silence for a minute or two after Anna had left, as if fearful that she might come back. Finally Mrs Marsh got up, went into the kitchen and put on the kettle. All the washing up still to do, she lamented. Next weekend I really must be free.

'What did you think of her?' she asked, coming back with a tray.

'Funny little thing,' said Philippa cheerfully. 'I loved her suit, didn't you? Nice for you to have her around, Mother. You've got her telephone number. Well, I don't see why she shouldn't do your shopping, when you don't want to go out. She seems very fond of you.'

So we are to go through life hand in hand, thought Mrs Marsh. 'Unfortunately, I find her rather tiresome,' she told her daughter. 'And I have the strangest feeling that she doesn't really like me. I get an occasional whiff of antagonism. Naturally she is far too polite to show it, or even to feel it. But there is something not quite right about her.'

'You're too censorious,' said her daughter, helping herself to an apple. 'I should make use of her if I were you.'

Philippa sees a way of discharging her responsibilities, observed Mrs Marsh. Well, she has been a good girl. And there is quite obviously a man in the background: she looks different. Suddenly and acutely she wished happiness for her daughter, a second marriage, nothing too precipitate or unsuitable, of course: something appropriate to her age and station. It seemed to her, then and later, that the worst fate in the world was to grow old as Anna would grow old. She imagined Anna and her friend Marie-France imprisoned by the shades of dead and dying relatives. *Mes ancêtres, dans des appartements solennels, tous idiots ou maniaques.* She was always grateful to the poets for giving colour, and authenticity, to her darker intuitions.

4

Anna Durrant had a recurring dream, which seemed to have been going on for many years and which must date from some time in her adolescence, since it bore all the marks of an adolescent fantasy. But over the years it had become more solemn, more mysterious, so that now it had achieved the status of a myth or a fairy tale. In the dream she was seated tidily and expectantly before a slice of cake, but not an ordinary cake: this was a dream cake, iced and filled and crowned with crystallized grapes. She took up her fork and plunged it into the cake, which immediately fragmented and revealed a gold wedding ring. Time and time again, in her dream, she heard the ring clatter on to the plate, while the cake, uneaten, vanished into thin air, its purpose achieved. It was somehow important not to eat the cake for fear of swallowing and therefore missing the ring. Since the advent of this dream, which she could no longer date or situate, she had shied away from too avid appetites, though she still possessed them, and had approached food cautiously, sometimes renouncing it altogether. While her ideal remained food of luscious sweetness and unctuosity – jellies, puddings, custards – she trained herself to eat only what was natural, and little enough of that. Fear of missing the ring kept her teeth closed before the fork could penetrate them, kept her eyes on her plate, seeing in one rapid survey what the food might conceal, and raising her head at last, as if to say, there is nothing for me in this, knowing that the dream would go on, and more, so that she could visualize the cake and the ring even when she was awake, so that if she longed for sweet food, as she frequently did, she would immediately see the ring falling on to the plate, after which the food would be irrelevant.

Walking home through the dark silent Sunday streets she reflected that Mrs Marsh did not really like her, did not even mean to be very kind, having no real sympathy with her situation, but remaining a decent woman, with the decent habits of a lifetime, had extended some sort of hospitality, and had thus got the upper hand of her reluctance and her uncertain temper. It was important never to mislead oneself as to the motives of other people, those who insisted on being kind, and those who, as was usual in her case, manifested a concern which was quickly tinged with irritation. 'If only she would do something to help herself,' was the habitual lament of those in the second category. So few people could be found who would understand or even try to understand a woman of her age and uncertain status, with no job, no profession, and no apparent avocation apart from caring for her mother. At this stage of the twentieth century mothers were supposed to look after themselves, even if elderly and frail, and to join keep-fit and self-help classes if they were not, thus sometimes appearing more vigorous than daughters who were beset with husbands and lovers and who had not yet rid themselves of menopausal anxiety.

A mother such as Amy Durrant had been was almost unheard of, anachronistic: plaintive, pleading, gentle, a victim of her poor heart in more than one instance. This came constantly to mind, even though Amy was dead. The envelope in her bag, given in a last despairing attempt at understanding to a woman whose mediation could be trusted, reminded Anna disagreeably of the matter in hand. She had no desire to read it, having some knowledge of what it contained. She had heard it so many times, that plea to be understood, although she understood all too well. She had only to consult her own hidden feelings in order to do so. Discretion and her own situation dictated then as now a smiling ignorance of what was intended, a determination to maintain the formalities of a relationship, even if it now had a worm at its heart. And she had done so, had repulsed the confession her mother seemed so impelled to make in the teeth of the decorum so prized by her daughter. They had loved one another despairingly: that was their undoing. And despair in love merely prolongs its intensity, as well as its duration, which is for ever. Now she must make do with mere acquaintances like Mrs Marsh, who thought her tiresome. She in her turn pitied Mrs Marsh for having avoided full knowledge of a mother's love, a mother's despair, for living what she saw as a limited emotional life. She saw all this, saw too Mrs Marsh's instinctive rejection of her, yet liked Mrs Marsh none the less for it. She saw her as a decent reliable sort of woman, much as her mother had: one who could be trusted.

But what coldness now, without that hellish and absorbing love, which had been her life for all of her life and which she now had to live without! They had lived, the two of them, in those dark rooms, as if the outside world no longer existed, as if life, in some mysterious fashion, had been renounced, although at the time of her widowhood Amy Durrant had been a young woman. Growing up with that sadly smiling mother had impressed upon Anna the duty of protecting that mother against further hurt. And she in turn had enjoyed protection, devotion, the fiercest dedication, without thought of self. It was natural for the two of them to walk arm in arm, for the daughter to hear stories of her parents' brief happiness, and to feel respect for its completeness, rounded as it was by a painless death and prolonged by an indefinite period of mourning. This was the sustenance of their innocent days, and even now, in the light of full knowledge, she did not regret the innocence.

To try to explain this innocence, which had marked her

fatally, was impossible. To the outside world the couple appeared touching, but heads were shaken over the outcome of such closeness, and it was confidently predicted that Anna would never marry. Was it for this reason that Amy Durrant's heart began to falter, to accelerate its uneven rhythm, and then to drop back into a throbbing so profound that both the throat and the stomach were affected? And if this happened at a time when Anna left the university (London, of course, so that she did not have to leave home) what more natural that she should undertake a piece of not too demanding research which would serve them both as an additional alibi? And that time was not problematic, for they were bound together in love and care, and eventually thought as one. Anna, raised in innocence and ignorance, had no desire other than to love and be loved, in this instance by her mother, for whose sorrow and frailty she felt responsible. To ease that pain she would give her life, for easing her mother's pain meant easing the pain in her own heart, bringing her cheerfulness and satisfaction. She was not unaware of the pitying glances, not from her own contemporaries, oddly enough, but from their mothers, mothers more battle-ready on their daughters' behalf than her own mother had ever dreamt of being. At about this time she began to have the dream of the cake disintegrating to disclose the wedding ring. The dream brought her joy. In spite of everything that had happened it still did.

Yet how was she to marry? No stranger entered that flat, where small pleasing rituals were enacted and peace reigned, because there was no discord between them. So hermetic was their existence that Anna's childhood was curiously prolonged into her early twenties. She was aware of this, having trained her mind to observance, yet felt it almost as a virtue. She attended her friends' weddings, although her mother was indignant that she was never asked to be a bridesmaid, still thinking in terms of a cortège of adult bridesmaids such as she had had at her own wedding to Anna's father, still hoping that Anna might meet a wedding

guest and fall in love with him, such a love affair being sanc-
tioned by the atmosphere of romance and her own fantasy of
the event. In other respects she could not see her daughter
making independent plans, nor was she anxious for her to
do so. She knew her to be as idealistic as she was herself,
and could not bear the prospect of disappointment for either
of them. And Anna, consoled and supported by the dream,
did not grieve too much when friends married and deserted
her, thinking her irrelevant to their new lives, and aware of
experiences which she could not share, aware too of their
newly discovered contempt for her virginity. They tended
to be sorry for her, but she herself was full of hope. She
had a belief in her destiny which verged on mysticism,
and throughout the long years in the silent flat, reading and
watching television with her mother, her cheerfulness was
entirely natural, and she did not notice the years going by.

It was the mother who ended all this. That was what she
now had to remember, that and the years which followed,
until her mother's death put an end to the bad faith which
had taken the place of the earlier trust. Feeling faint, as she so
often did, outside Harrods, being brought home in a cab by
a man in a camel-hair coat, with polished silver hair, whom
she introduced as 'Mr Ainsworth, darling, who very kindly
looked after me when I was feeling poorly. You'll stay to tea,
of course? Anna darling, will you get us some tea?' They were
deep in conversation when she returned from the kitchen,
and at once she had felt foreboding, not on her own behalf
but on her mother's. He was too glossy, too plausible, and
her mother was too flushed, too pretty. She was aware of a
disturbed scent in the air, as if her mother were warm and
excited, just as she was to be aware, later, of Ainsworth's brutal stink in the bathroom and the bottles of cologne he poured
over himself in order to become the lover and to dispel the
natural man. For he was to become her mother's lover, and
even her husband, or so they thought. Overnight their unity
was lost, although it was some time before Ainsworth moved
in. 'I do wish you'd call him George, darling,' her mother

had said with charming insouciance, and a resolute refusal to explain herself. She seemed to have recaptured the coquetry of her youth, when she had been hardy and capricious, before the marriage to Anna's father and the death which had changed her into a recluse. And inevitably there was a ceremony of sorts, and then Ainsworth took his rightful place in her mother's bedroom, whereas before he had only been a whispering visitor. Often she had gone into the hall late at night, tormented by doubt and heartache, and had seen his camel-hair coat and his pigskin gloves still lying over the chair, his umbrella propped up by its side.

He was dapper, she thought with distaste, not quite daring to think of his decisiveness which had conquered her mother. She sensed that he was a silent and energetic lover, and that he had had her mother in his sights since he had rescued her outside Harrods and brought her home to Albert Hall Mansions. Not exactly a fortune-hunter – another character from her mother's archaic repertoire – but sizing up the situation, the pretty, flattered, defenceless woman, whose very defencelessness excited him, so that in turn he drew from her an excited response. For the daughter he immediately felt a hunter's contempt, sensing that no one had ever breached her defences, relegating her almost to the status of a servant, aware of her dislike. They had lived like that for two years, until Ainsworth disappeared as abruptly as he had entered their lives in the first place. At first she had feared that he might return, until her mother revealed to her the circumstances of his departure. He had left the country, having extracted money for the journey from Amy Durrant: it appeared that he was already married, to a Belgian woman, with whom he was still sporadically in touch. All this they learned much later. At the time Amy had taken it on herself to disguise his disappearance. 'Why, yes, Anna and I are on our own again,' she said bravely to the few people to whom she still spoke. 'One shouldn't get married at my advanced age. But women never learn, do they?' Of Ainsworth's whereabouts they remained determinedly in ignorance, although living in fear that he might choose to enter their lives once more. And the fear, the shock, and above all the disappointment, the sudden withdrawal of his bodily vigour, drove Amy Durrant into a full-scale heart attack, and accelerated her long decline into invalidism.

She remained wistful: there was nothing she could do about that. She tried to hide it, aware of Anna's furious resistance to her plight. She could not see that Anna was the victim, for in her own mind she was inconsolable. She tried to placate her daughter, and sometimes succeeded. Anna remained good-humoured but now it was the good humour of the hospital nurse, and indeed as Mrs Durrant's hopes vanished the flat began to take on the appearance of a hospital room. Anna marshalled her mother's fading energies and strove for love and forgiveness. In this she was finally successful, but it was a success born of total renunciation. With what hope, with what avidity had her mother welcomed the doctor, Lawrence Halliday, seeing in him a last chance, an only chance for her daughter! And after each visit she urged Anna to lead him into the drawing-room and offer him a glass of sherry, taking good care to remain in her bedroom, and glad to do so, re-buttoning her blouse after the examination with shaking frightened fingers. And Halliday had seemed so well disposed, so polite to Anna, so concerned for her. By that time Anna could not easily leave home. That was her excuse. Her mother knew that her vigilance was part love, part revenge. Of such harsh truths does the emotional life consist.

At the end they were as one again. Death, and the prospect of life without one another reunited them as birth had once done. But who could feel pity for the poor unfledged creature left behind? She knew she was an object of concern and fought against it, took care to be well dressed, impeccably turned out, as if all depended on her appearance, kept a smile on her face, tried to think well of everyone, including those who were indifferent to her. The time passed slowly, that was all, but she was sure that it passed just as slowly for men and women imprisoned in offices and factories, and she was also sure that sooner or later she would find something to do, find someone to whom she could explain herself, and who would understand her, with all her diffidence and her complexity. Until then she took pleasure in small homely things, as if only these had the power to quell her enormous fear at being adrift in this cold world. Even now, she thought, as she was putting her key in the door, she would make a cup of tea, and write to Marie-France. They wrote frequently, elaborately, the journal of their respective lives. Over the years both came to see this correspondence as their main production. Yet as she put her purse back into her bag she once more encountered the stiff envelope, which she withdrew and held in her hand for a minute, debating with herself whether to throw it away. She already knew, or thought she knew, what it contained.

She made the tea and drank it greedily, cup after cup. She looked round the small room, willing herself to find it pleasant. In fact it was pleasant, and she usually took pleasure in it, but tonight she was too aware of the letter, which now lay on her desk. This would be the final confrontation with a mother whom in life she had never reproached but had refused to understand. She got up and pulled the red and white striped curtains, switched on the fire, creating an illusion of warmth and comfort. Finally, and with reluctance, she opened the stiff envelope, drew from it two sheets of paper, both of them creased and much folded. The first was her birth certificate: Anna Mary Pauline Durrant. This, she knew, was to confirm her status and her rightful place in the world. The second was a letter, written obviously with great difficulty, but, she saw as she read, as a last attempt at self-justification. Her hand reached once more for the teacup, as if to be put into last touch with her present reality. 'My darling,' she read, in her mother's pretty, schoolgirl's hand. Even the imprint of the words on the page seemed soft, tentative. 'I am afraid that you will never forgive me, and also that you will never understand. Perhaps when you are married you will realize what a temptation love can be, or even the pretence of love if one is lonely enough. Of course you were all in all to me, but to a woman like myself, not very strong, not very brave, a second marriage seemed like a gift from Heaven. And it brought me to life again, Anna: never forget that. I never tried to explain this to you, thinking that in so doing I might offend your dignity, for we never discussed these matters, and indeed there would not have been much to be gained from such discussions between a mother and a daughter such as we were. I tried to protect you, because I knew that you were hurt and angry, but I told myself that you would forgive me once you were married and had a home of your own. I am sure you will understand what I mean by that. For my punishment – and I have been greatly punished and greatly humiliated – I felt that I was making you unhappy, and that something between us had undergone a change. I do not reproach you, since the whole thing was my fault, and indeed you have been a perfect daughter. It is only because I sense that little change in you that I want to reach out to you one last time.

'My darling, it is my wish that when you marry you will understand even more than you do now, and when you reach my age you will reflect that even when one is old one may still want to commit a folly. Lawrence Halliday seems very fond of you and when I am gone I hope and pray that he will be there to look after you. This is the last letter I shall ever write, to you or to anyone else – indeed I hardly know anyone else – and it is only fitting that I should say my few last words to the daughter whom I have prized above everything else in this world. I hope that she will forgive me for a weakness which I cannot bring myself entirely to regret. I want her to know that I have had moments of great happiness in my life and I pray that she will have the same throughout hers. Mother.

'P.S. I have had George traced. It seems that he is living in Louvain with the woman I must call his wife. It is possible that he might try to contact you, in which case it might be better for you to move. If he does come back on no account are you to give him any money.'

But she had not waited for those last instructions. She had moved as if she were taking flight, and even now did not feel quite safe. She did not fear George Ainsworth or his possible reappearance; she discounted him entirely. What she feared was the stain of her mother's defeat, the contagion of her mother's timid hopes, which she had seen confounded. The hurt she had sustained she had concealed from her mother, just as she had concealed the news that Lawrence Halliday had married Victoria Gibson, a pretty, silly, energetic woman with far more visible attractions than she herself possessed. The last conversation she had had with him, as they stood in the shadowy drawing-room (and she had not invited him to sit down) was dry, unemotional: she had asked him not to tell her mother of his marriage, to leave her that last illusion in her long decline. His fair handsome face had flushed, as if he were caught out, but that was the only allusion Anna ever made to his desertion, if desertion was what it was. They had both kept their promise, and Amy Durrant had cherished one faint last hope when she died. Since then Anna had maintained her ambiguous poise, although she knew that it was brittle. What mattered to her now, above all else, was to repair the imperfections in her own conduct, to obliterate the rancours of the past which had so nearly ruined her innocence. Now it was important to think well of everyone, to behave as if there had been no flaw in the fabric, even to visit the same doctor, who, after all, knew her well. And why should he not be reminded of her? She meant no harm, had never meant him harm. It was only her mother's expectations that had done them a disservice.

Simply, now, she would like to be good, hopeful, humble, cheerful, as if the promise of her strange dream might yet be fulfilled, and as if good fortune, when it came, might find her worthy to receive it. Of her poor mother she thought with love, with regret, perhaps not entirely with sympathy, thinking her tactless to open her heart, as she had done in the letter as in life, yet longing for her none the less. She repressed the letter, shutting her mind against it. At the same time she knew a moment of stupor at being so far from home.

But all that mattered now was to live in the present, even on the surface, if that helped, to love with a different sort of love from that which she had been taught, to love Mrs Marsh, to love her neighbour (but that is not what I am looking for, she protested inwardly), and to live as the Bible told people – other people – to live. There were good things in this world, after all. She was in her own flat, safe, if not quite warm enough; she was in good health. It had been a pleasant day, almost. Now she was tired, and no wonder. She put the letter away into the drawer of her desk, pulled back the curtains, stood at the window easing her back with both hands, the gesture of a much older woman. She would write to Marie-France tomorrow, not tonight. Tonight she would go to bed early. There was no need to eat anything, although the fruit looked appetizing in the blue bowl she had brought from Albert Hall Mansions. Mrs Marsh had observed that the pears were good this year. As she turned out the lights she took one last look at the blue bowl. It seemed important to observe, at this moment of small consolations, that it had been a fine year for apples too.

5

Mrs Marsh was immersed in her daily exercise of scanning the Deaths column in *The Times*. The Births she brushed aside as no longer being of any relevance to her. The Deaths were a different matter. Not that she expected to see the names of anyone she knew on a daily basis: her life was too circumscribed for such surprises. Her few old friends were contacted at Christmas, and she would have heard directly if any one of them were ill, or more ill than usual. A daughter or a son would send a note, or perhaps telephone, just as she supposed that Philippa or Nick would do when she, in her turn, succumbed. What fascinated her was the tiny detail included in some of the announcements ('Suddenly, whilst playing golf') which set her thinking of the arbitrary nature of death, and its occasional playfulness, so infinitely more to be desired than the regrettably familiar 'after a long illness, borne with her usual indomitable courage'. Sometimes the name of one of her husband's colleagues cropped up, and these eminent persons were given obituaries heavy with honours and with occupational landmarks. In death as in life such people tended to occupy more space than others less fortunately endowed. She had known them once but had lost touch when her husband died. Their wives, those who had survived, sent a card at Christmas.

The second stage of Mrs Marsh's morning activity was thus reached, and she lapsed into rather puzzled memories of her late husband, a man whom she always thought she did not know particularly well. They had had a perfectly sound marriage, she reflected: both were sensible healthy people, both had enjoyed their life together. But it seemed to her now that they had never had a serious conversation, and she wondered if that were wrong. On the whole she thought not. Their home life had been optimistic, fortunate, if not particularly or comfortingly familiar. She had seen him off in the mornings, thinking how handsome he looked in his city clothes, had handed him his briefcase, and had looked forward, with a mild and containable pleasure, to welcoming him home again in the evening. Their house in Pelham Street had been pretty – she had loved that house – but she had not wept at leaving it, after Bill's death. She was too obsessed by that stage with the changed sound of his voice when he said to her, from his hospital bed, 'I'm done for, old girl,' and when they had trembled on the verge of a new intimacy, which, as he died, escaped them both. Cancer of the pancreas: no arguing with that. She had sat out her mourning in her first-floor drawing-room, filled with a new thoughtfulness: a spring sunlight had trembled on the walls and on a corner of the ceiling, and the bulbs she had planted earlier flourished on the window-sills. These signs of renewal seemed to her so inappropriate that she had immediately thought that she must relinquish the house, to Nick, who was then married, and go somewhere else. At sixty-two she was not too old to make new friends among her neighbours, and if she lived to a great age, as both her parents had done, she would be better off in a flat, where there might be a porter to look after her needs and to find her a daily woman.

So she had lived for twenty years, stoically, as her situation demanded. She thought of her husband these days without grief, but with a sense of gratitude, and also of frustration. How he would hate the life she lived now, in the dark flat, without too many visits from the children, and hardly any from her two grandchildren. She was sadder now than she had ever been in the months following her husband's death, a fact for which she reproached herself. What else could she expect at her age? She could even have married again, but had turned away from the suggestion, as if it had been tactless, inaesthetic, in any case not sufficiently compelling. And when there had been a further proposal she had rejected that as well, having decided that by now she was too awkward to combine either physically or mentally with a new partner. She had surveyed her gaunt face, her increasingly wiry hair, her large feet, and the body which now looked almost sexless, half-way, as she had thought, to extinction, and had decreed that enough was enough. The physical life, for which she had been grateful in the past, had left her with few memories. She supposed that she was a lucky woman, yet even in her heyday she had thought that too much fuss was made of sex, and too much nonsense talked. One outlived it, that was all: no amount of philosophical argument could overcome that fact. The young never believed it, of course. But then the young had many surprises waiting for them.

But there was too little to do when one was old, and feeling one's age, reluctant to venture further than the shops and the library, and then faced with a long afternoon at home. If she was at all nostalgic it was for her earlier vigour, when she had thought nothing of being out all day. She did not mind the silence, for she had come to cherish it, but there was a certain lack of human nourishment about her days that distressed her. Not excessively, for she was not an excessive woman, and not at all given to unnecessary regrets. She simply wished for the occasional conversation, the occasional stimulus of another personality. She was careful not to brood on this deficiency, but rather to face it squarely. She was, she knew, fortunate: she was not in need, did not depend on her children, had suffered no serious illnesses. Nevertheless she felt she was preparing mentally for her own death, for surely this daily immersion in the deaths of others, complete strangers for the most part, was no accident. Mrs Marsh believed that nothing in this life was accidental, thereby allying herself with many great thinkers of the past: it was the feeling which drove her, an unbeliever, to church on a Sunday. Something was taking place, some kind of preparation being made. She derived a bleak intellectual pleasure from charting her downward progress, about which she was without illusions. There was no question of going to rejoin Bill in a better place, as some of the death notices so confidently proclaimed: Bill had been incinerated before her very eyes. It had seemed the cleanest thing to do with his poor body. She had no sense that anyone was waiting for her, or indeed that her children would mourn her for very long: she had always been too sensible to cherish such comforting notions. She supposed that she must put up with whatever was coming as bravely as she could. In the meantime her strong old body carried on in its own way, which was pretty well, considering the poor use to which she now put it.

She thought that on the whole she had had a charmed life, a good husband, healthy children. But sometimes, now, the days proved unexpectedly long, particularly in the winter when it never really got light. If she craved anything she craved light, a fierce light from a yellow sun, such as she had seen in certain paintings in the days when she went to the National Gallery, Turner's sun, emerging from streaming vapours to conquer the waiting earth. And at the end she would like a vague blueness to descend, as in the painter's *Evening Star*, where a solitary boy leaves the deserted beach for home. That would be acceptable, she thought. But hardly likely: such phenomena were part of the living imagination, and were not produced with the intuition of the dying, nor even for their benefit. The creative life is a law unto itself.

There was no pressing need for her to think of dying, yet all her thoughts tended in that direction. She had received no warning signs. She was simply more reclusive than she had ever been, was drawn to evidence of disappearance, extinction, and to wondering how it would be. 'Peacefully, surrounded by her family', she read, when the doorbell unexpectedly rang.

'Mrs Marsh?' enquired the smartly dressed woman, with the fashionable shawl draped over her raincoat, and the air of a prospective Conservative candidate, or at least his agent.

'I am Mrs Marsh,' she said.

'Mrs Duncan. Peggy Duncan. Anna said you might be wanting someone to help out.'

'Mrs Duncan, how good of you to call! And how good of Anna to have remembered. I must thank her. Won't you come in?'

On closer examination Mrs Duncan proved to be a small woman in the indeterminate range of late middle age, with a strikingly white skin and fine brown eyes. She appeared to be fairly heavily made up, although this impression was largely conveyed by the fine grain of her thickly powdered face. She had beautifully cut champagne-coloured hair, and her gaze was loyal, implying fidelity, even on so short an acquaintance, as if she had stepped from a photograph of servants in days long gone by. Not that she looked anything like a servant – she was too well turned out for that – but the brown eyes were trusting and unwavering, and the voice was soft. She must have been a pretty girl, thought Mrs Marsh, and been treated like one all her life.

'I was just going to make a cup of coffee,' she said. 'Won't you join me?'

She led the way into her kitchen, put on the kettle, and hunted out a new packet of biscuits, although she knew that her tin contained chocolate digestives, a relic of Nick's last visit. 'This is very fortunate,' she said. 'Do sit down. And won't you take off your coat? Although I dare say it's not very warm in here. I hardly notice it myself.'

'I shan't stop, Madam.'

'Ah,' she said, deflated. 'Do help yourself to sugar.'

'As I say, I thought I'd call for a chat, to see what you wanted. But I have to make one thing clear, before we start. I can only do the job for a few months, well, not more than a year. In a year I'll be sixty. And I always promised myself I'd retire at sixty.'

'Very sensible,' said Mrs Marsh crisply. 'It sounds as if you've made plans.'

'My husband and I made our plans when the children left home. We've always been savers, never spent a lot on ourselves. That's how we were able to buy our house, you see.'

'Anna said that you lived in Paddington, if I'm not mistaken.'

'Well, that's part of the plan: no more Paddington, no more Star Street. Our house is on the Isle of Wight. That's where we're going when we retire, or when I do, rather. My husband retired last year, from the Post Office. Now he makes a bit extra window-cleaning.'

'How very interesting,' said Mrs Marsh, who did in fact find this interesting, and was excited by the prospect of possible access to a window-cleaner. 'And will you like retirement? Won't you miss London?' She did not ask Mrs Duncan if she would miss her work, for that she thought too stupid and potentially offensive a question, although Mrs Duncan was so obviously superior that she probably regarded herself as being almost in the professional class. I hope she won't be insulted when I bring the conversation back to money, she thought.

'It's our dream home, you see, something we've always wanted. Nice garden, patio, French windows, *en suite* bathrooms, the lot. So, you see, I don't mind working flat out for those little extras.'

It is the enterprise culture, thought Mrs Marsh, and it is admirable. I should have done something like that, but on a fixed income it would hardly have been possible.

'I won't say it hasn't been hard, sometimes,' Mrs Duncan went on. 'But the children have been very good to us. Luckily they're both doing well. Louise is in computers and Keith's in hairdressing. They've got their own places now, one in Fulham, one in Wandsworth. And there's room for both of them, when they come down, until they marry, of course, though there's no sign of that. "I want to make my mark first, Mum," Keith says to me. "I don't want to interfere with my career while I can still give it all I've got." '

'Did Keith cut your hair?' asked Mrs Marsh. 'It looks most beautifully shaped.'

'That's my Keith,' said Mrs Duncan proudly. 'Salon treatment. Of course I can't expect him to do it all the time. Saturdays I go round to Edgware Road. I know the man there, known him for ages. "Do everything," I say to him. Laugh! But when Keith does it everyone remarks on it.'

The hint of vulgarity had brought a tint of animation to her velvet cheeks. Mrs Marsh's wintry features relaxed into a brief smile. Yes, a pretty girl, she thought. And never thinking herself out of the running.

'You were with Anna, I believe,' she said, reluctantly calling the business to order.

'Still am. I was with her mother for ten years, no, more like eleven.'

'Ah, yes, poor Mrs Durrant.'

'Ainsworth. Mrs Ainsworth.'

Mrs Marsh looked at her in surprise. 'I knew her as Amy Durrant.'

'She was Amy Durrant, all along,' said Mrs Duncan confidentially. 'But when I went to her she called herself Mrs Ainsworth. Married this man, you see, or so she thought, until he told her he was already married.'

'Good heavens,' said Mrs Marsh slowly. 'I had no idea.'

'Well, of course, it was terrible for her. He was after her money, wasn't he? And I dare say she had to pay him off. Two years it lasted. I suppose he got fed up with her finicky ways. The sad thing was that I think she really loved him. A woman like that, on her own all those years. And there's the frustration, you have to reckon with that, don't you?'

'I dare say.' Mrs Marsh's tone was distant. Nevertheless,

she had to hear more. 'What kind of a man was he?' she asked.

'Good-looking, nicely turned out, well-spoken. Very clean, always smelled lovely. Always had a bit of a chat with me, before he went to work. Didn't leave the house until about ten, sometimes ten-thirty.'

'What did he do?'

'Mystery. Said he was a wine merchant, or so Mrs Ainsworth or Durrant or whatever she was told me. But I once saw him behind the counter of an off-licence when I was doing my shopping in Queensway. Luckily he didn't see me. I went past a few days later but he wasn't there any more. And shortly after that he was gone altogether.'

'Good Heavens. Poor Amy.'

'Of course, she went right down after that, didn't she? "My heart is broken, Peggy," she said to me. She used to pour it all out. Many's the morning I've just sat there and listened to her. Well, she couldn't talk to Anna, could she? Anna hated him. And if you ask me Anna's the one who really suffered.'

'Poor Anna,' said Mrs Marsh slowly.

'She took it very hard. Of course she's always been a bit fussy, like her mother. But look what her mother fell for! I shouldn't be surprised if Anna did the same thing, one day, fell for someone, I mean. Her mother hoped it would be the doctor.'

'Halliday?' Mrs Marsh was startled.

'She was fond of him, I know. And he seemed fond of her. But he just couldn't take it on, do you know what I mean? Anna, and her mother, and that flat.'

'Yes, I see. Poor Anna,' she said again. 'And you still keep an eye on her? I'd like to think she had someone she could turn to.'

She noted with interest, and not a little shame, that she had consigned Anna to Mrs Duncan instead of taking her on herself. Anna was the victim of multiple derelictions, she thought, hardly a person any more in her own right.

By the time they took their leave of each other, having agreed that Mrs Duncan was to come for three mornings a week, starting on the following Monday, each was experiencing a slight sense of disappointment. Mrs Duncan had hoped for an answering conviviality, for confidences from another witness to Amy Durrant's disgrace. She thought in the lurid terms of her girlhood reading, when women paid the price for giving in to the snares of men. It pleased her to think of Amy Durrant as a victim, for were not all women victims, saved from their fate only by marriage to a good man? Her own husband she had long classed as this archetypal good man, of the kind who would not try to deceive women, and in whom infidelity was unthinkable. Her own safety made her sympathetic to Amy Durrant, whom she nevertheless regarded with appalled fascination. She had understood, much as she had a general if vague understanding of catastrophe, the lure to which Amy Durrant had succumbed, but had not felt its echo in her own flesh, so comfortably catered for, so noticeably safe. She was not embarrassed by any sense of impropriety, although she realized that the burden of this fell on Anna's unprotected shoulders, a fact which made her more uncomfortable than the dilemma which had brought this about.

Mrs Duncan would not have been averse to discussing this problem with Mrs Marsh, but this was apparently not to be. What to do about Anna would have been a theme they could both have pursued on Monday, Wednesday and Friday mornings, over coffee. For she was anxious to hand Anna over to someone else, feeling uneasy in her presence for reasons which she could not define. She found her heart beating a little too strongly when she put her key into Anna's front door on Wednesday afternoons, and was always relieved to find that she had gone out, leaving the money on the kitchen table. She found that she usually worked more quickly on Wednesday afternoons, as if anxious to escape before Anna made her reappearance.

Anna was worrying, but not sufficiently attractive to

be ostentatiously worried over, and Mrs Duncan was astute enough to know that condolences over Anna's plight would not be welcome. There was, she told herself, no reason to worry; Anna was not a child. She had sensed Anna's antagonism during the Ainsworth affair, had sensed too that the antagonism would be turned against anyone who was a witness to her mother's weakness. Yet sensing the antagonism, she was at the same time unable to dismantle it, or even to identify it, for Anna's feelings were masked by her terrifying all-purpose goodwill. Occasionally Mrs Duncan saw a faraway look on Anna's face, a look of contained suffering and patience so adult that she felt ashamed, all her horrified and righteous sympathy banished. That expression of Anna's had always recalled her to her senses. No confidence had ever passed between them, and thus no truth was ever unveiled. She would have liked to be kind, yet it was clear that no kindness was expected, and if offered might be quietly refused. This knowledge, with which her reading had not equipped her to deal, made her uncomfortable, rendered her without resource. She continued to tidy Anna's flat, with an instinctive reluctance which she did not quite understand. She regarded Anna with a disfavour which made her almost fretful, and was always relieved not to have to encounter her.

Mrs Marsh was disappointed in herself because she had given in to the temptation of gossip. She regarded Mrs Duncan very firmly as a servant, and she had grown up with the knowledge that one never gossiped with servants. Not that she had imparted any information of her own, but she had listened fairly avidly to what Mrs Duncan had to tell her, and she was aware that any future association would depend on further discussions of a similar nature. How was she to bear this for three mornings a week without transgressing her codes? She looked round the kitchen, which seemed to her dingy: it probably needed painting, but at her age she regarded this as a needless extravagance. She went into her bedroom, ran a finger over the glass top of her dressing-table, disturbing a light film of whitish powder. It was shabby, she conceded, dusty, perhaps not too clean. Perhaps Mrs Duncan could see to all this. There were attractions to having someone in regular attendance. If she were ill, if she were to have a fall, as happened to so many women of her age, she had no doubt that Mrs Duncan would be invaluable. She raised her head to look out of the window at the grey empty street. Oh, the sun, the sun!

Later, having digested the morning's business in her usual efficient manner, she conceded that Mrs Duncan's revelations had not been without interest. What had been particularly interesting had been the woman's feelings about Anna, which she recognized as ambiguous, pessimistic. Mrs Marsh supposed that, had she been a good woman, she would have made Anna her concern, and regarded the settling of Anna as part of her responsibility as an elder of the tribe. But I am not a good woman, she told herself firmly, or if I am it is purely by default. Anna is too burdensome a project for a woman of my age. Her contemporaries must take care of her. I will introduce her to Philippa's two (but of course they are much too young). I will even introduce her to Nick. She can come to my Christmas drinks party. After that I wash my hands of the whole affair, which remains faintly distasteful to my mind. Mrs Duncan must see that she pulls her weight. But by this stage in her ruminations it was time for the News, so she gave Mrs Duncan and Anna and even poor Amy Durrant no further thought. So nice, she reflected, so refreshing, to hear a man's voice.

6

'*Bien chère* Marie-France,

'This comes to you with my Christmas greetings and all my hopes and wishes for a peaceful New Year. I suppose you will be going to Meaux for the holidays (I think you mentioned that Emmanuel and his family were joining you) and I hope that this letter arrives before you leave. I shall be staying here, quite happily, and catching up on my work, and on my sleep, for I have been having a very busy time. Christmas seems to have come round more quickly this year, and the shopping is a nightmare. On Christmas Day I shall take Aunt Vera to church, and then come back here for a quiet afternoon. After a light meal I shall settle down to read. There will be a great deal to think about. You may even get an extra letter.

'The great event of the week was Aunt Vera's Christmas party. She gives one every year, for the members of the Residents' Association, of which she has been chairwoman, her daughter and son, her two grandchildren and their partners, and the doctor and his wife. My Mrs Duncan was there to help out. It was a tremendous success and I enjoyed it enormously, although I knew no one except Philippa, Aunt Vera's daughter, and of course the doctor. I was interested to take a closer look at his wife, of whom more later. It was quite obvious to me, from various remarks dropped by Aunt Vera, that I was invited to meet her son, Nick. In any event I took care to look my best, though not for the famous Nick, I should emphasize, but because I love to dress up. I wore my brown corded silk suit with the gold buttons, and my gold ear-rings. I may even have looked a little too formal: Lucy, Philippa's daughter, wore a tiny leather skirt, and Michael, her son, a very bright yellow cashmere pullover – to show he was in advertising, I imagine. The doctor's wife, Victoria, or Vickie, as I am supposed to call her, although I have only met her once or twice, wore a short red dress with enormous shoulder pads. I thought she looked ridiculous, but she was so animated and so sure of herself that she soon had quite a crowd round her. All the elderly men from the surrounding flats thought her marvellous. We exchanged a few words and she announced that she was going to ask me to dinner, "to meet some new people" – hardly the most tactful greeting. Aunt Vera was in black and looked very dignified.

'The famous Nick turned out to be a sardonic-looking man of fifty-odd, which I suppose made him suitable for me – trust Aunt Vera! I can't say I took to him, but then first impressions are misleading and I told myself I was being a little unkind. He is certainly very presentable, tall and well dressed, but with rather disappointing hair and a distinct blue shadow round the chin, one of those men who needs to shave twice a day and who hadn't bothered, thinking he'd be meeting his mother's usual crowd. As we were meant to be partners – for there was no one else there who was unattached – I stayed with him more or less for the whole evening, although at one point we were rudely interrupted by Vickie, who seemed to want Nick all to herself. Now I must confess that this is a woman I really cannot like. She struck me as infantile, all petulance and smiles; one felt one had to win her back into a state of good temper from what-ever tantrum had recently claimed her. She is supposed to be delicate (I can't remember who told me that) which I suspect means that she cries and has headaches and various upsets and that all physical manifestations come easily to her, without ugly signs or after-effects. I have often found that these childlike women come from very happy families: they have been Daddy's girl or Mummy's little princess, and are spoilt ever after. The man they marry takes over from the parents in many ways. Poor Lawrence! But men seem to love it and take all those tears and smiles for a sign of temperament. Maybe they *are* a sign of temperament. But when I see it being paraded like this I become very calm and quiet, too quiet perhaps, but really I find such performances profoundly embarrassing. Would you believe that Nick was smiling? She is very pretty, of course, and immediately started to tease him. "Hallo," she said. "I'm Vickie Halliday. And you are?" "Nick Marsh." "Oh, of course. You look as if you could do with a great deal more to drink." "Oh?" "Positively ferocious! I've been watching you – *such* a ferocious expression. I'm not being tactless, am I? Take no notice if I am. I'm just sensitive to atmospheres. Hypersensitive, in fact." "I'm perfectly happy," he said. "But I've a hard day's trading behind me," (he is in the City like his father). "I can't say the same for you," he said. "You look quite radiant. I like your dress. Red suits you." "That's very gallant of you. Much better in fact. I'm just terribly lucky, I suppose." At which point I had had enough and moved away. I collected a handful of glasses and went off to the kitchen to wash them. I had a word with Mrs Duncan, then I freshened my make-up, and, still calm, went back into the drawing-room. I thought it was about time I paid some attention to Aunt Vera who had been on her feet the whole evening. Across the room I could see the two of them, still in conversation. I said to Aunt Vera that I must soon be going, but she told me to wait. "Nick will drive you home," she said. "I'm sorry he can't give you dinner," she added. "He is coming back here for a light supper and a talk about my investments – all much too boring for a guest. So you will have to excuse us. But Nick will drop you off first."

'So we drove back to Cranley Gardens. It was quite amusing. He told me that he usually has a dog in the back of the car, but that he had had to leave the dog at his place in Berkshire, something he doesn't care to do but has to when he has evening meetings. I told him how fond I was of his mother, which pleased him. I said that I would always keep an eye on her. Then I suddenly felt extremely tired: I suppose the evening had been a bit of a strain. I asked him in for coffee, which seemed to amuse him. "I must get back," he said. Then he kissed me. So you see, my dear, interesting things happen all the time . . .'

This surely was the right note, the note they always seemed to strike: feminine, intimate, critical, high-spirited. They had both read their Jane Austen, and prided themselves on keeping a cool head. She had in fact felt achingly unwell on the evening of the party. In the hallway of Mrs Marsh's flat (reached all too soon) she had arrived as Lawrence Halliday and his wife were taking off their coats.

'Hello, Anna,' Lawrence had said. 'You remember Vickie, don't you? Vickie, Anna.'

The small dark woman he was with turned to her thoughtfully.

'Anna,' she said. 'How *are* you?'

Her voice held deep, almost parodied compassion, but her gaze was withdrawn almost immediately, as more guests arrived, forcing them into uncomfortable proximity.

'We'd better go in,' said Lawrence, putting an arm round his wife's shoulders: she assumed an expression of spotlit festivity. A star, thought Anna. But Lawrence's gaze was mild, detached, polite, withdrawn: he was not thinking the same thoughts as his wife. It occurred to her, by an instantaneous insight which she could not verify, that he did not love her, that it was only sex between them, but that that was considerable. A small pulse beat in her head, signalling a future headache. Smiling, she had followed them into the room.

She had felt alarm and despair when she was introduced to the grimly smiling Nick, sensing, as she always did, that some sort of explanation for her presence had already been offered, and that it was not entirely favourable, or not entirely imaginative, or not entirely generous. She sensed criticism everywhere, but had perfected a condition of calm good humour, which she employed for every occasion. She saw at once the impossibility of having anything to do with this Nick, against whom her most intimate fibres instinctively protested. That secret and most censorious of voices told her that here was a man who would have to be cajoled into loving a woman, would not condescend to look at a woman unless she amused and entertained him, would expect salacious performances in private and a high level of sophistication in public. He was not, nor ever could be, that profound silent loving man whom she sought and had never found. From the dead father, whom time had effaced, to the absconding Ainsworth, to the disappearing Halliday – all men had come to represent absence, the absence which they could not or would not fill.

With Lawrence Halliday, who had taken over attendance on her mother when Dr Howarth, the senior partner of the practice, retired, she had thought that all would be well. It was not quite love, but for the first time in her life she had felt an untroubled sense of appropriation. This, she imagined, was how other women felt when they met their future husbands. Professional propriety had stood between them, and nothing had taken place, either inside or outside the drawing-room, but she could see his deference, could see that he was impressed by her demeanour, and had indeed, on those occasions when they drank their sherry so thoughtfully, with talk only of her mother, eyed him impassively, objectively, acknowledging that he pleased her, but not yet inclined to break the spell of good manners that lay on them both.

He was weak, she could see that: he flushed too readily, was uneasy when not being a doctor. Although his accent and speech were classless, she sensed a lifetime of scholar-ships behind him, and an eager mother in the background to whom he occasionally spoke roughly but to whom he was devoted. She sensed that his arrival in the Cheltenham

Terrace practice was the realization of a lifetime's dreams and ambitions, and that he was on his best behaviour, impressed, in spite of himself, by the massive shadowy comfort of Albert Hall Mansions. She could also see that he would need to shed these good manners from time to time, would seek noisy company, might have tastes which did not quite accord with his professional dignity. She felt that she could take care of all this. He must be cultivated, he must be guided, he must be made to feel comfortable. She would be happy to make him comfortable. In return he would make her into a married woman, and together they would both look after her mother. For it was unthinkable that she should abandon her mother, now that she was obviously failing, and Albert Hall Mansions was big enough for all of them.

It was not quite love, but it had seemed like destiny. What he felt she never knew. She could see that she impressed him, that he too thought in terms of what was fitting. She thought gravely about what might unite the two of them but sought to contain her mother's too obvious enthusiasm. Love came later, when he in his turn disappeared, and disappeared in the company of another woman, whose confident and confiding tones had made him bold. Then love took over, together with desolation and a sense of failure. She had sat in the drawing-room for many evenings, alone, after her mother had gone to bed, and fought hard with herself for control and mastery of her feelings. She knew what she had to do. What she had to do was to be perfectly courteous, always, to convey to him no sign of disappointment, to make no violent gulping scene such as a lesser woman might make. She saw that the effort she would be demanding of him would have been too much for him. Nothing was said; everything was understood. 'Don't upset my mother,' she had said. 'I will tell her later.' He had been relieved. But she had told her mother nothing.

'You're terribly thin, Anna,' he had said. 'Are you sure you're looking after yourself properly?' 'You're terribly thin,' he had said again at Mrs Marsh's party. 'You'd better come and see me.'

That was what she had brought home from the party, not the promise of pleasing Nick, for she knew that he found her ridiculous, with her flushed face and her careful clothes. And with this realization came an increasing coldness, as if the eager feelings with which she had anticipated the party had been overcome by reason and by hard fact, against which they had no defence. He did not even dislike her enough to feel antagonistic, as she suddenly and shockingly did. As if to disguise this unpleasantness she sought to please him, as that imagined other woman would have done, assumed a look of sparkling animation, darted forward, as Mrs Marsh, in black, with a crescent of dusty diamonds pinned to her left shoulder, came trudging in with a tray of slightly burnt sausages and a dish of mustard. Briefly they wrestled for control of the tray until Mrs Marsh moved inexorably on.

'Where do you live in London?' she had asked.

'Notting Hill Gate,' he had answered briefly, spraying her with his meaty breath.

His breath changed to cheese, as Lucy, his niece, offered tiny Welsh rarebits, and then to garlic as Mrs Duncan came by with the *crudités*. All this time he kept his eyes firmly in front of him, as if in implacable refusal of her presence.

'Have you any children?' she had asked desperately.

His dark jowled face swung briefly in her direction, one eyebrow lifted, the eye expressing surprise.

'None,' he replied. 'Have you?'

She was aware that she was uncomfortable to be with, had little to offer but her maidenly accomplishments and her letter-writing and her too careful clothes. Nothing there for a man like Nick, or perhaps for any man. But that is not what I am looking for, she thought. What she was looking for was a man to whom explanations of her position would be unnecessary, for he would be so interested that information would flow between them, with no effort required on either side. Instead she was presented, as if he were

65

a treat, a prize, with this Nick, whose costive utterances and implacable reserve she was supposed to find rewarding, as she supposed some other women might, women to whom a man resembled a safe waiting to be cracked, and the reward all that the safe contained. But that kind man, that teacher, lover, friend, who remained indistinct, would be generous with words; she imagined their life together as a long conversation, equally shared. For it was many years since she had spoken freely. She had grown up with the knowledge that she must protect her mother from hurt, and that meant from the truth. They had lived in a pleasant collaboration of unrealities, each secretly knowing that she was making a sacrifice for the other. Amy Durrant had pretended to feel more cheerful and certainly stronger than was the case; only once had she blithely disregarded their pact, when she let the stranger in, and the resulting devastation, when he left, was almost enough to hasten her end. They took it as a warning, paid more careful attention to their fictive life together, and presented a façade of optimism to the last. 'Such a marvellous spirit,' said neighbours, who sometimes commented, and who were briefly sympathetic when Amy died. 'Devoted. Such faith.' They had done it all without faith of any kind, but the discipline sometimes amounted to a kind of religious observance. And now it was too much part of her life to be discarded.

Within that carapace she was an adult woman, but one who had no voice because of her lifelong concealment, which no one now would question. She was represented by an exterior manner which she herself found burdensome, as if she were only just learning what other women had always known, so that she made too many efforts, and all of them inept. This strenuous task of engaging the attention of a man who secretly appalled her filled her with sadness, yet she was bound to persevere with him, as another woman might, as if some part of her still wanted to prove that she might make a conquest, and because of Lawrence Halliday being in the same room. She hated Nick Marsh, hated his cruelty, and

66

was determined that he should notice her, that he should acknowledge her in some way. All this was exacerbated by the public nature of the encounter. She was almost pleased when Vickie Halliday interrupted their conversation, halting as it was, and immediately began sparkling and dazzling like a firework in her red dress, with her red nails, and Lawrence's diamond on her finger. She had had a certain amount of champagne to drink, enough to make her silly and tactless, and an answering smile had spread over Nick's face. This was what ordinary, normal women did, Anna had thought: they issued a challenge, even if that challenge were only one of availability. And never mind propriety, decorum, good manners: all these had to go, and that was the whole point . . . 'Hypersensitive,' she heard this child-woman say, her eyes widening at the drama of her own life. Yet at the same time, when Lawrence had come up and touched her arm and said that they must leave she had accorded him a brisk no-nonsense attention, briefly grown up, like the woman she might be in thirty years' time. That was when Anna had moved to the kitchen. When she returned it was to hear Vickie inviting Nick to dinner. 'I'm a very good cook, even though I say it myself.' Turning to Anna, whom she had previously ignored, she had said, 'And you must come to one of my parties, Anna. It's time you met some new people. Lawrence has told me how good you were to your mother.' Lawrence had briefly drawn her away.

'You're very thin, Anna. You'd better come and see me.'

'Yes, I will,' she had replied.

'Will you go to her dinner party and eat her fabulous food?' she had asked Nick with a touch of asperity, once the others had left.

He had accorded her a brief glance of interest.

'Probably not,' he said.

'You two seem to have a lot to talk about,' said Philippa merrily, coming round with more champagne despite her mother's warning glance.

'It's time to go,' she said to him. And, to kind Philippa,

67

'It's been a lovely party. I must say goodbye to your mother. Although of course I'll ring her tomorrow.'

They had travelled back to Cranley Gardens in virtual silence, once he had looked round to see if his dog were comfortable, and then to explain the dog's absence. She had felt very cold, very tired. When the car stopped in the silent frosty street he had leaned over and kissed her on the mouth. She had kissed him back, knowing that this was his way of dismissing her. They had looked at each other, momentarily absolved from their mutual antagonism. Then, without a word, she had got out of the car, slammed the door, and walked away.

He had thought her a virgin, as did everyone else, as had her mother, but she had had her modest adventures during her year in Paris, students, as young and unspoiled as herself, two French boys and the more sophisticated Austrian who had told her to wear gardenia scent, as she had done ever since. They were so sweet, so friendly – part of her youth which now seemed to her archaic, as if the trusting creature she had been then were now under sheet ice. If her mother had guessed she had said nothing. Neither had said anything; that was part of the pact. No confessions, no confidences, nothing to disturb or to threaten their closeness. And now there was nothing to say, to anyone, only a letter to finish, with that faint distortion in the presentation of events at which she had become so expert. She was tired, very tired, as she always seemed to be these days, and her bed was her greatest comfort. She went to bed earlier and earlier, for the night thoughts were precious to her. Only then, in her solitude, did she seem to join her mother, whose presence was always in a corner of her consciousness. Lying down she found not only peace but her essential self, her loving self, when love came easily and was met with equal love, before cruelty and loss had taken their toll.

She turned back the bed, and went to the desk to finish her letter. 'I shall be thinking of you all at Meaux on Christmas Eve. How nice that Emmanuel and his family will be with you instead of with Solange's parents. How I wish that I had a nephew, or a niece, or best of all a sister! But I have many good friends, for which I am grateful, and above all I have you. Don't forget — I shall be coming to Paris to celebrate your sixtieth birthday! In the meantime my love to Papa, and my fondest love to yourself. I am thinking of you.

'*Grosses bises,*

Anna.'

7

'She is virtuous,' said Mrs Marsh. 'She is a good woman.'

'Hardly a recommendation in this day and age, Mother.'

'I'm obliged to correct you, Nick. People take too ribald a view of virtue, in my opinion. It is not necessarily very intelligent of them. And do stop saying "in this day and age". Anyone would think that goodness was simply an item of fashion. It is rather more than that, I should hope.'

'Nevertheless, you are doing her no favours by describing her in that way.'

'I find your attitude quite extraordinary. Is this the generation gap I have always heard about?'

'You started it, Mother.'

Mrs Marsh was tired and therefore combative. She was also appalled to see how tired she had become; far more so, surely, than after last year's party. They sat amid empty glasses and plates of congealed sausages, and she hardly had the strength to clear them away. Mrs Duncan had gone off smartly, saying that she would see to everything on the following morning. She could have stayed, thought Mrs Marsh, but I suppose she wanted to get her husband's meal. Philippa would have helped, but I did not want her to be late for the opera. She looked so nice for once: there must be someone in the background. The children, of course, think that I am immortal. And Nick would never dream of doing my washing up. Not that he would be unwilling, but he would simply never dream of doing it: the thought would never enter his mind. He grew up with servants, and he married a competent wife. I loved him the best, of all of them, Bill included. And yet nowadays he pleases me less. He looks self-satisfied, as if he might be a menace to women, meaning them no good. Ever since the divorce, ever since Sonia's remarriage, he has been taking his revenge. Her fault, both technically and morally, yet there is something unattractive about a man who divorces his wife on principle, because she has been unfaithful to him, when with a little magnanimity it could all have been settled. Whereas he had to punish her by making public the adultery.

I liked Sonia, so beautiful, so witty. There was never any intimacy between us, but I enjoyed her flying visits. She made me feel younger, although we had nothing in common. I was always a dull woman, and she was prestigious, with something a little unreal about her, as if her status and her beauty and the private income she had always enjoyed protected her from knowing painful truths. But they gave her a certain grace. I admired her. She never quite neglected me, although she was certainly of no use in any practical sense. Those flying visits of hers cheered me up, but when the visits became even more flying and even more brief I thought nothing of it, until the day when she rushed in, and after a few breathless enquiries, said she must use the bathroom and came down smelling of scent, saying she was late for a meeting with a friend.

That was her only clumsiness; ordinarily she was very graceful, knew how to organize these matters. That little trail of excitement gave me pause. Nick was unapproachable at this time. He took the whole matter more seriously than I did, than any of us did. And he found out, of course, because Sonia had no concealment in her. She was in love: that was what he could not forgive. So they divorced, much to my regret, and eventually she married again, not the man who caused the divorce but someone much older, to whom she was an ornament and an entertainment. And we lost touch:

I never blamed her. It was a sort of tact in her, although I missed her. Nick has borne a grudge ever since, as if he has it in for all women. It is high time he married again. I imagine he is not short of companions, whom he treats jocularly, without compassion. He defends himself against hurt, but what sort of a man is frightened of being hurt?

She heaved herself to her feet, collected the few glasses and plates which were left and took them out to the kitchen. She put the remaining canapés on a clean plate and went back with them into the drawing-room.

'You might finish these,' she said. 'We are only having scrambled eggs. I couldn't think of anything else. The kitchen is still in a state of siege.'

'What I meant was,' she said, seating herself again, as if reluctant to leave this important subject, 'that good women are an investment that many men refuse to make. Why should this be?'

'Don't hedge, Mother. You are talking about one particular good woman, as you call her, and I refuse to be drawn.'

'There is lipstick on your handkerchief,' said Mrs Marsh sharply.

'Blame yourself for that, Mother. There was no other way I could say good-night, knowing that I never wanted to see her again.'

'I dare say you insulted her, when she is so obviously virtuous.' A virgin, was what she meant to say, but it seemed too unkind.

'It is the obviousness that I object to,' he said.

Prudently, each observed a short silence. Neither wished to be drawn. Nick was uncomfortable, feeling vaguely in the wrong, but only because his mother made it clear to him that in this matter she opposed him. It was so rare for him to be admonished by his mother. For the rest he could not see that there was anything about which he need feel guilty. He had cancelled so many women with a kiss: in his view it signified that he did not wish to take matters further, the kiss itself conveying recognition of the woman's appeal. He thought of it as a form of chivalry, a way of saving both their faces. He saw no harm in it, rather the contrary. A man in his position – in any position – owed it to himself to make his intentions clear. It was even more important to make his lack of intentions clear, otherwise there might be telephone calls, invitations of an unwelcome nature which he must answer with a more brutal refusal. He had always known that he lacked a certain grace. He had inherited something of his mother's rectitude but simply misapplied it. Consequently he mishandled most emotional situations, cut them short, laughed at them, or refused to forgive. With a little more finesse he could have retained his wife. Yet he did not see how he could have continued to live with her after what he considered to be her unforgivable lightness. He thought of her a great deal, with regret, but also with rage. No woman, in his opinion, merited consideration after the suffering she had caused him.

The trouble is, thought Mrs Marsh, that people continued to think in terms of love and marriage as the great adventure, when there were so many more important matters, like work and death and the existence or non-existence of God. It was death which preoccupied her now: her work as a magistrate, which she had greatly enjoyed, was long over, and God, despite her repeated and fruitless attentions, refused to show His face, and must for ever keep His own counsel. How was death to be faced? More urgently, how was it to be managed? Who would find her if she died in her own bed, as she hoped to do, and get in touch with the children? Mrs Duncan had a key, but if she were going to die while Mrs Duncan still called three times a week she had better get it over and done with straight away, before Mrs Duncan went off to the Isle of Wight. Despite the difficulty presented by the arrangements she knew that she would not fight death when it came. On these quiet evenings, when there was no sound from the street, when neighbours as elderly as herself remained prudently indoors, she would switch off the television or the radio, lean her head back, and think of the past, not her adult past, when she was a married woman with small children, but the remote past, when she had a mother and a father and a nurse and was lovingly cared for. She saw faces which she had never consciously remembered: the grocer in the village shop, whose wife was immensely fat and somehow disabled, or a friend of her mother's, whose lavish kisses and lovely violet scent had always delighted her, or the gardener with his toothless mouth to whom, as a small child, she used to sing, in the hope of bringing a smile to his face – all gone, all dust now, yet imprinted on the memory in a way which was out of all proportion to their importance in her life. Never beautiful, never attractive, always too tall and too thin, she had nevertheless led the sort of life a young girl of good family was supposed to live, had married at a suitable age a suitable man and in due course had had suitable children.

When had it all disintegrated, so that now at eighty-one, nearly eighty-two, she sat alone in a gloomy flat on a quiet street, with children who were no longer children but complex adults, whose secrets she sensed but could not understand? Why did Philippa not produce her lover for her mother to welcome and examine? Why did Nick not love openly and whole-heartedly and perhaps bring children into the world? At night, in her bed, which in truth she never wanted to leave, she mentally urged her children on, with something of her old irritation, so that she could leave them to their fate and get on with the business of dying. She was half-beguiled by those images of dead faces which came unbidden into her mind, was even intrigued by the possibility that their owners, now forgotten, might be her guides into the next world, that in fact one did not go to join one's loved ones but rather a random selection of all the people who had ever figured in one's own life, on however temporary a basis. In the same way that she saw the face of the grocer, or smelled the violet scent of her mother's friend, Dolly, she might suddenly and without warning see a Chinese vase, one of a pair which had stood on the landing, or the shape of an ivory-handled fruit knife as it lay beside her plate on the family dinner table. Both vase and fruit knives had disappeared from her life decades ago, had vanished from sight long before she left her parents' home to get married, yet here they still were, in her consciousness, as if they had never gone away. And even a metal spoon, which the cook used to skim the fat from the soup . . . In many ways, in those dark hours, she longed to relax her hold on what life she had left and let these images come unbidden into her mind, to do with her what they would. They were so painless, so benign! She hoped that her husband had had similar visitations in the hours when he lay dying. His lips had moved in a faint smile at the end: she had leaned forward over his hospital bed, pressed his hand, and then he was gone. For this reason she had not grieved for him unduly, feeling obscurely that he had gone to a safe place.

'You're very quiet, Mother.'

She glanced up in surprise, and saw that her son was looking at her with some concern.

'I believe that this evening has tired you. Would you like me to clear off and leave you in peace? Your woman can get rid of all this, can't she?'

She took no notice. 'Go and sit at the table,' she said, as she had done when he was a child. 'The eggs won't be a moment. And I'll make some coffee – we could both do with some.'

She went into the kitchen. Of course, she thought, that's what I meant to consider. That was the real item on my agenda. And now I've left too little time and he will be annoyed if I mention it. He will be annoyed anyway: he finds me something of a nuisance these days. But there is so little time left for discussions of this nature that I may have to risk it.

'Eat your eggs while they are hot,' she said. 'And there are stewed pears if you want something afterwards. I'm

75

sorry there's nothing more substantial. I hope you filled up with the smoked salmon. I thought it all went quite well, didn't you? But quite a shock, all the same. One sees these people vaguely all the time, and expects them to go on being the same, whereas some of them looked terrible. Arthur Hoskyns, for example. You don't know him, of course. And Phyllis Martin was leaning on her stick all the time. Normally she only uses it when she goes out. Still, they all made the effort. If only it didn't leave such a mess.'

'Your woman is coming tomorrow, isn't she?'

'And that's another thing. She could easily have stayed on and cleaned up this evening, but, no, she has to offer to come in for an extra morning tomorrow. It seems to me that I am paying her a great deal of money for not very much, but as she keeps telling me it is all going towards something, a new set of towels or saucepans for her house. I told you about her plans, didn't I? So enterprising. But I do rather object to the expense.'

'You've got the money, Mother. And now you've got the help.' Enjoy it while you can was the sentence that came unbidden into both their minds; neither, however, was rash enough to speak it out loud.

'You may smoke,' said Mrs Marsh, who loved the smell of a cigar. She looked fondly but critically at the blue-jowled face opposite her, its lips puckering as it drew in the first lungful of smoke which emerged again heavy and fragrant. She could see that he was attractive to women, with that suggestion of ease and also of mastery, as if he would be easy to please, but only when he got his own way. Why would a woman not want to please such a man? For she did not think, much as she loved him, that these days he would set out to please a woman. He lacked the humility, thought too much of his damaged pride ever to be eager and hopeful again. Therefore a woman must be found for him who would be so fond and so respectful that she would hardly notice or care if he were not overly fond and respectful towards her

76

lesser self. For in this equation it was her son's happiness which overran all other considerations in Mrs Marsh's mind. Which brought her back to her major preoccupation, the one which she knew would annoy her son but which she must voice before the opportunity slipped away: Anna.

Slightly ashamed of herself, yet with a growing sense of urgency, she thought that if Anna were her daughter-in-law she would be able to die in the full knowledge that attention would be paid. For Anna, with her cloying affection, would be assiduous, telephoning twice a day, visiting regularly, doing shopping, fetching library books, passing on messages. This might be difficult to tolerate, at least until she was finally enfeebled, but in the end she would be grateful. What made Anna so difficult a proposition in the present was that she behaved like a daughter-in-law already, but a daughter-in-law without a husband. It would be difficult to think of Anna as any sort of close relation: she was too unassimilable for that. She was presentable, had been well brought up, well educated, and was virtuous. Ah! That was it! That was what her mind had been telling her ever since her guests had left, and before Nick had come back. She had seen his bitter smile and had not liked it. But there was another problem, one which came in the wake of that secret sardonic smile of his: he had not liked Anna. And if the truth were to be told she did not care for the girl either.

To Mrs Marsh's generation all unmarried women were girls, whatever their age. Yet when she thought of Anna as a girl she thought of a particularly unfortunate sort of girl, the sort of girl she had known when she herself was a girl. Such girls sat out at dances with a bright fixed smile on their faces until somebody's brother was despatched to rescue them. They were girls who saw their chances diminishing, and who showed their panic, determined always to be jolly and to do the right thing. Of course Anna was not like that, was in many ways a sophisticated woman, one who lived alone and managed her own affairs, and had the presence of mind always to look impeccable. Yet Mrs Marsh had only to think of Anna to see the slightly pitted complexion, conscientiously enlivened, see the ardent loving smile, feel the soft lips gliding over her cheek, perceive – and this was curious – a reserve there almost as great as her own. There was the possibility, not so far considered, that Anna's feelings of estrangement mirrored those of Mrs Marsh herself. For I am too temperate in my affections, she thought, and she is used to great and overwhelming devotion. The world must seem a cold place to her, and Nick's secret smile a mockery of all she once felt. She could almost hear the girl say, 'That is not what I'm after,' and aloud she said to her son, 'Will you be seeing Anna again?'

'Why on earth should I?' he said, in some surprise.

'It is just that I feel responsible for her. I thought you might take her out. She is a good woman,' she fatally added.

'Mother, I am delighted that she is a good woman. Delighted for her, delighted for you. I found her a crashing bore. Why do you keep going on about her?'

'I should like to see you marry again,' she ever more fatally stated.

'And you are suggesting that I might marry that bore? Thank you very much.'

She could see that she had annoyed and insulted him, for he must only be offered pretty women, women who knew all the ancient arts, and with whom he did not have to make too much of an effort.

'Of course not,' she said, more weakly than she meant to. 'You may do exactly as you please. You hardly need me to give you permission.'

But he was too annoyed to pay much attention to her, got up and found his coat, drew his scarf round his neck, the stump of his cigar still in his mouth. She thought he looked ruthless, handsome: despite herself she admired him. Of course it would not work, she thought, he deserved a woman as powerful as himself. My dying does not concern him. Why should it?

'We shall have to talk about your affairs another time,'

he said. 'I must leave it for now. I promised to look in on a friend.'

Mrs Marsh thought she knew the sort of friend her son might call upon at past ten o'clock at night: one of the Dianas or Janes he sometimes mentioned, throwing them at her in bulk, as it were, so that she would not suspect any one of them and would thus be still further occluded from his life.

'What will you do about Christmas?' he asked, bending his cigar-smelling face to kiss her.

'Philippa said something about Blakeney. I expect she'll ring tomorrow – I'll ask her then. I do love it there.'

'Good-night, then, Mother. I'll be in touch next week.'

'Good-night, dear. It was good of you to come this evening. I know it was a bore.'

Suddenly she genuinely knew this, saw that he had been charitable, forbearing, a good son. Saw too that she should leave everything to Mrs Duncan and go to the haven of her bed and the comforts of the World Service. Everything was quite simple, after all. She was tired, but she was perfectly well. She had no further thoughts of dying. And as these thoughts receded Anna faded quite naturally from her mind.

The following morning, as Mrs Duncan was Hoovering, Mrs Marsh had two telephone calls. One was from her daughter, Philippa.

'Mother? I thought it went very well, didn't you?'

'Not too badly at all, considering how all my friends are getting old. How was *Don Giovanni*?'

'Sublime. Marvellous performance.'

And are you happy? Mrs Marsh wanted to ask, but remembering the embarrassments of the previous evening preferred not to.

'You're coming to us at Christmas, aren't you? And staying for a bit? We thought we'd go down to the cottage on Boxing Day. Michael will collect you, if you don't want to drive yourself.'

'Oh, I'll take my own car. I'll even take the children, if they can put up with my driving.'

'Terrific. I'll tell them to get in touch. And if you could bring one or two things with you? Some mince pies from M. and S., and one of their Dundee cakes, in case anyone drops in. And some nuts. Dates too: Lucy loves them. I'll check with you next week, shall I?'

Mrs Marsh felt an unaccustomed glow and an access of love for her daughter. To be used, to be useful! It was a feeling she had nearly forgotten. Moving less heavily she went into the kitchen to prepare coffee for Mrs Duncan and herself. She could hear the Hoover whine as it was switched off.

When the telephone rang again Mrs Duncan answered it. She came into the kitchen with a studiedly neutral expression. 'Anna,' she said.

'Anna, my dear, good-morning.'

'Aunt Vera, such a lovely party. I can't thank you enough for inviting me.'

She recognized the soft gushing tones with something of her normal irritation.

'I'm glad you enjoyed yourself,' she said conclusively.

'It was so nice to see Philippa again,' the voice went on. 'And to meet Nick.'

'Ah, yes.'

'He's very attractive, isn't he? You must be very proud of him.'

'Yes.'

'Perhaps a *little* difficult until you get to know him. But awfully nice, really.'

'Yes.'

'And what are you going to do for Christmas, Aunt Vera? I expect you'll want to go to church on Christmas Day. I'll come and collect you, shall I?'

'As a matter of fact, Anna, I shall be going down to my daughter's in Norfolk.'

'Philippa? Oh, how wonderful. I expect you'll have a lovely time.'

80

'And what will you do?'

'Oh, don't worry about me – I've got tons of things to do.'

'In that case I'll wish you a Merry Christmas, Anna. I hope you won't be too lonely.'

There was a pause.

'No,' said the voice eventually. 'I certainly shan't be lonely. Merry Christmas, Aunt Vera.' Then the telephone was put down.

I have angered her in some way, thought Mrs Marsh. But really, there is no need for me to treat her so warily. I expect it is Nick she is really angry with. But in the light of day Nick's imperviousness to Anna seemed more understandable. She really is rather tiresome, thought Mrs Marsh. And one never knows what she is thinking. I am almost frightened of her, she thought, with surprise. But this was so ridiculous that she shook it off and went into the spare bedroom, where Mrs Duncan was putting on her coat, to give her her money and a small present.

'The Isle of Wight for Christmas?' she asked.

'Yes, both the children are coming.'

'I shall be with the family too.'

They preened slightly, enjoying their good fortune. Then, 'Until Friday,' said Mrs Marsh, and shut the door thankfully behind her.

8

Although programmed both to be good and to do good Anna felt at ease only in solitude, when no duties should be required of her. Her nurturing instincts thus in abeyance she could contemplate the future quite calmly and see it for what it was, a long succession of empty days, when no one would call her by her name and ask of her such tasks as she was usually eager to perform. With her mother gone she alternated between loss and hope. When loss prevailed she made herself into a smiling helpmate, although there were few deserving cases, few in real need. For she had known real need and could not excuse the indifference of those she clamoured to help. She knew that they did not love her, found her tiresome, but could not see why she should abandon them for that reason. Only hatred stung her, the hatred of Nick Marsh, of Vickie Halliday. For they had hated her, she knew, hated her bland surface and her patient smile, projecting on to her, as onto a blank screen, their unresolved conflicts, and finding no purchase for their aggressive defensiveness. Or was it defensive aggression? Something sharply sexual in both cases: an avidity, an instinct to destroy, and all disguised by a set of manners which commended themselves in society, good humour, slyness, the intimation of possession, the performance of actual or potential ownership, or the enactment of its opposite . . .

She could see that Nick was a mass of hurt pride, that

he resented the presence at his side of a woman whom he found unattractive, and who was making a clumsy attempt to aspire to companionship. Yet she had seen no way of leaving him: his very rudeness indicated injury, his averted face an awareness of grievances sustained. Her instinct was to put him at his ease, to play the pleasant party game, and, what was more important, to play it innocently, without becoming entrapped by the dubious undercurrents. It was only when she became aware of his impatience, his contempt for her simple and no doubt timid manners, that she had hardened slightly, for she recognized the sexual insult behind his elaborate performance of indifference, and her surprise had turned into anger before she was able to conquer what was for her so excessive a reaction. His final kiss was injurious: there was no doubt about that. Fortunately, no one would ever know about it. She was quite proud of the way she had got out of the car, slammed the door, and walked off without once looking back. Yet her hand, when she had reached for her keys, was trembling, and she was glad there were no witnesses.

Vickie Halliday was another matter, one in which she felt no pangs of conscience. She had always known that Vickie was her enemy, although it had never occurred to her that she herself might be seen in the same light. She had disliked Vickie on sight, by instinct, seeing in her the sexual predator who would inevitably emerge victorious from any engagement, and who had carried off Lawrence Halliday almost without a struggle. Yet surely that was history now: there was no need to indicate, without much subtlety, that she was the wife, the chosen one. Anna remembered the night she had sat alone in the drawing-room in Albert Hall Mansions, after Lawrence had informed her of his forthcoming marriage. She had settled her mother in bed, had kissed her, had said that she was not yet tired, that she would read for a bit. 'I expect you've got a lot to think about, darling,' said Amy Durrant, with tremulous complacency. 'Lawrence stayed a long time this evening, didn't he?' Calmly she had borne away the empty cup which had contained her mother's tisane, and closed the bedroom door behind her.

In the drawing-room she had switched on a single lamp, and then switched it off again: it seemed to her appropriate to sit in the dark, and she had allowed herself this little touch of drama. Besides, she could see quite well in the light of the street lamps, and she was not going to exaggerate her hurt. It was not yet despair. She recognized the rules of the game, saw that in any contest the more brightly coloured of the species would carry off the prize. Simply she was sorry that Lawrence had succumbed to so obvious a woman: she thought less of him for that. Vickie with her permanent air of excitement and suspicion, her urgent little body, her impermeable self-confidence, her air of conveying her understanding of a man's needs, her own greediness . . . Lawrence had looked hapless as he had told her of his plans, almost a victim, as if he were sorry for what he was doing, but was in no way able to change his mind, having been taken over by a will greater than his own. She had behaved simply and with composure, had not expressed surprise, had wished him well. In the drawing-room that night, in the dark, she was grateful for the memory of that dignified parting. It had not been easy. But nothing in her life was easy, and she had had to learn to deal with the constraints. Her mother had had to be kept in ignorance: another constraint. She was proud that she had not caused her mother additional hurt and disappointment. In comparison with her mother's wistful frailty, her exaggerated sensibility, she herself was calm and strong, so calm, throughout the months which followed, that she had felt herself growing immeasurably older, becoming a parent to her own mother, and as if she had no business to think in terms of a marriage of her own, as if whatever feelings she had left must be put on one side. For the duration, she thought, measuring the duration of her mother's life, but in time meaning the duration of her own.

This blind calm, this stoicism, had encountered, at Mrs Marsh's party, a Vickie to whom Lawrence must have made admiring references to Anna Durrant's strength of character. From such exchanges Vickie had retained not the tribute but the admiration, and had been on her guard, even against so humble an adversary. Bad skin, she had noted, no figure to speak of, and in her relief, in her contempt for the woman's evident spinsterhood, she had greeted her with a tone expressing deep commiseration, as if her sympathy were not only manifest but entirely natural, and appropriate in the circumstances. If others noted this, so much the better. But Anna was simply bemused: why was Vickie so anxious? And was it not strange to affect such a tone of intimacy in such crowded surroundings? There was an invitation to confidences there to which she had no intention of responding. She sensed that Vickie would be quite happy to have her as an acolyte, a pensioner, provided that an unseen audience would commend her for her generosity: these considerations apart, Vickie's hectically darting eyes conveyed her entire lack of interest. The meaning of this encounter was not lost on Anna, who put any discomfort felt on either side down to the fact that Vickie was some years her junior and had not yet acquired the smoothness of manner necessary in such a context. She recognized also that women of Vickie's temperament cannot deal with unhappiness, even if it is felt by others: she would be hopeless in a bereavement, impatient, urging recovery. 'Look on the bright side,' she would say. 'It was over so quickly, he could hardly have felt a thing.' In the same way she had looked askance at Anna's composure, aware that it was built on unhappiness, an unhappiness in which she herself had played an active part. Hence her dislike.

These thoughts accompanied Anna on Christmas Eve, when she sat at her window looking out at the dark street, now devoid of the slightest signs of life. No passers-by, few cars, everyone safe at home. In upper windows some lights still shone, as reluctant children refused to go to sleep. An empty taxi passed, its wheels greasily indicating recent rain. Rain was forecast for the following day, and for the day after that. Neatly, thoughtfully, she turned away, back into her own living-room, a pleasant room, with its striped taffeta curtains and chaircovers, its oval mirror over the fireplace. Never quite warm enough – but she had felt the cold ever since her mother's death. As this was Christmas Eve, and she had no duties on the following day, except perhaps to look in on Miss Carter (who would not be pleased to see her), and to invite her neighbour, Eric Harvey, for a cup of coffee, she would allow herself the supreme luxury of a sleeping pill, one of a dwindling stock given to her after her mother's funeral. These represented a problem: soon she would have to obtain another supply. For she could not now do without them; they made all the difference between loss and hope. On days following her nights of natural sleep she would feel weighed down by her deficiencies, shackled to the past, but after a sleep of artificial depth and duration she would not be able to suppress a certain childish expectancy. For who was now to cast her down? She was free, she was healthy, she had survived. She would feel buoyed up, a lightness in her step. And the anticipation of such a state was part of the benefit of the medication itself, to which she attached a small ritual. Bathed and cleansed, her hair down, she would prepare the cup of camomile tea with careful gestures, and then, seated on the side of the bed, she would place the tiny pink pill on the back of her tongue and take a sip of the hot tea. It always went down easily. She thought it entirely anodyne, as perhaps it was. And even if it is habit-forming, she thought, what of it? I have no other bad habits.

Her waking was beautiful. If she had any regrets they were for the darkness of the windows, the earliness of the hour. On such a day – Christmas Day – she could have slept until ten had she wanted to. But she was always early: that was seemingly inevitable. The day stretched before her, endlessly, yet she was not unhappy. She looked at the luminous dial of her clock: five forty-five. Presently she would make tea and bring it back to bed, perhaps even stay there. But she knew that once she was awake her bed would soon become intolerable. Reaching for her dressing-gown she got up and went to the kitchen, aware, as she had been on the previous evening, of the oppressive silence of the streets.

The hours promised to be long. When she could stay in bed no longer, she pushed back the covers, collected her teacup, ran a bath, and tried to visualize the coming day. Dressed, she sat down to breakfast at half-past seven, the windows still black. The chemical benefits of her beautiful night's sleep had bestowed on her a very slight optimism, even amusement. She would go through the charade of this day, she decided, but without taking it too seriously: it would be under-populated, devoid of conversation, but otherwise no worse than any other. She had never been sentimental about Christmas. She and her mother had exchanged gifts – usually exquisite, usually expensive – and had then retired to their rooms to dress. Lunch had been a mild affair, a roast chicken, salad, cheese, a little fruit. In the afternoon her mother rested, while Anna went for a walk. They came together again for tea, after which they read or watched television. Fatal alliance! There was no strain, no frustration, no untoward longing for other company. They had enjoyed a day of rest and were in perfect harmony.

This harmony was something which she was still able, as now, to recapture. But the long days she found wearisome, and the even longer winter, and the bad light, and the absence of conversation. Then the marvellous thought struck her: but there is no need to live like this! She was, by her careful standards, a fairly rich woman. She was not bound to this flat, which was never warm enough, to this house, to this silent street. She could escape; escape was within her means, and she need explain herself to no one, need not offer excuses or explanations, since no one would be curious enough to make enquiries. She could live in Paris, near Marie-France; she could go south to the sun. Excited, she began to make plans. A season in Paris to begin with: she could revive that almost extinct plan of research, begun so long ago, and dwindling into insignificance in the light of more urgent matters. And perhaps she would look up those old friends who had been her lovers, thirty years ago. There had been much sweetness there, no rancour; they had met as equals. Long walks beside the Seine, or in the gardens at Versailles, would end in a simple meal, and then a walk home, arm in arm. She would meet them now as adults, and they would remember their youth, and then say a fond goodbye, glad to have been reminded of each other. She would walk by the Seine, alone now, but no longer lonely. The possibilities were infinite. Then she would take the train to Nice and spend some days warming her chilled mind and body, until she felt free and lively again. She saw a southern market in her mind's eye, its colours, its promise of plenitude and of health. She would rent a flat and stay there until it got too hot (but could it ever get too hot?) and then move back into the green heart of France, perhaps to Bourges, until she found a town or a village in which she might want to live. A house, this time, on a street, with big windows, through which she would hear the sound of bells. She looked out of her own windows in Cranley Gardens, and laughed at the pretence in which she was somnolently imprisoned: one crawling taxi, coming off duty, grey dusky air, a light sprinkling of damp, and in the distance the mournful sound of a car on a wet road. Good-humoured now – for even if nothing came of it the fantasy would have served its purpose – she got up, put the flat to rights, and carefully made up her face. The day no longer held any terrors for her.

At ten o'clock she rang the bell of the neighbouring flat. There were two on this floor, and she was on nodding and greeting terms with Mr Harvey, who had her spare key, as she had his. A small neat meek man, some years into retirement, he was the ideal neighbour, virtuous, discreet, and silent. Sometimes she thought that she would have welcomed a more forceful presence, but this man, with his bald head, his short neck, his short legs, and his high round stomach, was peaceable, did not object to her radio, and kept his own television sound fairly low, wincingly aware that behind the party wall there lurked a presence which registered his own. Their relationship was built on caution; neither desired to know the other particularly well. Anna thought that a brief seasonal gesture might be offered, had indeed arranged a tray in readiness, with her mother's best coffee cups and some shortbread biscuits, but Mr Harvey came to his front door wearing an overcoat, a faint additional flush of animation on his submerged cheekbones, the surrounding flesh strongly perfumed. Beyond him, in the hall, she could see two plastic carrier bags filled with small parcels wrapped in Christmas paper.

'So kind of you, Miss Durrant, but I am just off to my sister in Mill Hill. Was there anything I might do for you? I expect to be out all day, but I shall be back this evening. Can I give you a lift anywhere? But perhaps you are not going north?'

'No,' she said. 'I am going to Brompton Square, and I think I'll walk.'

'Oh, but I could easily drop you off at Brompton Square.'

'No, please don't bother. I should like the walk. I hope you have a pleasant day.'

'You're sure there was nothing you wanted?'

'Perfectly sure, Mr Harvey.'

She could see that he was becoming agitated, fearful that he might have annoyed her, yet agonizingly aware that every minute spent in her company made him late for his sister, whom he had promised to take to church. The dilemma was resolved by Anna's wishing him a Merry Christmas, and turning back to her own flat. He heard her door close and waited a prudent five minutes: another meeting would be embarrassing. When he judged the coast to be clear he silently opened his door, took his carrier bags, crept out, and then recklessly pulled the door to and locked it with a flourish. Anna, standing behind her own front door, hands in pockets of her raincoat, registered that the coast was clear and smiled with relief. This day was to be full of surprises:

her own hilarity, Mr Harvey's embarrassment, and above all the enriching fantasy of escape. Unfortunately there was little she could do to implement this at (she checked her watch) ten twenty on a lowering Christmas morning. She had no cooking to do: she had nothing much of anything to do, and she was too restless to read. That left Miss Carter, in Brompton Square. She was grateful to her for providing a suitable excuse to offer Mr Harvey. Miss Carter, in this instance, was her alibi.

Miss Carter had been her mother's dressmaker, not a very good one, but invaluable in Amy Durrant's later years when she could no longer go out to the shops. It was Miss Carter who had taught Anna to make her own clothes, and had then jealously withdrawn her favour. She had insisted on a monopoly of Mrs Durrant's needs, and they had not liked to deprive her of her visits, of the cup of tea and the glass of sherry, and of her frequently angry outpourings. Miss Carter was endemically angry, sometimes for no reason they could divine, but although quite old, in her late seventies, was still useful if hems needed to be taken up or buttons to be changed, small tasks which she was happy to undertake. A dry spry woman, with badly tinted black hair, she had been on the stage as a girl, and had on one occasion shared a dressing-room with Jessie Matthews. Now she lived in a basement in Brompton Square, and still did occasional work for increasingly elderly patrons.

She had turned up at Amy Durrant's funeral, dressed in black from head to foot, and had seemed so badly affected that Anna had invited her back to Albert Hall Mansions afterwards, when the few mourners had dispersed.

'I'll make some coffee,' she had managed to say, warming her frozen hands, and longing for someone else to take over. 'Or would you rather have a drink?'

Two glasses of whisky later Miss Carter had seemed disposed to stay for the afternoon, but Anna had pleaded a headache, and her visitor had reluctantly got to her feet. 'I shall miss her,' she had said accusingly. Anna had patted her arm, seeing tears in the small eyes. 'I'll keep in touch,' she had said, although she knew that Miss Carter had no affection for her. And now here she was, keeping in touch, just in case Miss Carter should lack for anything on this festive morning. She had bought her a tin of biscuits, and a plant, and felt ashamed that nothing more lavish had come to mind.

The windless air made walking almost a pleasure, although the sky was low and grey. Once past South Kensington there was a little more animation in the streets, although the day seemed preternaturally calm, vowed to silence. In Brompton Square a stray balloon was tied to a railing, and there were a couple of empty lager cans in the gutter. Otherwise it was as still as Pompeii. Miss Carter's basement door opened very slightly on to Miss Carter's suspicious eye; they took stock of each other over the chain which she kept fastened day and night. 'Oh, it's you,' said Miss Carter finally. 'I suppose you'd better come in.' The door closed and opened again, giving Anna time to ponder the cause for Miss Carter's animosity. But it had always been there, she reflected: Miss Carter had always been a contentious woman. It was her devotion to Amy Durrant which had stood her in good stead. But that is over now, thought Anna. And really it need no longer concern me. Her smile, as she handed over the biscuits and the pot of hyacinths, was kindly, for the reality of Miss Carter was beginning once more to be obscured by her earlier vision of the south, made all the more radiant by the darkness in which Miss Carter chose to live, sacrificing everything to her cats and their comfort, keeping the fire burning at all hours, turning out bags of scraps for them to play with, jealously loving them, as she did now, one clasped tightly to her face, the other occupying the seat of the chair on which Anna had supposed she might be invited to sit.

'Were you on your way somewhere?' enquired Miss Carter. 'Only we don't often see you round this way.'

Although obviously anxious for Anna to leave she thought it politic to blame her for not coming sooner. She was more timid than anyone knew, and was really only comfortable when undisturbed. This pleasantly smiling woman was a nuisance. She had never had much time for her.

'I just wondered how you were going to spend your day,' said Anna. 'Yes, don't worry, I must be off in a moment. Will you be all right?'

For she recognized a lonely person when she met one.

'Don't you worry about me,' said Miss Carter indignantly. 'I'm invited out! Upstairs, on the ground floor. Christmas drinks, eleven thirty. Then I shall come back here, and me and the girls will have our lunch.'

'You'll be all right on your own?'

Miss Carter took her time. 'I think my time will be adequately filled,' she said. She was by now furious. This was habitual. Amy and Anna did not know, but they suspected, that Miss Carter was ashamed of her excesses, and frequently went home to clasp the older of her two cats and weep into its fur. 'I don't want to hurry you,' she said, feeling the slow onset of shame, 'but I want to get changed.'

'Of course.'

'Nice of you to come. Thank you for the biscuits.'

The cat darted off the brown velvet cushions and made for the front door.

'Don't let her get out,' cried Miss Carter, scooping the heavy body into her arms.

'Goodbye,' they said. 'Goodbye,' as if for the last time. Before Anna turned to make her way up the basement steps she heard the sound of the chain being replaced.

Resigned now to the empty day, but still strangely comforted by her earlier thoughts, she turned into the park, where a few determined joggers were to be seen. She walked now to tire herself, so that she could go home and stay indoors with a good conscience. She walked for a couple of hours until the rain started. Bleak, bleak, she acknowledged, under the leaden sky, with the steady rain soaking her hair, but I never need spend another winter like this. Even if the weather is bad elsewhere it need never be as cheerless as this. Around her the park emptied, as the joggers and the men with dogs went home to their lunch. Tired now, and wet, she turned towards the Alexandra Gate and into Exhibition Road. The last mile seemed very hard, and she fancied that the sky was darkening towards evening, although it was not yet two o'clock.

In the flat she took off her wet clothes, and made tea. An afternoon to oneself, she thought, would be luxury for some: I shall make it so for me. She boiled two eggs for her lunch, but could only eat one: she felt as if a yellow stain were hardening on her lips. She tried to recapture her earlier vision of the village street on which her house would stand. She washed up, averting her eyes from the traces of egg yolk on her plate, then went into the bathroom and washed her hair.

In her dressing-gown, her hair spread over her shoulders, she sat listening to a concert on the radio and felt almost at peace, but dangerously so, as if waiting for death. It was now quite dark. She got up and pulled the curtains, brushed away a speck of dust from the arm of her chair, then went to her bedroom to put up her hair and to dress, in her peacock-blue suit, in case anyone called. This day would end, like all the others, and she would look back in pity at the person who had endured it. She made tea, forced herself to eat a few biscuits. Sweet food was easier to swallow. Yet she was in perfect health, untroubled by her body, as she supposed few women of her age had any right to be. Extreme discipline kept her in check, while demons, she knew, circled and waited. But she had been given this dispensation of a calm temperament, and had outwitted many a fear.

When she judged it late enough she prepared for bed, her chosen moment. It was understood that she would take another pill tonight. That left only two. To obtain more she would have to see Lawrence Halliday. The inevitability of this thought brought warmth to her cheeks, made the prospect of other days like this less onerous. One to one, she thought, without those others. Suddenly, Nick Marsh,

Vickie, even Mrs Marsh, seemed to her a band of grotesques. The beautiful peace began to loosen her limbs, and she lay back on the pillows, a smile of anticipation on her face.

9

Mrs Marsh, in Blakeney, fell heavily, and cut her knee on the stone step of her daughter's cottage. Hauled to her feet by Philippa and Michael she appeared dazed and fretful, more concerned with the state of her lacerated stocking than with what might have caused her accident. They took her indoors and sat her in an armchair, wondering aloud whether to call the doctor, when, 'Don't *fuss*, Philippa,' said Mrs Marsh in her normal voice, to their great relief.

'What was all that about?' asked Philippa, a little too heartily.

'Your new doormat,' retorted Mrs Marsh. 'Must have skidded away from the tiles. I should have warned you about that. Better to weight it down at first. Well, at least nothing's broken.'

But she was glad that Philippa was there, and would have stayed in her chair, resting for a little, had not Michael said, 'You'd better get that stocking off, Gran, or it'll stick. I'll help you upstairs – lean on me.'

Philippa, seeing the two tall figures humping slowly up the stairs, thought how old her mother looked. She quickly assembled bandages and antiseptic and hurried after them. Later, seated downstairs again, the knee thickly bandaged and forming a bulge under a clean stocking, Mrs Marsh was silent, reviewing in her mind the consequences of her fall if she had been alone. Uppermost in her thoughts was the fear

95

of burdening her daughter, of being an embarrassment to her grandson: she had felt ashamed of her thick torn stocking, and had no desire to reveal more of her heavy underclothes. The disgraces of old age were best kept to oneself. She felt an unaccustomed warmth across her forehead, the vestiges of a retrospective blush, and longed to be in her own bed at home, with her radio for company, rather than in Philippa's guest room, with its sloping ceiling and its window that did not quite close.

'We'll go back to Norwich in the morning, if you're feeling up to it,' said Philippa.

'Actually I'd rather go home,' said Mrs Marsh. 'I'll have to go eventually, so I might as well go tomorrow, if Michael wouldn't mind driving my car.'

'You can't be on your own,' objected her daughter.

'What absolute nonsense. I'm not ill. I took a toss, that's all. And you're not to come fussing up to London. I'll call the doctor, if I need him. Don't look so worried,' she added, regretting that she had never made a habit of endearments, for she felt unconsciously fond and regretful, as if she were seeing Philippa for the last time. 'I'm a tough old bird.' Indeed I am, she told herself. But she was glad to be helped up the stairs, for all her limbs seemed to have stiffened while she had been resting in the chair.

'You see,' she said, forcing a little energy into her voice. 'There are no stairs at home. I shan't have to put any weight on it.'

The knee was throbbing now and the bandage felt too tight. In bed, when Philippa had left her, she leaned her head back, and let two hard little tears chase down her cheeks. It is the shock, she thought: delayed shock. What a fool I must have looked. Her one wish was to protect her daughter and her grandson against further unattractive sights. Whatever indignities were to follow she preferred to keep discreetly concealed. She thought she might keep up some sort of pretence of normality until she reached home, and trained all her considerable will-power to that end. Several times, during the following morning, when, leaning on one of Philippa's late husband's sticks, she took a turn round the garden to show them how well she was, she felt the threat of tears once more. She could not remember crying since Nick had announced that he was divorcing Sonia, and those tears had been more of anger than of sorrow, a shameful hurried episode thankfully forgotten. If I were at home, she thought, I could cry all I wanted to, but then being at home I might be more relaxed, less melancholy. I am homesick, she thought with surprise. Homesick for that dark flat which I have never much liked, homesick for my own chair and my footstool, for that brown kitchen teapot which I brought from Pelham Street (Beatrice swore that it made the best tea, and she was right: I often enjoyed a cup in the basement with her), homesick above all for my bedroom, so gloomy in daytime, so comfortingly womblike at night.

'What time were you thinking of starting out?' she asked her daughter, in a tone as light and agreeable as she could manage.

'I thought after lunch, not that there is much of anything left.'

'Why don't we go now? I will give you both lunch at that nice place we passed, the one you recommended. Then I could be home in time for tea.'

'If you're sure . . . In that case I won't come with you. I'll stay here and lock up. Take Michael to lunch by all means, he'd love it. Gran is giving you lunch at the White Rose,' she called to her son. 'Nothing to drink, mind,' she added. 'You're to drive very carefully back to London. Will that be all right, Mother?'

She looked so anxious, a frown creasing her broad fair forehead, that Mrs Marsh once again regretted that she was so undemonstrative a mother.

'Perfectly fine,' she said. 'Thank you for everything. My dear,' she added awkwardly.

In the car her knee throbbed, but she was determined to see this through. She even managed a lamb chop at

97

the White Rose, while Michael ate his way through potted shrimps, salmon fishcakes, and treacle tart. She admired his appetite. A decent fellow, she thought, more to him than to his sister. He has a look of Bill about him. She smiled at him, remembering motoring with her husband in the early days of their courtship. I enjoyed being engaged, she thought: one got out so much.

'Have you had enough, dear?' she asked, finding the endearment easier the second time. 'Then I think we should make a move.'

The rest of the journey was uneventful. She thought she might have dozed a little: certainly her head came up with a jerk as they entered London, in time to notice that the weather was dark and damp, a slight drizzle misting the windscreen. She felt tired and stiff, and wondered how soon she might decently be alone. Michael helped her into the flat, which had a blighted air, as if it had been deserted for some time. The bad light seemed to lay a filter of neglect over her chair, her lamp, her little table: an abandoned library book, with a Christmas card marking her place, lay askew on the footstool, which she now cleared, glancing at the book to see if she wanted to go on with it, and then remembering that she had read it before, feeling nothing but relief, all other considerations secondary.

'Don't let me keep you, Michael,' she said, cheerfully, she hoped. 'I'm fine now. And I expect you're busy this evening.'

'Well, if you're sure, Gran. I might give Sophie a ring. Surprise her – she's not expecting me till the weekend. Take her out to dinner, or something.'

No, that is not a good idea, thought Mrs Marsh. Ground rules should be observed, and he was still a novice at the game. But perhaps this Sophie was a good girl, if there were any left, and would be pleased to be surprised in this way. In any event the treat which she had promised herself ever since the previous painful evening – a cup of tea from her old cook Beatrice's brown pot – could not be postponed any longer. She felt restless at the thought of having to wait for it, and it was with a slightly distracted affection that she saw Michael to the door. Left alone, her face sagged, and she had to rest in her chair for a while before she could summon up the energy to make her way to the kitchen.

Her night was agitated. She woke several times and had to get up: feeling her way into her bedroom, and unsteady on her feet, she knocked over her glass of water. Back in bed, but lying rather awkwardly, she could hear the last drops pattering on to the carpet. And Mrs Duncan was in the Isle of Wight until the following week, she remembered. She promised herself that she would review the situation in the morning, but the morning dawned dark and discouraging, and she felt too tired to get up. Dragging herself to the bathroom she was shocked by the sight of her grey face and wild hair. A very slight return of pride forced her to get dressed and even to make her bed: she was not sure whether she could face another night like the one she had previously endured. The arrival of *The Times* cheered her slightly, and she managed to make tea and a slice of toast for her breakfast. Then she left her plate and cup in the sink, hobbled into the sitting-room, and waited for the day to begin.

She sat down heavily, propped her leg on the stool, and, through the bandage, palpated her knee. It did not seem to be any worse, was, if anything, less swollen and less sore. The trouble was that she felt rather unwell in herself: a generalized ache, a coldness, which made her rather fearful. There was no one she could call. Nick was in Hong Kong on business, and in any event she would not wish him to see her like this. Her neighbours were too decrepit to carry shopping, although she did not think she would want to eat much; there was a tin of soup in the larder which would do for her lunch. Perhaps it would be wise to call the doctor, just to reassure herself. There was nothing she really needed, and yet the length of the day before her left her disheartened. Still only nine o'clock . . . And she found that she could not settle to *The Times*, which she put aside for the evening, when she might be able to concentrate a little better, and she had quite rejected the library book, which she did not wish to read again, and she had no hope of getting to the library. It was then that she thought of Anna. Anna might be problematic in herself but she would certainly be an excellent person to perform a few small tasks, a little shopping, a change of books, the newsagent (she would treat herself to *Country Life*). She would not want her around for company: indeed Anna was too odd, too uncomfortable for that purpose. But Anna was used to performing such small tasks as these, and would no doubt be grateful for the opportunity to perform them once again. Mrs Marsh hauled her bag on to her lap, found her diary and her glasses, and eventually the slip of paper on which she had noted down Anna's telephone number. Within seconds the remote voice answered her own. She could almost imagine that she saw the abstracted, almost archaic smile. 'But that is not what I am looking for,' she thought, as if the thought had been transmitted from Anna's head into her own, and she made her voice sound warmer than usual, because the fear which she had banished by the act of getting up and getting dressed now threatened to return, and she found herself anxious for company.

'Anna? It's Vera Marsh. I hope I don't disturb you?'

The silence at the other end seemed dreamy, as did the voice when it spoke.

'Aunt Vera! How nice to hear from you. How are you?'

'I'm well, but I had a silly fall when I was down at my daughter's, and I think I'd better stay put for a couple of days. I was wondering if you'd be kind enough to . . .'

'But of course.' The voice sharpened, became competent. 'I'll come at once. Have you called the doctor?'

'No, I don't think I need a doctor. I'm a strong woman, always have been.'

'Call him,' said the voice, warmer now. 'He'll just be starting his surgery; he can come round afterwards. It's the sensible thing to do. You probably need a couple of good nights' sleep to get over the shock.'

'You may be right,' said Mrs Marsh humbly. The pleasure of being taken in hand was gratifying, but alarming. Is it to be downhill all the way now, she thought, no more independence, no more cherished little habits, little eccentricities, no more quiet brooding life with my own thoughts, my own silence? She felt the onset of tears once again, took the stick which she had brought up from Philippa's, stumped into her bedroom, and wiped a swathe of pale pink powder over her face. She looked round the room: the water, she was glad to note, had disappeared into the carpet and left no trace. She wiped up the few drops on the bedside table with one of Bill's handkerchiefs which she stuffed into the sleeve of her brown pullover. She congratulated herself on having made the bed. But she did not look forward to the coming night, and she hoped that the doctor might be persuaded to leave her a sleeping pill, or a prescription which Anna could take to the chemist. She prided herself on never using sedatives, but with the memory of the previous night's nightmares fresh in her mind she was prepared to make a temporary concession. Just for once, she thought, putting down the telephone. The doctor would be with her as soon as possible.

Anna, when she came, was flushed, almost attractive. She took off her raincoat, revealing a cashmere sweater of palest cream, and a tan tartan skirt: a strong and agitated smell of gardenias filled the room. Mrs Marsh, restored to something of her usual authority by the presence of another human creature, noted Anna's extreme thinness, resolved to speak to her about it, flapped her hand slightly in the direction of the scent, and, suggesting a cup of coffee, prepared to endure Anna's company for the price of the pleasure of being waited on.

'Did you ring the doctor?' asked Anna, coming in with a tray. She had found a packet of biscuits from somewhere, or maybe she had even brought them.

'He's on his way. I wonder if I might ask you to change my books for me? And I suppose I should eat something, although I'm not in the least hungry. If you could get me some eggs, perhaps. And bread, of course. Milk. Tomatoes, perhaps. A few bananas. You see, I only came back last night. If you could let me know how much you lay out . . . Or take my purse.'

'That won't be necessary,' said Anna, with her maddening smile. 'Do you want me to go now? Or shall I wait?'

'No, go now,' said Mrs Marsh, who had no desire to reveal her leg to Anna when the doctor came. In her mind the doctor – any doctor – did not count as a man, and could therefore be allowed to witness her physical disgrace, but the presence of another woman could be critical (she could imagine the younger woman's eye on her thick rolled down stocking, on the ugly old-fashioned suspenders) and she was anxious to get her out of the flat. She was grateful to her for coming, but felt something like the onset of her old impatience. The girl's forbearing smile, her way of standing with her ballet dancer's feet in the third position, her clasped hands, like those of Seurat's *Poseuse*, were beginning to annoy Mrs Marsh, who was anxious now for the doctor's visit.

'If he leaves a prescription you could perhaps get it later,' she said. 'I should be so grateful to have the books as soon as possible. I am lost without something to read. If you could get me a couple of biographies, nothing too political. Perhaps something to do with the theatre, or travel. I'm sure you'll think of something.'

Alone, she had time to hobble to the bathroom, and to hobble back to her chair. The leg was notably less stiff, but she still felt chilled. When the doorbell rang she started, but got up eagerly, looking forward to the treat of a masculine presence.

'So good of you to come,' she murmured. 'I had a silly fall . . . Won't you take off your coat?'

The graceless stocking was once again rolled down, the crude and unravelling bandage discarded. Mrs Marsh looked down on the fair head bent over her knee. An attractive man, she thought, although he will lose that hair fairly soon. It is already thinning on the crown. He looks as young men used to look in the early days of the war, when they were so handsome and so brave. Not that this one is brave: he has a troubled look. I believe Phyllis Martin told me that he comes from somewhere in the Midlands, although there is no trace of an accent. Impossible to tell where he went to school. About the same age as Nick, perhaps a year or two younger. Yes, definitely attractive: the women must be falling over themselves. Not that there's much chance of anything there. He longs for a quiet life, I should think. Not a happy man, perhaps. Beautiful hands.

'Does that hurt?' asked Lawrence Halliday, raising his eyes, meeting Mrs Marsh's amused glance, and blushing.

Mrs Marsh was restored to good humour by this exchange. He must have read my thoughts, she told herself, or else he is beset by women. She felt cheered by this evidence of a spark of life still in her: her face relaxed, and a little warmth came into her cheeks.

'No, it doesn't hurt,' she said, with all of her old brisk-ness. 'If you could just strap it up for me, that will do nicely. Oh, and if you would be so kind as to leave me a couple of sleeping pills? I shall be as right as rain tomorrow.'

'I'll leave you a prescription. Can you get someone to go out for you?'

'Oh, yes, I have a friend coming. Do forgive me for not offering you coffee. And thank you for coming. You've put my mind quite at rest.'

And he has, she thought with surprise, watching him shrug himself into his coat. Good figure, she noted, and still neat around the waist. That hangdog air must stand him in good stead, as if women were to be his ruin, or as if he were waiting to be punished. I doubt if he is happily married: his wife seems shrill. But then she probably has a hard time keeping an eye on him.

The bell rang. 'I'll go,' he said. 'I'm on my way out anyway. Give me a ring if you're worried about the leg, but you shouldn't have any more trouble. Just rest for a day or two and you'll be fine.' The bell rang again. 'Goodbye now.'

She heard his stifled exclamation, 'Anna! What are you doing here?' heard Anna's composed voice saying, 'Good morning, Lawrence.' That was all she heard before the door banged shut.

'I got you a life of Somerset Maugham,' said Anna, the brilliant flush fading into patches on her cheeks. 'And Noël Coward's *Diaries*. And this album of English landscapes which I thought you'd like. I'm going to make you a little lunch, nothing too heavy. Did Lawrence leave a prescription?'

'I didn't realize you knew him so well,' said Mrs Marsh, remembering the use of Christian names, also the very slight discomfiture in Lawrence Halliday's voice, as if unprepared for the sight of her.

'Oh, yes. After all,' she said, in a reasonable tone, 'he used to look in on my mother. Although we switched to Grantley towards the end.'

'Grantley has since retired.'

'Yes, the two older partners left at about the same time, at least within a year or two of each other. That leaves Lawrence. Dr Halliday, I should call him.'

'I believe he has a young woman joining him, so Phyllis Martin told me. Very wise of him, I should say. The books are excellent, Anna – how I shall enjoy looking at those pictures! I shan't want anything to eat,' she added.

But in the kitchen Anna had grilled some bacon and a couple of tomatoes, and arranged them on toast. She had bought a slice of apple strudel from the bakery counter at the supermarket, and made a pot of strong coffee.

'Why, how unusual,' said Mrs Marsh. 'But aren't you joining me?'

'No, thank you, Aunt Vera, I'll have something later.'

The flush, Mrs Marsh noted, had quite gone, leaving an impression of startling whiteness.

'I'll just clear away. I've cut some brown bread and

butter for later – it's between two plates on the kitchen table. I'll go to the chemist's in a minute. Is there anything else you want?'

'*Country Life*, perhaps,' said Mrs Marsh a little drowsily. She was quite looking forward to a quiet afternoon with her thoughts. Anna could now leave her. It would not be proper to speculate about Anna and the doctor in Anna's presence: it would be too unkind. The poor girl, with her flat figure, blushing like that. As if he would ever look at her! Mrs Marsh was as cruel in her judgements as a woman who has never lost a moment's sleep over a man can be. He would be frightened by a good woman, she thought agreeably. He needed to be taken over, possessed against his will. Ravished, she thought, with a touch of humour. Poor Anna. But then she probably blushed like that whenever a man spoke to her. With Nick, for example, she was just the same. And she is rather tiresome. Very kind, but somehow one can't quite relax when she is in the room with one. A man would find her impossible.

'If you could just put the things through the letter-box,' she said, her eyes half closing. 'And of course you'll let me know how much I owe you.'

She thought she heard, 'That won't be necessary,' felt in the atmosphere that offence had been taken, wondered if she had imagined all or any of this, just managed to remove her glasses and lower them to the side table, and fell into sleep, as if sleep were once more her friend.

When she awoke it was as if she had dreamt the last few days. The room was dark, although when she peered at her watch she saw that it was not yet four. She had an impression of emptiness, of dereliction. Yes, that was it: the flat was empty. Anna had gone, eccentrically, without warning her, as if acting in accordance with a judgement to which Mrs Marsh had no access. No note on the kitchen table, but a tray laid with a cup and saucer, and the bread and butter, as promised, between two plates. Mrs Marsh felt cheered. At last she could enjoy a cup of tea from Beatrice's pot.

And *The Times*, not yet read. She stumped out into the hall, hardly wincing at all. Yes, there was *Country Life*, and a small white box which must contain her pills. Very decent of her, she thought. Poor girl. What an impression of loneliness she gives, and yet she never complains. I shall have to ask her to lunch again, perhaps when Philippa next comes up. Philippa is kinder than I am. But at that moment her kettle boiled, and she gave Anna no further thought.

10

Anna dreamed that she was talking to her mother, who was flushed, animated, and in perfect health. They discussed various matters of an intimate nature, with no constraint on either side. 'I was very attractive to men,' said her mother, with a fine smile. 'Even the doctor . . . And when I was expecting you I did not put on weight. Only a little here.' She touched her breast. 'You will be the same.' In the dream Anna did not protest, for she felt young and strong. 'How lovely to see you looking so well,' she said to her mother. 'Oh, I was always well in those days,' her mother replied. There was something coquettish about her, as if she were still prepared to make conquests.

Then what happened? Mother, what happened? Waking with a violent shudder, she wanted urgently to confront her mother and ask her what had led to her long claustration. But my mother is dead, she thought, with immense surprise. She has been dead for months, and we never had this type of conversation. Was she like this before I knew her? And what had she to say to me? How did the dream end? Why was she so vividly present, when, in the daily life I live now, she is so strikingly absent?

The fine smile which her mother had worn in the dream reminded her disagreeably of the time when Ainsworth had been in residence in Albert Hall Mansions, and the very great strain it had been to keep her face and voice calm in the presence of what she considered to be her mother's folly. Amy Durrant had been rejuvenated by the physical life which had been restored to her, but at the same time it had made her vulnerable, as if she thought it might be withdrawn again at any moment, as indeed it had been. Even Ainsworth had been roused to tenderness by her hectic fragility, though he was a man whose sexual tastes were fairly primitive: he liked to conquer. His contempt for Anna was roused by her nun-like patience about the flat, as if she were determined not to notice the sexual games that were being enacted. To Ainsworth this attitude signified benightedness, to Amy Durrant a precious virginity: in fact it masked disgust, more than disgust, horror. To have to admit the intruder was bad enough: to see her mother so reduced, so grateful was worse. To see her hurry out into the hallway when Ainsworth put his key in the lock, to greet him in silent ardour while closing the drawing-room door behind her so that there should be no witnesses, to whisper, to flush, and to conceal, or to attempt to conceal from her daughter a certain tremulousness, a momentary impression of dishevelment, brought simply to Anna's face a calm smile, as if she had noticed nothing amiss, no change in their relationship, merely another place to be laid at the table, as if Ainsworth were a guest who had turned up unexpectedly, the duration of whose visit was uncertain. She waited on them at table, willing herself to unreflecting service.

'Well, Anna, what have you got for us this evening?' Ainsworth would jovially ask. 'Something delicious, I've no doubt. You've taught her well, Amy.'

He did not quite say that she would make a fine wife for someone some day, for she was already long past the age of youthful encounters, but in general it suited them both to treat her as a child, a virtuous and innocent minor who would be unable to comprehend the violent attraction which they had for each other. For the attraction was violent, even perverse. Shamelessly they touched one another: Ainsworth, passing behind Amy's chair, would bury his face in her neck, while she, her head thrown back, her eyes closed, would surrender, palpitating. Anna, who was sometimes in the room when this happened, could not avoid feelings of shock and sadness. Once, Ainsworth had raised his head from Amy's throat and his eyes had met Anna's. His gaze hardened; he had straightened up, removed his hands from Amy's shoulders, and said, 'We are shocking your daughter.' His dislike was manifest.

Her role was to be a neutral presence, expressing neither disappointment nor disdain. Thus had begun the years of concealment, after so many years of trust. She took to spending the evenings in her room, on the pretext of reviewing her almost extinct research project, and in the daytime she managed to be busy, reluctant to witness her mother's dangerous flightiness, ashamed to be so level-headed in the presence of so much ardour, feeling like a governess or a prison wardress, terrified of what was to come. She knew that her mother was giving Ainsworth money. This was known as 'investing in George's business', and the need for capital was explained by the bankruptcy of his former partner. 'George has virtually had to start again,' her mother said happily. 'But don't worry, darling, your capital is intact.' In reply to her questions as to what George's business actually was, her mother was vague. 'It is a holding company,' she said. 'He has various interests – finance, property . . .'

'I thought he was a wine merchant,' she had said.

'That is a sideline, darling. When he relaunches the company he will put the wine business side of it under management.'

'And whose name will this company be in?'

'George's, of course. Why are you asking me all these questions?'

'Perhaps because you are keeping me in the dark.'

Her mother was indignant. 'There is no concealment, Anna. As I said, your own money is in your name. Perhaps I shan't be able to leave you as much as I had hoped, but you will be well provided for. In fact George was saying to me the other day that he wondered why you didn't try to get some sort of a job.'

'Really? What did he suggest?'

'Well, something artistic. Interior design, or fashion. After all, I'm quite well now, and anyway I've got George to look after me.'

And after your money, thought Anna, whose fears kept her at home, as if George might start selling her mother's jewellery in her absence. For she had never doubted that he was a crook. His very glossiness counted against him. That well-brushed grey hair, those full frank brown eyes that could narrow so suddenly and so suspiciously, the mobile mouth and the plump connoisseur's fingers, that air of pre-emptive bustle, the camel-hair coat flapping open over the well-cut grey suit, the immaculate shirt . . . And where was he going, leaving the house in an aura of scent? For he had sybaritic habits, as if he had been separated from life's pleasures for far too long. Or as if he had suddenly come into money. Sometimes he tried to behave as a family man, inspired by uncharacteristic prudence, but the effect was parodic. Meeting Anna's expressionless eyes his own would, just for an instant, imply a sneer. She understood him very well: he came to be a little afraid of her. For although he had obtained money from Amy Durrant there was much that had to be concealed. Questions would be asked, were already being asked, as to premises, office staff, the registered name of the company, for the Durrants' family solicitor had been strangely obstructive. Telephone calls were made very late at night, yet he received none. And that final day of absence, the front door closing behind him at five in the morning, Amy's explanation that he had gone abroad on business, and even then her utter belief that he would be back . . . Over the ensuing days the belief had changed to bewilderment that there was no word from him, and then to fear that there might have been an accident. Then finally a letter came, in a thin foreign envelope, with no forwarding address. Even that was ambiguous: business in Europe would keep him absent for some time, perhaps indefinitely. Amy was not to think of him again. Perhaps it would be better if they rebuilt their lives separately. He said – and this was strange – that he had loved her. Perhaps he had.

The following day Anna had the locks changed, and went to see the solicitor, who shook his head.

'I'll put a trace on him, of course,' he said. 'But I doubt if much will come of it. I advised your mother against transferring capital, but she wouldn't listen. Fortunately your own money is intact.'

At the sound of the locksmith hammering Amy Durrant had tearfully accused her daughter of enmity, even of jealousy. Then she retired to bed, distraught. It was not until her solicitor called with the grave news that George Ainsworth had previously been imprisoned for fraud, and that his prison record showed him to have been married to a Marguerite Luthier, a Belgian woman, that she gave up hope and entered into her long decline, restored to her unpartnered state and incurably diminished, so that from that day they began to think of her as menaced.

There followed a period of closeness, but it was not the closeness they had previously known, trusting and unreflective. This was the closeness of fear, of impending tragedy. Anna became her mother's nurse, her comforter. Not a word of reproach escaped her, for Amy Durrant's humiliation was too great. Together they confronted the days that remained to them, and now it was to Anna's hand that Amy clung. She seemed to spend her time consumed with grief for her daughter, as if only now conscious of the wrong she might have inflicted upon her. For she could see now that she had been unthinking, that she had been a corrupting influence. Never had her daughter looked so plain, so immature, her slight figure concealed beneath her bright colours, her make-up heightened to cover her paleness. Her odd bedizened appearance was the outcome of an enormous if misplaced courage. Belatedly, her mother knew this, yearned for her, but was too frightened and too ashamed to open the discussion which they had never had, too careful of her daughter's dignity to try to justify herself, too uncertain of the degree of her daughter's experience or lack of experience to trust her possible comprehension, or worse, her look of condemnation. So they had come to an unspoken mutual decision: they would be cheerful, they would be polite, they would love each other unreservedly, but it would not be as it had been before, for there would be shame, and to cover the shame the cheerfulness, the politeness. Neither yielded to confession, and as the months passed, and then the years, they were drawn together by a conspiracy which no one else could ever enter, each determined to protect the other. In Amy Durrant's last days they had lived on an exalted plane: the pact had been kept. Each played a not inconsiderable part: how could they relate their experience to the rest of the world? They had an impression of triumph, of constancy rewarded. Odd and archaic as their bond might have been, their anachronistic and exclusive closeness had somehow seen them through. Amy Durrant's death was easy. Anna had not appeared too stricken, had not collapsed, fallen apart, had a breakdown, as the few people who knew her had predicted, for by that time the circle of their friends and acquaintances had, by their unspoken decision, been voluntarily reduced, and when Anna moved from Albert Hall Mansions it was quite a while before anybody noticed.

She had escaped as from a prison cell, and she was determined never again to be imprisoned. But she was to discover that determination had a great deal to do with it, and that vigilance was needed if she were to enjoy her freedom. She was quite free: her mother's posthumous letter had given her permission to be free, and if she were ever, by the remotest chance, to run across George Ainsworth again she would walk straight past him without acknowledgement, knowing that her mother had nothing more to fear. For the fearfulness of her mother in her later years lingered like a stain in her memory: the physical shrinking that had taken place, her startled reaction if the doorbell rang, the way her lips occasionally moved as if she were talking to someone who was not there, as if she were rehearsing a speech to be made on some future occasion – all this overlaid, perhaps for ever, the earlier natural memories of a loving mother, whom widowhood had restored to her essential innocent self. Why then had her mother appeared, in that curious dream, to be so complacent, so frivolous, so unaware of what had happened to her? To be the girl she must once have been, beyond knowledge, beyond all possible memory?

To break her mother's spell had been the work of a lifetime, and now here she was in yet another disguise to pose additional questions, insinuate further complexities. That strange coquettish look . . . The more she tried to recapture the dream the more she was aware of a certain slyness, a complacency, the look of a woman to whom conquests came easily. This was both relevant and not relevant, in a manner she had yet to decipher. Quite simply, the dream had left her with a headache, as did most of her dreams these days. Only on the nights when she took a pill was she granted sleep without dreams. How she now longed for that chemical sleep, the depth, the totality of it! Such a sleep seemed preferable to life itself, for life was proving problematic.

Nothing had prepared her for the life she seemed called upon to live, a life in which all choices seemed possible but none desirable. She thought fleetingly of the fantasy she had entertained on Christmas Day, of a house on a street in the centre of France, and the bells which would sound through her renewed days and nights, but in fact this fantasy was overlaid by the memory of Christmas Day itself, and the very real grey streets through which she had walked with such determination. For it was, once more, determination which had seen her through that long day, and the remnants of a good-heartedness to which she clung. In middle life, she knew, the feelings wither slightly, rancour and disappointment replacing earlier hope and expectation. And now that she was in middle life herself she must expect a certain

113

coldness to replace the earlier warmth. Yet she rejected the coldness she now felt, thought it pitiful of her to feel no love simply because she herself was unloved, prized the innocence which had not quite left her, mourned her youth only in so far as it had taken a certain whole-heartedness with it. She reminded herself how fortunate she was, of how she might make her freedom work for her instead of letting it weigh her down. Freedom brought with it anxiety, or should do: choices must perpetually be made. Yet lying in bed on a dark morning, with an aching head, she felt in no way enabled to make choices. Her mind would have been easier had she been in the grip of some iron routine. Once more she regretted her comparative idleness. For her previous life had been one of full employment. Such a person as she had once been was now called a 'carer', and no status attached to the work, which was thought to be anonymous. She rejected the label. She had acted out of love and had felt the time well spent. Her present problem was not lack of work but lack of love. With all its complications she had understood her mother's life and had not rejected any part of it. What they had lived through may have been painful, but in a curious way it had been complete, a complete sentimental education. Now she was left with nothing but superficialities, chill acquaintances, doors shutting behind her retreating figure. The onset of self-pity shamed her and gave her the energy to push back the bed-clothes and reach for her dressing-gown.

She raised the window and leaned out, trying in vain to catch the smell of turned earth, to sense an emergent spring, but it was too early in the year: the air was sour, lightless. Yet with the prison of her bedroom behind her her spirits rose a little. She was free, she was well, she could still feel a vestigial enthusiasm for the day. Mrs Marsh might need her again, and again she would strive to please her, knowing that her efforts would somehow always fall short of the mark. She knew, she was sure she knew, that there was goodwill on both sides, but that each thought the other strange, too foreign to the life they had always known to be entirely trustworthy. Each was solitary: that should have been a bond. But Mrs Marsh preferred her solitude, which she filled with the reminiscences of old age, not used to sharing the time with others, having fallen out of the habit, or perhaps having relinquished it with gratitude. Anna could see why this way of life should make Mrs Marsh brusque in manner, but could not devise a set of responses which Mrs Marsh would think in any way appropriate. All that was required of her was a telephone call, to see whether Mrs Marsh needed any more shopping, and in due course she would make that call. It was just that she herself felt so tired, so stale after her bad night that she felt no desire to leave the flat. She told herself that she would feel better once dressed, chose a white silk shirt, a brown cashmere pullover, a narrow brown and white tweed skirt. Surveying herself in the glass she felt mildly restored.

Mrs Marsh, on the telephone, sounded more or less like her old self. It was possible to detect in her tone something of her habitual annoyance.

'Aunt Vera?'

'Oh, Anna.'

'Was there anything you wanted? You sound better than you did yesterday.'

'Nothing, thank you. Philippa is coming up today. She wants me to go back with her, but I'd rather stay here. So difficult to make people understand that.'

Anna laughed. 'People do tend to worry if you're on your own. I'm glad Philippa's coming. Do give her my regards, won't you?'

'Oh, and Anna, thank you so much for being so kind yesterday. I was most grateful. You must come to lunch one day soon, when I'm on my feet again.'

'Of course. I'd love to. But in fact I may be going to Paris in a week or two's time, to see my friend Marie-France. I usually try to go for her birthday. We've been friends for years, ever since I left school.'

'Very nice,' said Mrs Marsh, losing interest. 'Well, I

won't keep you, Anna. You must have a lot to do. Perhaps we'll see each other when you return.'

'Of course. I'll telephone you. And you're sure there's nothing you need? Oh, no, Philippa's coming. Well, good-bye for now, Aunt Vera.'

'Goodbye,' said Mrs Marsh.

So that was all right. The day was hers. She might go out, book a ticket for Paris, although she did not intend to leave for over a fortnight. She might have one of those days of which she had occasionally dreamed in the dark sanctuary of Albert Hall Mansions: a morning looking through her notes, and an afternoon of art galleries and a visit to the London Library. Yet the grey air repelled her, and the sad sound of cars passing mournfully on wet roads. There was something which prevented her from leaving the flat, something which had nothing to do with the dimness of the January day and the silence of this street. She stood at the window for a moment longer than was necessary to survey the weather, then turned and sat down, leaning her head back in her chair. She was still oppressed by the fragments of her dream, now fading, going to join all the other dreams in which her mother appeared to her, sometimes admonishing, sometimes cajoling, always young and pretty. There had been a remark she could not quite recapture, something to do with that same youth and prettiness of which her mother had always boasted. Even when she was quite old a compliment on her prettiness would bring a smile to her face. Yet she had known only two men in her life, one fleetingly, the other disastrously. Perhaps she had missed her true vocation, which was to be cherished by a strong man throughout her lifetime. She had never quite lost her look of expectation, as if that strong man might still appear.

In the dreams she was different, bolder, less scrupu-lous, perhaps. She had alluded to her prowess, which Amy Durrant had never done, would never do. 'I was very attrac-tive to men,' her mother had said. And then something else. Of course, that was it. 'Even the doctor . . . ' How strangely the mind works, she thought. I had no idea that I would telephone Lawrence today, and yet that is what I am going to do. What could be more obvious? I need a prescription; I can no longer waste my life dreaming of my mother. And yet it was she who prompted me, as she would have liked to do had all been as she wished it to be.

It is all quite innocent – I may not even see him. Mrs Marsh said there was a woman doctor joining him. But perhaps it would be nice to see him, to re-establish contact, to show him that there is no ill-feeling. After all, what harm could I possibly do? He is a married man, and I am a spinster whom no one would think to compliment, as they so dutifully complimented my mother. Sleep is what I need, not Lawrence Halliday. But when the receptionist gave her an appointment for that afternoon she was not in the least surprised. The whole episode had the smoothness of a dream, which was where it had had its origins.

Memory now played its part, together with an ambience of shuttered rooms, of lowered voices, of hands fleetingly held. He had been concerned for her, curious about the life she led. Perhaps his concern had been professional, but she had never thought so. In any event the attraction had been kept in check. It was the attraction of the strong for the weak, and she had been the strong one. His dilemma had been quite clear to her: whether to surrender to the comfortable and comforting atmosphere of the flat and its endowments, or to continue to make his way in the world unfettered. He had chosen the world, or perhaps the world had chosen him. Yet his expression, when she had last seen him, had been preoccupied, almost listless, as if the world, in the shape of his wife, were too much with him, as if he missed his original home, with its simplicity and its loving mother.

He was betrayed by his looks, as she was by hers. If life had typecast her as a wise virgin, he was destined, by his irresolute blond handsomeness, to be the prey of women who would be excited by the prospect of appropriating him, not necessarily for his own good. She knew that she was unbending, that in some respects she intimidated him, knew too that when he was away from her he would revolt against the respect he all too obviously felt for her, and would assume a brutality, a boisterousness, which would just as suddenly desert him. Part of him wished nothing more than to be taken in and cared for, as he had once been cared for, in the days before he had embarked upon his arduous upward climb away from his origins, away from earlier simplicities. At other times he felt like a man, with a man's appetites and impatience.

She had known all this, but had not known how to resolve his difficulties for him, or how to bring him to a decision. She had been courteous, gentle. It had even crossed her mind that her apparent sexlessness stood her in good stead, denoting as it did absolute lack of pressure on him. For the decision was his: her own mind was made up. Because of this mistaken attitude the move was never made, and she had subsequently wondered whether she had imagined that he felt for her anything other than admiration. For she had his admiration, that was never in any doubt: she thought that she had his tenderness as well. He felt regret for her, as if at some time in the future, when he had made all his decisions, decisions in which she no longer figured, he might miss her.

She had not changed. The two dramas that had consumed her life had left her intact, as if they had conferred as much as they had taken away. The idea that she might have discarded them, discounted them, seemed to her impossible. She saw that the whole purpose of her existence was to keep affection alive, even at the risk of living imperfectly in the present. She looked forward wholeheartedly to her meeting with Lawrence Halliday. She would say nothing other than what the situation required. Yet she hoped to see in his eyes that look of admiration and of tenderness – now quite legitimate, no longer dangerous – which had once been there, and which she might take home with her, to link her life now as it had been in earlier more hopeful days.

She felt a moment's coldness. I am ridiculous, she thought. Women no longer live like this. They live like Vickie Gibson, or Halliday as she is now, decisively, avidly, indignantly even: they go down into the marketplace, whereas I pay the price of staying out of it. Her exalted mood evaporated, and once again she felt tired and uncertain. She regretted her appointment, and only the prospect of uninterrupted sleep prevented her from cancelling it. In a moment of discouragement she felt her affections slip from her, for which she immediately reproached herself. It occurred to her that her major failing might be an absence of anger: she could not remember ever feeling anything so simple as anger in her life. It is only a visit to an old friend, she told herself, as she pulled on her raincoat. No harm can come of it. But it was a feeling of sadness which accompanied her along the street.

II

Halliday flushed slightly when his secretary showed him his appointment book, with Anna's name in it. This rapid and elusive colouring was a habit he had retained from adolescence, one which signified uneasiness rather than embarrassment. He had flushed when he was introduced to his future wife at a party, this time from a mixture of confusion and dread, for he knew in an instant that he was violently attracted to her, and sensed that she was shallow and more problematic than she appeared at first sight. In a word he knew that he might marry her, for he was lonely and tired of inventing his own amusements when he came home in the evening. He hoped naïvely that a woman might comfort him. Vickie Gibson also flushed when she was introduced to him, but this signified very little, as he came to discover: her emotions were hectic and unreliable, although she possessed in her calmer moments a suave common sense which continued to disconcert him.

After five years of marriage his own emotions had cooled, and he felt lonely again. His physical life was still violent; he sometimes wondered if his wife intended that it should be so for ever. He himself was finding it somewhat of a strain to meet the challenge of his wife's conscientious provocation, her insistence on experiment, her publicly demonstrated assiduity. Privately he put this down to the onset of an early menopause, and wondered whether he would have the patience to deal with it when the time came. He was used, by now, to her juvenility, which caused her to fall into extreme emotional attitudes. If anyone disagreed with her with any degree of firmness, she would flush ominously and bite her lip. Later, in their bedroom, there would be tears, and the familiar query, 'Why does everyone hate me?' For she desired to be loved by everyone, but above all by men, as she had been by her father, whom she in her turn adored. Halliday had learned to deal with her emotions, but was still unprepared for her apparently effortless transition to hard-eyed practicality. It was not quite what he had desired. Anna Durrant's name in his appointment book reminded him that he had once had a choice, and the memory caused him to flush uneasily, aware of distant embarrassments and their ability to catch him out.

Embarrassment had been with him for as long as he could remember, with the exception of a few brief early years spent in loving communion with his mother and father. The only son of a Leicester newsagent, he had grown up in perfect happiness, or so it now seemed to him, a happiness which was threatened by the death of his father when the boy was ten years old. He remembered his mother, scrubbing her face with a rolled-up handkerchief, which she thrust resolutely into the pocket of her cardigan. She had taken his hand into her damp one.

'We shall just have to carry on, shan't we, son? Daddy would have wanted it that way.'

So he delivered the papers before he went to school, getting up at five in the frozen winter mornings, before it was light, and going home again to the fuggy warmth of the shop, with its cloying gas heater, and warming himself in the back room while his mother in the kitchen cooked him a huge fried breakfast. He was quite willing to serve in the shop, although his mother was against it: she would come running in from the back room or the kitchen whenever the bell rang, and was annoyed if she saw him chatting to a customer. She had plans for him: he was not to spend his life as she had done, tied to the shop and knowing nothing more extensive than the street in which the shop was situated, going no further than the baker or the greengrocer a few yards away, and enjoying a brief rest only on a Sunday afternoon, when she lay down in her dark bedroom for an hour and allowed her son to make her a cup of tea. Then she was up again, washing, cooking a joint of meat which they ate ceremoniously on Sunday evenings, the morning having been too crowded with Sunday newspapers to give them time for lunch. When she heard Lawrence's bicycle approaching, she would change the sign from OPEN to CLOSED: later she would come downstairs and clean up a bit, but for the time being she could devote a few hours to herself and to the son whom she adored. She counted herself a lucky woman, for the boy was a good boy, fond, docile, clever, and with the promise of exceptional looks. Tall, fair, and serious, he had long eyelashes, of which he was ashamed, and a thin mobile mouth which retained the attention of many girls. Already, in early adolescence, he was attracting the glances of women as well as of girls.

His mother was determined that he should stay on at school, and if possible go to university, although she did not look forward to his absence. But she was brave, had been high-spirited in youth, and still enjoyed a good laugh with her friend June Seager, who liked to keep her company in the room at the back of the shop. 'May and June, made for each other,' June would laugh, and indeed they got on exceptionally well. Lawrence would hear the sound of their laughter even before he wheeled his bicycle into the passage. 'Here's Laurie,' one of them would say, it did not matter which, for they both doted on him, and tea would be poured out, and his favourite jam tarts would be lifted carefully out of the tin into which his mother had put them, still warm, after her late baking session on the previous Sunday night, when he was already in bed and asleep. They loved to see him eat, would follow the progress of every mouthful, and then, when he had wiped his lips with his handkerchief, would ask him about school, and how he was getting on. Fortunately he was able to repay their loving care with satisfactory progress: it was important to him to do well for his mother's sake. He did not worry about her, knowing that June was there to keep an eye on her, but he longed to make her happy. Her happiness, it seemed, was to be his responsibility, and one which he had no wish to shirk.

May and June: sometimes he could visualize them even now, laughing together over one of their endless cups of tea in the shabby all-purpose room at the back of the shop, neither of them attractive or confident, usually dressed in an accumulation of cardigans, scarves and fleece-lined boots, but always beaming with love for him. They were like no other women he was ever to know: by the same token no other woman ever entirely matched up to them. He did not notice them growing older, although his mother occasionally complained of tiredness, but she was always prompt to put before him a plate of deliciously cooked food, and therefore he did not see that her tiredness was in any way incapacitating. The shop was getting shabby and needed modernizing, but they had their regular customers and they were not ambitious. For years, it seemed, nothing changed, nor did it seem likely to change.

He was a clever but not a brilliant boy, the kind who develops slowly and on whom teachers look approvingly but without great expectations. He surprised them all by putting on a great turn of speed in the sixth form and carrying off six prizes, including the prize for Latin, together with the offer of a place at Cambridge. His mind was made up: he would read medicine. In the year that remained to him before he went up to Cambridge he helped his mother in the shop and put himself through an advanced course in physics and biology. He also secured the appointment of a part-time manager to help his mother when he himself was away. Fred was a lugubrious man, past the age of retirement, who had previously sold his own ironmongery business and who could not bear to be idle. May Halliday was doubtful, but her son was firm. She let him have his way, as she had always done. Her grief at losing him was enormous. The night before he was due to leave she shed a few tears, then wiped them away, and set before him three beautiful lemon pancakes, his absolute favourite.

'You will take care, won't you, dear?'

'I'll be all right.' He was making the transition from 'Mum' to 'Mother', and feared that under the stress of emotion he might revert to 'Mum' once more.

'Take care of yourself,' they said to each other on the following day. He took her in his arms, then released her and hurried off, knowing that June, less cheerful than usual, was preparing a pot of tea in the back room as a restorative. Part of him longed to stay in their company, to be safe, to be looked after, to be loved as only they could love him, but he also knew that the needs of his body were becoming urgent and that these could not be satisfied while he was under his mother's roof. Nevertheless he was forlorn throughout the journey, and it was only when he got off the train at Cambridge and surveyed the beautiful pale city that his spirits rose. He had grown immensely tall, and his fair ingenuous looks made him the object of instant admiration. He was soon able to satisfy his appetite for girls, who adored him, longing to make him blush with embarrassment. He graduated from nurses and secretaries to fellow students, smart girls, smarter than he was himself, who took good care not to fall in love with him. This puzzled him, for he saw no harm in love, and was if anything sentimental by nature. But he was learning about ambiguity, and about ambiguous situations. In a short time he saw that the world was a more complicated place than he had ever supposed that it would be.

At Cambridge he ironed his accent out into an acceptable classlessness. To have gone further in this direction would have signified disloyalty to his mother, so he kept his voice as low and as neutral as possible. He did his best to work his feelings into a comparable classlessness, and enjoyed affairs with one or two girls whose material situation was markedly superior to his own. He saw no significance in this, but enjoyed being invited to their houses in the vacations, enjoyed the log fires and the sherry before lunch and taking the dogs out for a run. He knew that he could only repay hospitality with his agreeable presence, but this seemed to be enough, and so heady were these delights that he managed to suppress the thought of his mother in her dark bedroom, sleeping away her Sunday afternoons, while he cavorted with the dogs in the spinney behind his host's house. But he did not quite forget her, and when he did go home his heart, which had been growing colder, melted as she came running to meet him, like a girl. In those moments he thought of her as his girl, closer than all the Angelas and the Jennifers, with their high voices, and the baffled and occasionally resentful anxiety with which they surveyed his naked back as he got out of bed and reached for his shirt. He would leave them, these girls, and go back to his studies. When he wanted a rest he would go home to his mother and her lemon pancakes, her jam tarts, her rhubarb pie, all scenting the shabby house with sugary richness, the smell of home.

He went on to St Mary's, Paddington, and enjoyed the work. Although he had begun conscientiously he could not now imagine anything in life other than being a doctor. Nothing disturbed or repelled him, and he had acquired enough self-confidence to be looked upon kindly by his seniors. He was immediately popular with the patients, many of them women, for he preferred the women's medical wards: he saw in each worried face, each new pink bed-jacket, his mother or June, and he would hasten to reassure them, to replace a grimace of pain with a smile of gratitude. He thought he would like to bring comfort to women for the rest of his life, although he still blushed when any one of them pressed his hand and thanked him. But he was not fond of the hospital atmosphere, found his living conditions cramped, and longed for the wider world. He had decided on general practice, had in fact just made his decision, was going out with a couple of friends to celebrate, when he was called to the telephone.

'It's June here, Laurie. Bad news, I'm afraid, dear. It's Mum. Can you come home? She's in the hospital.'

'What happened?' he asked, his mouth dry.

But all she said was, 'Hurry, dear,' and put the telephone down.

He went to Leicester that night, went straight from the station to the hospital, saw her in the small end room into which they moved moribund patients. She had had a severe stroke, was deeply unconscious, but he thought that after a while she returned the pressure of his hand. He stayed with her all night, and was there when she died in the early hours of the morning.

June wept unreservedly; he himself was tearless. But from that moment on, he later reckoned, he took no comfort from his life, felt perpetually cold and disheartened. He sold the shop, said goodbye to June, and took the train back to London, where, with the proceeds from the sale, and the small amount of money his mother had left him, he bought a small flat on the top floor of a house in Barkston Gardens, off the Earl's Court Road. It felt strange being on his own, but he was too sad to want company. His only consolation was his work: he became dedicated. His friends saw less of him. Even the women fell away. The day he was taken on as a junior partner by two elderly Chelsea doctors was the greatest day of his life. His only regret was not being able to tell his mother of his success. But this passed, or almost passed, and as time went on he got used to his new life, and forgot Leicester. Only when he was exceptionally unhappy did he think of earlier days, and then with a complicated mixture of impatience and regret.

The doctors, Grantley and Howarth, let him deal with the chronic cases, with the old people whom they were too busy to visit. He enjoyed these visits, enjoyed in particular the old ladies, Mrs Finnegan, Mrs King, Mrs Marsh, Mrs Durrant, this last a grace and favour patient held over from the days when Dr Howarth had had his original practice in Kensington. Halliday enjoyed entering their houses or flats, and the welcome they unreservedly gave him. He glanced at their surroundings with a new eye: he was getting tired of Barkston Gardens. When he first went to Albert Hall Mansions he felt a deep peace descend on him.

'But your hands are cold, doctor!' said pretty silly Amy Durrant, chafing his cold hands with her own warm ones. 'Is it very cold out? I don't move from here these days. My poor heart, you know. But you must have some hot coffee! I insist! And some of my daughter's coconut biscuits. Anna, darling.'

But Anna was already bringing in a tray. He looked at her then, saw a pale slight figure in a bright blue suit, saw heavy hair giving some dignity to an unremarkable face. He accepted the coffee and the biscuits, and for some reason found it easy to answer questions about himself, although he only gave them the barest details: Leicester, his parents dead. They exclaimed sympathetically, or at least Mrs Durrant did; Anna was rather silent. Warmed by the coffee and the attention, he followed Mrs Durrant into her bedroom, where he ausculted her and took her blood pressure. There was nothing much to be done for her except to renew her prescription for Digoxin and to offer a few soothing words.

'You'll go on for years,' he told her cheerfully.

'I hope so,' she smiled. 'It's not myself I worry about. It's Anna.' Her eyes filled with the easy tears of old age.

'There's no need for you to worry,' he told her, and patted her hand. The tears vanished and she smiled gratefully.

'There's no appreciable change,' he said to Anna in the drawing-room. 'She seems in good general health. I'll look in again next week.'

'I'd be so grateful,' she said, and her smile lit up her rather plain face. Surprised, he looked at her again. She held out her hand, which was long and slender. 'It's been so good of you,' she said. He flushed then, and made his exit.

He returned the following week, and the week after that. His visits became regular, and on each occasion Amy Durrant drew him in lovingly, and he was welcomed by the sublime smell of fresh baking. For a while he began to fantasize that he was at home again, although the surroundings were very different from that shabby room at the back of the shop where June and his mother gossiped and drank tea. But this warm shadowy drawing-room was sufficiently symbolic for him to feel strangely relaxed, and when he followed Amy Durrant into her bedroom to examine her it was all part of the ritual, a ritual to which very little actual importance attached but to which both felt committed. He thought of it as dream-time. And then, leaving Amy Durrant to get dressed again, it was to Anna that he returned. He felt for her. He felt a tenderness in her presence. He sensed that she was good, that she was faithful, and forbearing, used to sacrifice. Like his mother. He felt nothing for her in any other way, yet entertained fantasies of living with her in that peaceful flat, where at last he would take his ease, away from the often discordant excitements of his too prolonged bachelor existence. When their hands touched he scanned her face, and saw that her gaze was without guile. Yet there was a sternness about her, as if expecting nothing less than the truth from him. That serious peaceful look of hers, as if she were prepared to wait for him, but only if he were to perform to the highest of standards, gave him pause. He was, after all, a mature man, with an active body. However tenderly he entered that flat he sometimes left it with a puzzled sense of relief.

And yet she was good . . . He thought this once more, regretfully, when he met Vickie Gibson at a party given by one of the elderly doctors, and began an affair with her that same evening. This he found disconcerting, for he had both desired and disliked her at first sight, loved her vulnerability, her excitability, loathed her social performance, which was that of a grown-up child showing off. He was invited, the following weekend, not to her own flat, as he had expected, but to a flat in Cadogan Gate, where her father, the director of a West End firm of chartered accountants, looked him over carefully, and her mother flashed him the occasional distracted smile, as if she were thinking of something totally different. She appeared to believe – and to give him to understand – that she had married beneath her, leaving her daughter to the care of her pompous prosperous husband. Vickie and her father were in close and indulgent accord; many were the private jokes which passed between them. He had felt himself irritated, and had wanted to carry her off, away from this petulant atmosphere. Dinner had been a strain, full of slippery food: cups of soup, rack of lamb, caramelized oranges. He felt an overpowering and futile fury when he realized that he was on probation as a future son-in-law, was shocked when Vickie allowed herself to be petted by her father. Yet all this aroused in him a powerful excitement, which was compounded equally of sexual impatience and sheer exasperation.

It was her father who saw to it that they married. Vickie was tired of her job – she worked, predictably enough, for a firm of smart estate agents – and she already had the complacent air of a married woman. He had not the heart to let her down. The engagement was celebrated with an outburst of tearful excitement from Vickie, and the promise of a house from Vickie's father. The house, in Tryon Street, was small, fashionable, uncomfortable, and conveniently near the practice. With death in his heart he had surveyed the tiny rooms, in which his head seemed almost to touch the ceiling, while Vickie competently took measurements, humming to herself as if he were momentarily forgotten. Yet when she stood up to kiss him goodbye her tongue slipped naturally into his mouth and she moved his hands to her full breasts. He tore himself away reluctantly, picked up his bag, and went on his visits. Albert Hall Mansions was last on his list. The welcome from Amy Durrant was as warm as ever, but there was anxiety in her eyes, as if she had hoped to be welcoming him in another capacity. His examination of her was as scrupulous as usual, but he could hardly bear to meet her gaze. He patted her hand by way of apology, then retreated to the drawing-room for what he felt was going to be one of the major ordeals of his life.

'Anna,' he said finally, after a painful silence, during which the only sound was that of his sherry glass being returned to a silver tray. 'I'm getting married.'

There was the slightest of pauses.

'Married? Then I must wish you well, Lawrence.'

'To Vickie Gibson,' he went on. 'I think you know her.'

'No, I don't know her.'

'Then you must meet her. I hope you'll be friends.'

There was a high colour in her cheeks, but otherwise no sign of emotion.

'Anna . . .'

'You won't mind if I don't tell my mother, will you?'

He gripped her hand. After a while she loosened it and turned away.

'And you will understand if we ask one of the other doctors to call?'

'Is this really necessary? I am very fond of your mother. And of you.'

'Are you?' She turned to him and gave him her full sad gaze. 'I wish you well,' she repeated. 'I have always wished you well.'

He felt crushed by such nobility, and also resentful of it. He felt that he had been dismissed, found wanting. That night he made love vigorously to his fiancée and was mollified by her loudly voiced satisfaction. He was to seek her company assiduously in the weeks which followed, as if fearful of what he might do if she were not there to protect him.

After five years of marriage he was resigned to half measures, his physical life as rewarding as ever, his brain and his heart untouched. He was successful, popular, established, yet he had moments of astonishing sadness. He had learnt, in his turn, to protect his wife and her frequent silliness, to smooth over her tactlessness, to pour the wine at her dinner parties, to accompany her fearfully elaborate cooking. Heavily spiced and garnished Mediterranean dishes replaced the simple roasts of his youth; he had retained his sweet tooth, and longed for his mother's baking, her apple pies, her jam tarts. He thought back a great deal these days when not loyally sharing his wife's anecdotes, the anecdotes – of a humorous or embarrassing nature – which his wife recounted to her dinner guests. He looked preoccupied; they admired his dedication. In fact he was longing for them all to be quiet, or for himself to be elsewhere.

He never thought of Anna, had not thought of her until he saw her at Mrs Marsh's party. Seeing her in front of him now, in his office, he was quite calm, free from uncomfortable memories. She too was calm: they might have been old friends. As indeed, in a sense, they were. He noted that she looked much the same, but that she was very thin: he remembered noting this before. Surely she was thinner than he remembered?

'What can I do for you, Anna?'

'I'd like another prescription, Lawrence.' She held out an empty bottle. 'Dr Grantley gave me these when my mother died.'

He took the bottle from her. That was all they had in common now, he thought: the deaths of mothers.

'Have you lost weight recently?'

'I may have done. But I'm very well. I'm always well.'

'Just step onto the scales, would you?' A pause. 'You weigh just over seven stone, Anna.'

'What of it? I've never been fat.'

'I'd better examine you,' he said unhappily.

Their faces remained neutral as his hands palpated her. He thought her body beautiful, fine and gracile, in sharp contrast to the rather coarse skin of her face. He was reminded of Degas's *Jeunes Spartiates s'exerçant à la guerre*. She lay on his couch quite peacefully, looking not at him but at the glass front of a small cabinet on his wall. His hands pressed firmly down on her abdomen.

'Does that hurt?' he asked.

'No. Nothing hurts.'

'You can get dressed, Anna.'

She came back from behind the screen with her hair dishevelled, which made her look older but more approachable, and sat down.

'You're going to have to put on weight, you know. But you know that, don't you?'

'Yes. I'll put it on in France. I'm going to France soon.'

'I shall want to see you when you come back. In fact I want to monitor any weight gain. Or loss, of course, but we won't talk about that. Can I trust you to come and see me? Or do you want me to make an appointment now?'

'That won't be necessary. And the prescription, Lawrence?'

'Oh, yes. Never more than one of these at a time, Anna. And only when necessary. Don't make a habit of them.'

'L. M. Halliday,' she read. 'What is the "M" for?'

'I hardly dare tell you.'

'Be brave.'

'Merlin.'

'I see,' she said. 'Yes, that is rather serious. But don't worry – I'll keep it to myself.'

He was grateful to her for bringing their meeting to so skilful a conclusion, for striking the right note – amiable, light-hearted, worldly, not heavy with reminiscence. He was grateful to find himself so light-hearted. She bore no grudge; she was not dependent on him. She was a healthy woman, with a healthy sense of her own worth. So he told himself. He held out his hand in a comradely fashion. For a moment she scanned him with her all-judging, all-comprehending gaze. You are too hard on me, he wanted to say. Not everyone can live like you – ascetically, devotedly, selflessly. It is not quite becoming in a woman: no man could put up with it. But his mood changed, and he was puzzled by the change, as if not realizing that she still had power to affect him. When the door closed behind her he sat for a while, looking at his hands. Then, rousing himself with a sigh, he buzzed his secretary to send in the next patient.

12

She was surprised to have heard nothing from Marie-France, to have had no confirmation of her expected arrival in Paris. When she thought back to the days before Christmas she realized that letters from Marie-France had been coming at longer and longer intervals, although when they came they expressed the same interest in Anna's life that they had done for the past thirty years. Her own letter containing the account of Mrs Marsh's party had not been answered, but she had supposed that Marie-France was with her family at Meaux, and had not therefore been especially disconcerted to receive no reply. She had simply written again with the details of her flight.

Telephoning was difficult, as Bertrand Forestier, Marie-France's father, kept the telephone in his study and insisted that it should not be used when he was working, which was more or less all the time, except for his ceremonious promenade in the late afternoon, when he drank a cup of coffee at the Deux Magots and read his newspaper, always hoping to be greeted by a colleague, a *confrère*, a fellow ruminant in the pastures of literature. This rarely happened, but Anna, taking coffee herself one day, had surreptitiously observed him: the fastidious manicured hands had flicked open the newspaper, the pale heavy scornful face had expressed various forms of contempt or disgust, and when the coffee was finished the cup had been filled with water from the carafe on the table until that too was finished and the interlude concluded. No colleague or *confrère* had greeted him, and it was easy to suppose that he was not much liked. His main weapon was sarcasm, which had served him well in the days when he had contributed a weekly *causerie* to a now defunct journal, but which was now a shield used to mask his affections. He loved his daughter, or so it was supposed, since they had never lived apart, but he imposed his iron rules upon her and upon his household as if he still expected to be obeyed unquestioningly. He was eighty-six and in immovably good health. Marie-France, at sixty, was as disciplined and submissive as if she were a little girl. This would no doubt explain why she had been unable to answer Anna's letter, and why it would be an act of grave irresponsibility to telephone her.

They had met many years ago, when Marie-France had been an *assistante* at Anna's school, and had formed a friendship straight away, the ten years between their ages being obliterated by a similarity of experience: widowed parents, comfortable circumstances, a general inability to see the world in anything but hopeful terms. Marie-France had been taken home to meet Anna's mother: Anna in due course had been granted an audience by Marie-France's father. Together they permitted themselves a little mild impatience with the demands of elderly parents, but this was offered humorously, as if to suggest any hint of rebellion would threaten not only the terms of their friendship but of their separate individual lives. The thought that they never voiced to each other, at least in each other's presence, although it may have been hinted at in a letter, was that one day they would be free. No serious consideration was allowed to mar this prospect, for example that they might be free but untrained for any other way of life, or that they might encounter difficulties which had never occurred to them in the days of their claustration. Marie-France, patiently smiling, sweet-natured in the face of various privations, rubbing her cold hands together in a gesture which was entirely characteristic, had long been a nun-like presence in Anna's life: absent or present, in her letters or in their too rare meetings, she was the same unchanging friend. Absent, she was present through the medium of her letters, which usually arrived at the rate of one every two or three weeks, and to which Anna replied with never failing pleasure.

The letters were elevated, amusing, giving no hint of loneliness or pain. They might have been written by two acquaintances who had met in the Pump Room in Bath, for it was Marie-France, whose English was perfect, and who was devoted to the works of Jane Austen, who best captured the tone. Lately Anna had felt the strain of such a correspondence, had felt unable to harness the carefree flippancy which masked their more serious exchanges. But their friendship demanded that each be forbearing and resilient, capable and good-humoured, that negative moods should never be voiced or even alluded to, above all that seriousness should be kept at bay. What united them was a long habit of celibacy. They were accustomed to regard themselves as spinsters, and gallantly shouldered the burden, knowing, but never acknowledging the fact to each other, that spinsterhood was the reason why Marie-France was despised by her family, why Anna had, finally, disappointed her mother. They extolled the joys of spinsterhood, never hinting at its pains. Anna had supposed that this would continue throughout the rest of their lives until at last, as she hoped, they broke through to the reality of who each of them was and remade their friendship on an entirely different basis. She found herself approaching that time with dread but also with some curiosity.

Marie-France, sweet friend, sweet sister, the only unmarried girl in a crowd of cousins, tolerated by all, feared by none. The cousins were the only visitors her father would allow. Each year a holiday was spent at the home of one or other of the cousins, or more usually in a villa at Les Sables d'Olonne, which had belonged to Forestiers since the grandparents' day and which was now shared between two families who found it convenient to occupy it for the month of August and to let it for the rest of the year. Every Christmas or New Year a cousin or two, complete with wife or husband, would travel to Meaux from Neuilly, from Viroflay, or from farther afield, from Montpellier or from La Rochelle. On Bertrand Forestier's birthday the same cousins, or their delegates, would bring greetings to the flat in the rue Huysmans, pay a few well-placed compliments, drink a glass of champagne, and depart with relief, having kissed Marie-France in the hallway and warmly pressed her hand. Marie-France's letters were filled with references to Aline, to Nicole, to Emmanuel and Solange, to little Julie who was so charming, and Anna had learned to distinguish them, although news of Marie-France's family left her feeling that her own life was underpopulated. The thought occurred to her that Marie-France's sixtieth birthday would probably be celebrated in a familial setting, and that she herself might not be entirely expected. But she had announced her impending visit some time ago and saw no reason to revise her plans. For safety's sake she wrote again, suggesting that they should meet at a tea-room in the rue Monsieur-le-Prince: there she could offer her invitation to lunch on the day of Marie-France's actual birthday, thus avoiding the idea that she might come to the flat. She would take Marie-France to lunch at the Restaurant Voltaire and leave her to her family for the evening. This slight evidence that she might, out of sheer tact, have to observe that others had the priority saddened her, until she reflected that it was an act of friendship on her part to comply with Marie-France's putative engagements, and that Marie-France would be flattered and grateful for her delicacy.

She telephoned the small hotel in the rue de Fleurus where she usually stayed and was astonished to be told by a disembodied voice that it was closed for refurbishment and that no bookings could be accepted until the spring. Thoughtfully, she replaced the receiver. She glanced out of the window at the icy sun which had replaced the earlier drab weather and reflected that that particular hotel had never been very warm or indeed very comfortable, that she was now a comparatively rich woman, picked up the telephone again, and, this time successfully, booked a room at an hotel in the rue du Colisée which she had read about in an article in a magazine. It was wholly uncharacteristic of her to stay on the right bank, so far from Marie-France, but she had a feeling, which she realized had been growing on her for some time, that nothing much would come of this visit. She might be left to herself a great deal, a prospect which did not frighten her but which had certainly not been foreseen. Some very slight feeling of dispossession, which she could not entirely attach either to the past or to the future, guided her to neutral surroundings, whereas had she been more confident she would have sought out a familiar landscape. But she reminded herself that no welcome had been forthcoming, that maybe she was not entirely expected, that it was more becoming, at a time of celebration to which she had not been invited, to keep her distance. It was with a slight feeling of coldness, as distinct from the physical coldness which daily oppressed her, that she set out for the airport. Her composure, which so disconcerted others, ensured that no one addressed a word to her throughout the early morning flight.

The reality of Paris unsettled her, as it always did, so different was it from the nostalgic Paris which she carried around in her head. Here on the right bank, near the Champs Elysées, she was more aware of rushing traffic than she had ever been in the rue de Fleurus. After her silent flat in silent Cranley Gardens it came as a disagreeable surprise, and her attempts to cross the few streets leading to the Rond-Point were clumsy. '*En arrière!*' yelled a policeman, blowing his whistle at her, and she nervously jumped back on to the pavement. The same icy sun shone over Paris, but its light was northern, cruel: it would vanish abruptly in a pool of carmine, to be instantly replaced by frost and fog. Momentarily cheered by the broadness of the space around her, by the brief brilliance of the light of early afternoon, she turned her thoughts to her forthcoming meeting with

Marie-France, wondering with a certain melancholy why she felt so unsure of her welcome. Nothing has changed, she told herself: nothing that she could see had changed. That she herself was growing older she did not take into account, for she had felt the same age for as long as she could remember, neither young nor old, because she was sometimes the one and sometimes the other. She had dressed as carefully as usual, and as far as she could see she looked no different. She was puzzled as to how she would spend the rest of her time, if Marie-France were too busy to see her every day. In a way their friendship proceeded better when they corresponded than when they met: she knew that once she got home again she would fashion even her melancholy into something amusingly philosophical, that she would describe this very bus ride in her most carefully chosen words.

There was always her work, of course, that not altogether invalid project to write a series of articles, or even, if she were capable of it, something more substantial, on the great salons of Paris during the Second Empire. The research had given her some agreeable moments, but she could not quite hide from herself the knowledge that until now the work had been more alibi than pastime, enabling her to escape, if only to Colindale, to read old newspapers, or to the library of the Victoria and Albert Museum, where she liked to sit and look over the formal garden while her hands lay idly on the notes which she had meant to transcribe. Now there was nothing to prevent her making this work the main purpose of her life, but she took no joy from the prospect. The moment for its completion had long passed, although she would dutifully visit a few museums while she was here. But more than work she wanted pleasure, and knew that she was no longer capable of procuring it for herself. She looked out of the window of the bus at the immensity of Paris. She remembered it as being so small, so intimate and charming, so warmed by the friendships of her student year, when it was still possible to be a student and not to be controversial, or *contestataire*. 1964: her wonderful year. And within what seemed like a brief space of time poor Marie-France, in the rue Huysmans, was sending bulletins of street battles and tear gas. They had asked her to stay with them in London, but she had replied that she could not leave her father.

Marie-France was there, suddenly, in front of her, the worn gold ring flashing briefly as she raised her thin brown hand in greeting. She half rose from the small marble-topped table, and then, laughing, subsided. They kissed, and ordered coffee, overwhelmed into wordlessness by being together after a year's absence. Anna felt comforted by the conventions of this friendship in which so little was demanded of her, and repressed the thought that on this occasion she was more demanding than usual, exigent even, that although she had so little to say she nevertheless wanted to be interrogated, interviewed, or at least subjected to searching questioning. She wanted a witness to herself, as she existed in this place, at this time. Someone should make it their business to find out how she was, how she felt, whether this or that pleased or displeased her. Her opinion should be sought on many subjects, and in an ideal state she would feel free to express distaste, rejection, as in fact she had never done in the course of her real but increasingly nebulous life. She felt a moment of panic as she realized that she was far from home yet still imprisoned by the silence of home, and that no one would seek her out or help her to break that silence. With an odd presentiment she felt that her recent interview with Lawrence Halliday had pre-empted the intimacy she had expected to feel in the company of Marie-France, or that Marie-France in her turn might confer. Something had imperceptibly changed, yet she could not imagine what it was. She looked at Marie-France: the same brownish unadorned skin, the same lightless brown hair. Only the fine brown eyes, her best feature, seemed wider and brighter, the wide thin mouth more ready to break into a smile. The red jacket was new, certainly, and a surprising choice in one so reserved by nature, so like a saint in her acceptance of her reduced share of the world's delights.

Aloud she said, 'You're looking well, *ma mie*. Surprisingly well. How are you?'

'Oh, I'm fine.' The English was still fluent, still barely accented, although perhaps the accent was a little stronger than it had been. 'Tell me about yourself, Anna.'

She could think of nothing to say, although when she got home she would write a decent account of herself. Again she felt a very slight surprise and alienation, as she watched Marie-France glance about her, as if their meeting were simply a pretext for drinking a cup of coffee in agreeable surroundings, a pleasant but unimportant interlude in an otherwise quite ordinary day. Her hand played with a necklace of small pearls, and then with the brown and red silk scarf inside the neck of her sweater.

'Yes, I'm fine,' Marie-France repeated, but her expression denoted a smiling absence.

'Marie-France, what has happened? Something has happened – do tell me.'

The absent smile grew blissful.

'Yes, Anna, something has happened. I wanted you to be one of the first to know. I couldn't bring myself to write: I waited until you got here.'

At once the conventions were shattered. For Marie-France to be unable to write was significant enough. There was a restlessness, a brightness about her that was even more significant; her hands were very slightly febrile, contrasting with the voice, which was an insistent monotone. Anna sensed that she was no longer a confidante; indeed, this had just been made clear to her. She understood now why this visit was to be so different from all the others, and why she had sensed this from the unusual silence which had greeted her last letter.

'Are you in love?'

Her tone was neutral, polite: she could not quite manage the collusive roguishness which might, she thought distantly, have been in order.

'Isn't it ridiculous? At my age?'

'I'm very glad for you. Who is it?'

She now had Marie-France's full attention.

'You remember I told you when Aline died? Early last year?'

Indeed this death of a cousin had been made the subject of a very affecting account, one of Marie-France's best letters. Aline had died of cancer in Montpellier: Marie-France and her father had gone to the funeral. And there, incredibly, the widower, Philippe, had cast his eye around in the search for a replacement, and in a very short time it had lighted on Marie-France.

'But Marie-France, wasn't that a little precipitate?'

'We are not children, Anna. Philippe is five years older than I am. We have known each other nearly all our lives; he tells me that he had always liked me. Naturally, when Aline was alive we never spoke of this. In fact I never suspected . . . But he needs someone to look after him, and he made his decision. *Et voilà.*' She smiled delightedly.

Yes, thought Anna, you will look after him, as you have always looked after Papa, and what man, seeing your loyalty, would not wish himself to be the object of a similar devotion? Why should a grieving widower not seek immediate consolation, particularly if he had nursed a secret affection while his wife was still alive? And what glory for Marie-France, the virtuous spinster, about to astound her family with news of her unsuspected apotheosis! Who could begrudge her her moment of triumph, even if it included this infinitesimal triumph in a tea-room in the rue Monsieur-le-Prince, on a day of sunshine as ruthless as the workings of the human heart? She could have written, thought Anna, and she knew that the thought would persist.

She said aloud, 'And when will you be married?'

'Oh, not until Papa . . . He is nearly eighty-seven, Anna. He relies on me for everything. He knows, of course. I told him, and I think he was quite pleased. But we agreed that I shouldn't leave him. Not yet, anyway. Of course, Philippe is impatient, but we agreed to wait. Aline has only been dead for a year. He had a Mass said for her a few days ago.'

'Marie-France, don't wait. Don't let anything stand in your way.'

Marie-France looked at her in surprise.

'But it is all agreed, Anna. After all, we are not children, not adolescents, although I feel . . . It is not as if there were anything physical between us, though there too I must confess . . . '

She laughed awkwardly, and coloured.

'In that case it would be quite wrong to wait,' said Anna composedly, although she felt Marie-France's confession to be untoward. But that is precisely what she wanted me to know, she reflected, and she is too excited to conceal it. She signalled the waitress for the bill, busied her hands with change for the tip.

'Where will you live?' she asked. 'And what must I call you in future?'

'Well, eventually in our flat in the rue Huysmans, when Papa . . . Dunoyer,' she pronounced, her face radiant, the humiliations of a lifetime forgotten. 'Mme Dunoyer.'

And do you love him? Or was the temptation so great that to resist it would have been unthinkable?

Aloud she said, 'I'm very happy for you.'

'But I want you to meet him, Anna. He is coming for my birthday tomorrow: he is taking me out to lunch. And we are having a few friends for a glass of champagne in the evening. Of course you are invited.'

'And of course I'll be delighted.'

'What will you do with your time in Paris? I expect you'll want to get on with your work, now that you're free.'

Anna reflected that Marie-France would not until this moment have made so brisk a remark. Marie-France evidently felt the same, for she coloured slightly.

'Where are you staying?' she asked.

'On the right bank,' replied Anna, pulling on her gloves. 'It's handier for the Louvre. Yes, I'll do some work. And I'll

143

see you tomorrow evening.' For there was to be no lunch, she thought.

'Six o'clock. Oh, Anna, I am so happy.'

But there was a note of panic in her voice, and for a second or two she looked her age, even haggard.

They parted resolutely, each striding off with great purpose in response to apparently ineluctable demands. For the first time in their lives they were embarrassed with each other. Anna thought with shame of the coy letter she had written about her encounter with Nick Marsh. It had been a way of saving her face, although everything about it had been false. This would have been apparent to Marie-France in her newly awakened state. Yet she was not as yet quite comfortable in that state, could commit errors of taste while under the influence of her so recent excitement, had had to let her friend know that she and Philippe were lovers. Anna struggled with the knowledge that their friendship would now end, for what place could she occupy? Their understanding was fragmented, an imbalance revealed that had not been there before.

She realized that she had a great deal of time on her hands. She walked down to St Germain des Près, and caught a bus across the river to the Louvre. She would look at the portraits of Ingres, calm, replete, satisfied with their immensely enviable situation in this world, and careless of the world to come. She wandered through the rooms, deserted at this time of day, past the great discordant machines of the Romantics, to those effortlessly authoritative presences: Mme Rivière, reclining fatly on her blue velvet cushions, the charming Mme Pancoucke in her white satin dress, Mme Marcotte, in unbecoming brown, her large sad eyes speaking of a physical rather than a metaphysical unease. For it was impossible to think of metaphysics in the face of such overwhelming bodily reality. Life on this earth, they seemed to say, is fulfilling: who could imagine anything being added to it? She remembered Baudelaire's remark that he found it difficult to breathe when faced with a portrait by Ingres: he felt as though the oxygen had been sucked out of the atmosphere. So insistent were the candid oval eyes that she could almost sense the processes behind them: discreet gurglings and shiftings in those flawless bodies, and in the minds an almost innocent sexual knowledge. Almost innocent . . . She turned away, to the window, and looked out on the Tuileries, empty now in the cold but unfriendly light. Viewed through a misty window from an upper floor, the perspective of the flower beds seemed rigorous, almost painful.

She walked back through the echoing galleries, down the great stone steps into an oncoming rush of school-children. Outside, in the cold air, she shivered slightly. The sun had gone, and the sky was now hazy. She made her way to the bus stop, wondering how she was to fill the ensuing days. But I need not stay, she thought. After tomorrow there will be no need for me to stay, and indeed there will be no grounds on which I can comfortably be expected to stay. Slightly cheered, and with the thought of her flat quite vividly in her mind, she made her way back to St Germain, looked at the titles of the new books in the windows of La Hune and Le Divan, and with a sigh sat down in the Deux Magots and ordered coffee.

The afternoon passed slowly. At four o'clock precisely Bertrand Forestier made his entrance, one palm briefly uplifted to signal his presence to the waiter. Seated, he gave his contemptuous attention to the day's news, visibly sneering when a particularly obtuse report displeased him. Please don't last much longer, thought Anna. Please enter a rapid and painless decline, so that Marie-France can be free. For it now seemed to her monstrous that her friend's happiness should be impeded in any way, and she could see that the old man would be implacable, that the flat in the rue Huysmans, and the inheritance, would be theirs only in the teeth of an immoderate resistance. Nothing stated, of course, nothing out in the open, but an assumption that the situation could only exist if he gave it permission to exist, and that the permission so far granted might be the only arrangement to which they could lay claim. She watched him drink his two cups of coffee and his three glasses of water, watched the manicured hands flick the newspaper back into shape, then place his hat securely on his head, and, the palm again upturned for the benefit of the waiter, he was finally gone. And so upright, she thought disconsolately: from the back he looks a mere seventy.

The following day passed meaninglessly, though not as unpleasantly as she had feared. Looking back afterwards she remembered walking a great deal, though in no fixed direction. She remembered eating lunch, which was unusual, and, even more unusual, ordering a glass of wine. Her very real sadness she now accepted as a natural accompaniment, almost a companion. She spent the afternoon in the hotel, which was hushed and silent, and lay on her bed, trying unsuccessfully to sleep. Then, with a sigh, she got up, took a bath, and dressed in the brown corded silk suit which she had worn to Mrs Marsh's party. She looked at herself blankly in the mirror, seeing only a shadowy evanescent figure. At five forty-five she took a cab to the rue Huysmans.

From behind the door of the apartment she could hear Marie-France's excited laughter. She rang the bell, waited, heard more laughter, and was finally greeted by Marie-France, looking flushed. She was wearing a red and white printed silk dress: despite the cold of the late January night she seemed to give off warmth. She took Anna fondly by the hand and led her into the salon, which was brown, as she herself had once been. Anna had time to wonder whether she would make any changes when the time came before being presented to Monsieur Forestier, majestic and all too upright in a grey suit, the jacket buttoned over a camel-hair waistcoat, the rosette of the Legion of Honour in place.

'Papa, you remember Anna, don't you?'

He gave an almost imperceptible nod.

'Mademoiselle.'

'And this is Philippe. Philippe, this is my dear friend Anna Durrant.'

Philippe Dunoyer bowed from the waist, said, '*Enchanté*, Mademoiselle,' and raised his eyes to hers. She found herself looking at a man who bore an uncanny resemblance to George Ainsworth. Unfortunate, she thought, her heart beating uncomfortably. Perhaps all men of that age have the same well-brushed hair, the same full frank gaze, the same glossy joviality. Yet there was something speculative in his expression that gave her pause. Yes, there was a certain resemblance, but only a faint one. She moved to the side of the room, leaving Philippe to various cousins. She supposed that this was a more or less official engagement party. Marie-France looked very happy.

Yet on two occasions she found herself being examined by Dunoyer, as if he feared a hostile witness and was waiting to disarm her. Unable to bear this, and the clash of personalities represented by the relentless father, the opportunist fiancé – for she now saw him as entirely venal, on no evidence better than the way his gaze hardened to meet her own – she waved goodbye, promising to write at length once she was back in London, and went to fetch her coat. As she made her way to the door she was aware of Dunoyer heading in her direction.

'Not going already?' he said, smiling steadily.

'Yes, I must. Good-night.'

'Good-night, Anna.'

The hand which he had placed in the small of her back slipped lower.

'Good-night,' he said again, giving her a little pat.

That night, in her hotel, she thought sadly of Marie-France. There would be no more brave civilized letters, for life had broken in to rescue her. The intimacy of their friendship must be sacrificed. They would meet again, but as acquaintances rather than as friends. She doubted whether Dunoyer would encourage close friendship between them; in any event, Dunoyer was dubious, and was better avoided. Those portraits in the Louvre, speaking of the sexual battle fought and won . . . How strange that art and life should coalesce like this, in the space of a single day!

There was much material for reflection here, although that reflection might prove disheartening. She slept little that night, and the following morning, as if this had been planned all along, left for home.

13

Mrs Marsh was taking tea with her friend Phyllis Martin, in Lady Martin's overfurnished flat two floors above her own in Cranmer Court. Lady Martin, as she so frequently reminded her visitors, was fond of colour. 'I have always loved colour. Colour means so much to me. I am particularly sensitive to strong vibrant colours – I love to have them about me.' In spite of these assertions she had chosen a harsh cold petrol-blue fabric to cover the sofa and armchairs in her sitting-room: the carpet was flowered, pink and grey, and the curtains were again petrol blue, with a suggestion of pink, and also green, in a complicated frieze motif which ran round their borders. Many lamps, in equally strong butter yellow parchment shades, shed an eager light. Further evidence of Lady Martin's sensitivity was to be found in various pieces of *faux bambou* furniture, and a tea trolley, in fake brass, bearing a plate of buttered scones and a silver teapot under a scarlet tea cosy patterned with white hearts.

Lady Martin herself, in contrast, was a small pretty woman who must once have been a small and exceedingly pretty girl. Even now she opened her round blue eyes wide at every remark addressed to her, as if she were being fêted or courted, as she had been in the old days. Her extremely narrow figure, in child-sized clothes, was always fashionably dressed: in the teeth of grave discomfort she wore tight high-heeled boots with her little fur coat and cossack hat, even though this necessitated her carrying a stick. Even today she wore them, as if to demonstrate her relative youthfulness, which she saw as thrown into relief by Mrs Marsh's large humble brown shoes. She gave off an air of dusty sparkle, all that was left of a career of effortless and successful flirtation. Her nails were a confident crimson, to match her red wool suit, although the knuckles of her small hands were now slightly swollen with arthritis. She bore her age well, largely by dint of ignoring it altogether; as far as she was concerned she was still the girl who delighted in scandals, who was interested in the love affairs of others, who was a high-spirited gossip, an intimate and confidante, a best friend who could easily pretend surprise when betrayal was on the cards, as it so often was throughout her life.

She liked women, but men were her business. She had been engaged many times, but to everyone's surprise had married only once. Yet even now she commandeered other women's husbands, led them off at parties, asked their advice about her investments, although she was a shrewd woman and capable of dealing with them quite well by herself, would lay her crimson-nailed hand upon their arms as if alluding to past intimacy, would arch her brows and widen her eyes if anyone expressed the mildest annoyance at these tactics. Women tended to mistrust her, but she was hard to dislike. She was artless, decorative, almost a period piece, dating back to the era of the flapper, of cupid's bow mouths, and eyelashes as symmetrical and perfect as the petals of a daisy. She managed a pleasant enough little life, although it was greatly reduced: her audience now consisted of the husbands of other elderly women like herself. She was seventy-nine, two years younger than Mrs Marsh, who appeared to be decades older, as both of them realized. This was a great consolation to Lady Martin. 'But then I've always looked after myself,' was her first thought, as she contemplated Mrs Marsh's looming figure and iron-grey hair. Her own hair was a mass of elaborate blue-white curls. 'Poor Phyllis, she has no dignity,' thought Mrs Marsh, who had learnt long ago, as a clumsy girl, not to set great store by outward appearance. 'And those arm rests could do with a wash. Maybe she doesn't notice.'

They sat at ease. It was something of a relief to each of them to be with a companion of her own age. All references would be easily understood; nothing need be explained, and no excuses need be offered for the sticks which lay beside each armchair, although allusions to bodily ills remained cautious. They took a certain comfort from each other, and it was necessary for them to meet fairly regularly. Not that either of them would be much good in a crisis, Mrs Marsh reflected: Phyllis Martin was the kind of woman who turns up with an armful of flowers when the illness or the accident is nearly forgotten, while she herself, though never a party to such stratagems, considered herself too bleak to offer much in the way of reassurance. But they could telephone the doctor for each other, a fact which remained close to the surface of both their minds. Out of a strange superstition Mrs Marsh had not told her friend of her accident until it was safely in the past. After all, she thought, I dealt with it myself. And there was something symbolic about a fall: Phyllis would probably wonder aloud whether it might not have been a slight stroke. So she had merely indicated the bandage under her thick stocking, and murmured in explanation, 'Took a bit of a toss at Philippa's. My own fault. But that cottage of hers is a menace.' The thought of Philippa was an odd comfort to her in these circumstances, for Lady Martin had no children.

'You always give one such a good tea, Phyllis,' she said, accepting another thickly buttered scone. They ate rapidly, greedily, recognizing this pleasure as one of the consolations of old age. Mrs Marsh took a long drink of tea from a frail flowered cup, and, her hunger and thirst slaked, prepared to put up with Phyllis's reminiscences, which had to do largely with her own gallant past and the men who had fallen in love with her and who had threatened to abandon their girlfriends and fiancées until she had laid a fragrant hand on a masculine arm and made them promise to do nothing of the sort. Many elderly men, married for years, remembered her fondly: should she encounter them again, after all those years, as she sometimes did, she told her friend, she would be shocked at how they had let themselves go: heavy stomachs, liver spots on the hands – here she spread her own hands prettily – baldness . . . How right she had been, all those years ago, to talk them back into a belated recognition of their duty! But they still thought about her, she averred: one or two of them wrote to her, quite affecting letters, which of course she never answered. This monologue ran its usual course until the ultimate sentence was reached, the signal for Mrs Marsh to come out of her dream and attend once more to the conversation in hand, for at this point Lady Martin's flippancy concealed a very real regret.

'. . . and after all that Archie was the one I married.'

There was a moment of silence as they contemplated their dead husbands. Phyllis Martin's glance strayed to the large silver-framed photograph of Archie, in Air Force uniform, as if wondering ruefully where he had gone. So must she have looked at him when he tormented her in this life, for he had been beset by girls when, as a Flight Lieutenant, he had led dangerous missions over Germany in World War II, to emerge unscathed from his plane, and ready at once to relax with whomever came to hand. One was not supposed to know about his infidelities, which was why Mrs Marsh kept silent at this point. He had matured into a likeable man, bluff, good-natured, not particularly interesting, much as he had been when younger: indifference to danger had been his most glowing attribute. The two couples had dined together a few times, when Archie was at the Air Ministry, and Bill Marsh was still alive. Bill had died first, leaving his widow marked in inconspicuous ways. Archie had survived him by a bare two years, when he succumbed to a fatal heart attack.

The two wives had kept in touch, although they had little in common, and Phyllis Martin had taken Mrs Marsh's advice and moved into the empty flat two floors above her own, when her house in Markham Square had got too much for her. Now, she supposed, they would never move out again, until death came for them in their turn. Death was never mentioned between them. If they spoke of their husbands it was as if they were referring to men they had once known, men who had inexplicably passed out of their lives. Only the brief seriousness accorded to the subject, and the regret that they took care to banish from their expressions as soon as they could manage this, indicated that much could be said, that much was being withheld. For it would have been the height of vulgarity to weep in public. Even Lady Martin's famed sensitivity took second place to the rules of behaviour, which had always governed those to whom she still referred as 'our sort of people'. The trouble was that there were so few of them left.

Both had been presented at Court, Mrs Marsh gloomy in white satin, with feathers in her hair, Lady Martin, predictably, the most beautiful debutante of two seasons. Both had married the man of their choice. That these men happened to be entirely suitable was, in their view, only to be expected: if broken hearts were mentioned they raised eyebrows in well-bred dismay. Love was embarrassing, unless crowned by a wedding, and of course no one in their set had a breakdown or an illegitimate child. They supposed such matters to be confined to the lower classes, with whom they were on excellent terms when the latter were employed as servants. Feelings were never much discussed, although with the advent of old age – of real age – they were diverted by the tricks which memory played on them, and trembled on the brink of discovery, of real information, after the years of well-bred subterfuge. 'Do you remember so-and-so?' one of them would suddenly ask, only to have the other reply, incredulously, 'Why, I was thinking of her only the other day. She died, of course.' But again, when death came into the equation, they turned resolutely to other matters.

For the moment, their appetites satisfied, they relapsed into silence. This was always welcome to Mrs Marsh, who found silence sympathetic these days, who chose silence above noise, and who was developing a special affinity with the night hours, when all the world, or as much of it as she could imagine, was silent. But she remembered her manners, knew how Phyllis loved to chatter, and pulled herself together.

'Do you get out much these days, Phyllis?' she asked politely.

The question seemed to call Lady Martin to order.

'As much as I can,' she replied. 'Bridge twice a week, of course: that keeps one in touch. And I still get to the shops every day. But I find I don't like to be out in the evenings, apart from the bridge. I'm quite glad to get home these days.'

'You used to be out every night.'

'Not any more. When I think of all the clothes hanging in my wardrobe, things I shall never wear again! I suppose my clothes will see me out now,' she said wistfully. 'No need to buy anything more. But then I don't like shopping either – I can't cope with crowded stores, and I used to love them.' She sighed.

Mrs Marsh looked down at her grey tweeds. 'No,' she agreed. 'No need to buy anything more.'

There was another brief silence, as they digested this discovery. Rallying first, Lady Martin decided to repair her own defences, which, she thought, had suffered in this recent exchange.

'That accident of yours, Vera,' she said. 'You're quite sure you're recovered? You want to be careful, you know.'

'Oh, it was nothing, Phyllis. I just use the stick as a precaution. It was just a silly fall, a lot of fuss over nothing. I only called the doctor because Philippa insisted.'

'Halliday?'

'Yes.'

Lady Martin began to sparkle. Vera Marsh could only admire her stamina. In the course of their friendship she had witnessed many lightings-up of this sort, usually when the name of a man was introduced into what was evidently considered to be the essentially predictable conversation of women.

'Now you must agree, Vera, Halliday is a very attractive man. Dishy,' she pronounced audaciously.

'He is quite good-looking, yes.'

'Of course, he has a soft spot for me. He came when I had bronchitis, last year, you remember. Such lovely hands, and such nice manners.'

'He appeals to women, that is quite clear. I dare say it helps him professionally.'

'He married that very amusing girl, Miriam Lloyd's daughter. She married that rather fat man, Miriam, I mean. I believe there's quite a lot of money there. Miriam was a cut above him, of course. But the daughter turned out to be quite attractive, don't you think? Vivacious. I do like a girl to be vivacious.'

'I don't know the wife – Vickie, isn't it? – all that well. To be honest she struck me as rather tiresome. But she made that little party of mine go off rather well.'

'That's where I last saw her. In a clever little red frock. Quite expensive, if I'm any judge. Do they get on well, do you know?'

'Do who get on well?'

'Halliday and his wife.'

'Really, Phyllis, how on earth should I know?' said Mrs Marsh with some distaste. Her friend's insistence on sexual speculation frequently pained her.

'Only a man like that spells trouble, in my opinion. Although I have to admit that his wife looks as if she could keep an eye on him.'

'Anyway,' said Mrs Marsh repressively. 'He didn't think there was anything wrong with my leg.'

'Oh, good,' said her friend, disappointed. 'But how did you manage? Getting about, I mean.'

'Well, I managed. I stayed in for a couple of days. All I wanted, really, was something to read.'

Anna, she thought, and almost blushed. How could I have forgotten her?

Aloud, she said, 'A friend went to the library for me. Anna Durrant,' she added scrupulously.

'That young woman whom Nick brought to your party?'

'Oh, he didn't bring her, Phyllis. She attached herself to him. He was longing to get away from her – I could see it. No, poor Anna is not Nick's type at all. He likes sophisticated women. Anna, I'm afraid, is rather simple.'

'Who was she with, then?' asked Lady Martin, losing interest.

'She came on her own, I expect,' replied Mrs Marsh, peering into the depths of her handbag and snapping it shut with a finality which signalled the end of the conversation. 'I must go, Phyllis. Nick said he'd look in this evening. Right in the middle of *The Archers*, I expect, although of course I love to see him.'

Both rose stiffly.

'You must come to me next time,' said Mrs Marsh, bending down to kiss her friend's soft powdery cheek, and inhaling the scent of *Jolie Madame* mingled with something a little older, the smell of age. This saddened her, for she knew from her own experience how it clung, was never entirely banished. She thought of it as not belonging to this life but as a sort of emanation from the grave, an indication that one's time on earth was coming to a close, and that nothing could save one from the approaching end. Chastened by this reminder that even one as determinedly sprightly as Phyllis Martin was vulnerable, she lingered awkwardly. She would have liked to have embraced her friend once more, but such expansiveness was not in her nature. I am old too, she reminded herself: there is not much to choose between us. We both of us smell of mortality, and there is nothing to be done about it.

She had noticed old people in supermarkets, hesitating over their frugal purchases, treating themselves to something sweet, an indulgence remembered from remote childhood, and smelt their careful poverty as she passed them. She had put this down to poor diet, poor hygiene, to the fatigue of old age, but now she knew that what she had witnessed was ineluctable decline, that inching nearer to the abyss against which one had no defence. She had, at the time, felt closer to the poor old men, the pugnacious old women, with their woollen hats, without knowing why. Now, bending to kiss Phyllis Martin, who was comfortably off and self-indulgent, she realized that both she and her friend were at one with those old people, instantly recognizable to the young, who would wrinkle their noses and long to escape from them. It should make one philosophical, she thought: one should be impressed by the ways of nature. Yet one felt sadness and fear. If only God would give a sign, yet He remained obstinately invisible. She then remembered that she had not gone to the Oratory, where she carried on her angry conversation with God, for some weeks, and resolved to go again as soon as the weather brightened.

Failing God, one turned to Nature. If only the year would turn, she thought longingly, as she plodded down the stairs to her own flat. If only I could smell grass and feel heat and see the sun! For now she craved only light, and thought that if she lived until the summer she would stare at the sun, taking its radiance into her very substance, letting her eyes burn until they were sightless. She would not mind dying, if it could be in the summer. She would have liked someone to expose her on a hillside, at dawn, and leave her there to die: she would endure the midday heat and the pitiless afternoon with exaltation, and then, when the light went, she would expire without regret. She glanced out of the landing window at the dry sticks of leafless shrubs, at the blackness of leafless branches. The grass below the flats had a sour sapless look, and the red of the Post Office van parked across the street provided a dull crude contrast, as if only the harshest of colours could be allowed to exist at this cruel time. She knew that spring would come eventually, but she knew that it would be too slow, too gradual for her needs. She was astonished to recognize desire, for that had long been dead. Now her desire was almost abstract, metaphysical. She desired transformation, and knew that it was not yet time, that winter was holding her prisoner, and that she must not let go until the order of release came with the returning sun. It is not yet time, she thought, as she put her key into the lock, and the thought, if anything, left her slightly cheered.

The stick impeded her, and she hung it over her arm, where it impeded her still further. Well, she could get rid of that for a start. She hung it in the hall cupboard and felt an immediate sense of relief. She would in future resist all attempts to turn her into an old woman. It was Philippa who had insisted on the stick, a kindly harassed suggestion which it would have been ungracious to resist. She had brought Bill's stick home from the hospital, when he lay dying, and had known that he would never need it again. She had appropriated it timidly when her leg was bad, wondering if she would feel any nearer to her dead husband, but had felt nothing but guilty irritation at his refusal to re-enter her life in any way. Even his memory was fading, yet she thought quite frequently of her parents, saw them in dreams as she had never seen them in life. They had been a serene but distant couple, whereas in her dreams they smiled at her eagerly, lovingly, as though she were a child. They must have worn those eager loving smiles when I was a baby, she thought, learning to walk. She marvelled at the circuitousness of time, which returned her nightly to babyhood, leaving her middle years untouched.

The thought interested her: she immediately felt the need to discuss it. But there was only Phyllis Martin with whom such a matter might be discussed: no one else was old enough. And poor Phyllis would take fright: she was basically a very fragile person. Take, for example, her refusal to offer one a drink, on the pretext that because Archie, her late husband, drank so heavily, she rarely kept any drink in the house, and when she did, for guests, almost hated to serve it. As if husbands could influence one from the grave! But Archie had made Phyllis vulnerable, as she had never been before she married him. In a way she was enjoying whatever freedom came with widowhood, but at the same time she would allow no encroachments on that freedom. There was no way in which Phyllis Martin would enjoy a discussion of memory, either recent or distant. Amazing really, she thought, that we get on so well. We have absolutely nothing in common.

She poured herself a large whisky and switched on the radio for the News, which, after a few minutes, she failed to hear. She picked up *The Times* and turned to the back page, where she scanned the weather reports from foreign cities. Then she let the paper fall, and rested her head on the back of her chair. She was quite comfortable, and even mildly regretted the prospect of being disturbed by Nick, to whom she would wish to give her full attention. He was proving more difficult in middle age than he had even been as a child, although Philippa had always been the easier of the two. Nick had been taciturn but obedient. Now he was taciturn and struck her as dangerous. This, she knew, had to do with his attitude towards women, which she saw as a civilized form of denial. He would pay them compliments, but expect these compliments not to be taken seriously. Everything must be a joke, a farce: the teasing tone, once established, must be sustained. She imagined women bound by sheer good manners to respond to this, yet thought they must be puzzled, even infuriated, by his prudence. For he was both laughing at them and protecting himself. She had seen this happening, had seen him flap a hand at a woman's importunity. She longed for him to change, to be married, yet knew that she was not to be allowed to intervene, was not even supposed to notice or to understand his stratagems. Look how angry he had been when she had mentioned Anna Durrant's name! And how angry she had been with herself ever since for dragging, even by implication, a woman such as Anna into a context in which she had no place. She

159

acknowledged, reluctantly, that Anna had been kind when she had had her fall, but it had been a remote rather than a familial kindness. There was no need to attach her further. And Nick deserved a real woman, a mature exciting woman, a woman with experience who would take him in hand and teach him some humility and gratitude. He needed, she knew, to be taught both. But he was a good son, if not a demonstrative one: he looked in on her regularly, even though it was out of his way, and in any event had more exciting things to do. With that one, admittedly major, exception, she would not want him changed.

She was listening to *The Archers* when she heard his key in the door. He had had a key ever since she had moved into the flat after Bill's death. It gave her some comfort to know that if she died without somehow alerting the children her body would eventually be found. Mrs Duncan also had a key, but she had almost ceased to rely on Mrs Duncan for this office. Mrs Duncan, it was clear, was interested only in Mrs Duncan and her exciting future. There was no faulting her: she worked well and efficiently, but there had been a slight falling off in intimacy after that so promising beginning. Once Mrs Marsh had been on the telephone when Mrs Duncan arrived. 'Oh, do excuse me a moment,' she had said. 'I want to have a word with my daily help. May I ring you back?' She had gone into the kitchen to put on the kettle, and had found Mrs Duncan stiff with disapproval. 'Is anything wrong?' she had asked. 'Housekeeper, if you don't mind, Madam, not daily help.' The 'Madam' had expressed not deference but its opposite. 'After all, I am a professional. "You're a professional, Mum," my son says.' 'I am so sorry,' she had apologized. 'You must forgive me. I'm afraid I'm living in the past these days.' She forebore to go into details of her former cook, parlourmaid, and daily woman – who really was daily – and busied herself with Mrs Duncan's coffee and biscuits. After a moment Mrs Duncan sat down on the other side of the kitchen table. But she seemed to eat her biscuit with pursed lips, and things had never been the same since.

She thought Nick looked swarthy, but put the effect of congestion down to an unhelpful overhead light. He sat down heavily, his coat unbuttoned. After a minute he handed her the evening paper. She could smell a faint emanation of whisky.

'I won't offer you a drink,' she said. 'You seem to have had one already.'

'Don't start on me, Mother. I'm not well.'

'You're not well?' she repeated, trying to still the alarm she felt. She moved over to his chair and put her dry old hand to his forehead.

'You've got a temperature,' she pronounced.

'I'm supposed to be going out to dinner.'

'Ring them up and cancel it. You're staying here tonight. You can wear Daddy's pyjamas and dressing-gown. The spare bed's already made up. I'm going to get you a hot drink and a hot-water bottle.'

He protested feebly, longing to be overruled. He was already collapsing into illness, trailing after her, coat unbuttoned and dragging on his shoulders, his voice regressing by at least three decades.

'It is only flu,' she told him brutally. 'You had better get into bed. Let me know when you're ready for your drink.'

For he had never, even as a boy, wanted her to see him undressed.

He allowed her to sit by him and to watch him as he took his aspirin and drank his tea. I must buy lemons tomorrow, she thought. She was energized by this reprieve, which had removed the sad thoughts of old age plaguing her earlier in the evening. She put his light out firmly, although it was only eight o'clock. Then she crept from the room, as she used to do when he was young. That night she lay half awake, listening for him. Yet in the morning she felt brighter than usual. So all is not gone, she thought, with something like a return of optimism, and wondered if he could eat a little toast and marmite for his breakfast.

14

Halliday rested his folded hands on Anna's case notes.

'You've lost more weight, you know. Oh, very little, I agree, but every weight loss is significant. Do you feel quite well?'

'I'm not ill . . .'

'But?'

'I feel a heaviness, a drowsiness. I long for sleep, yet I wake up exhausted.'

'Do you have a temperature in the evenings?'

'Oh, no.' She looked at him, surprised. 'I'm not ill, Lawrence. But sometimes I feel I can't go on as I am.'

'Perhaps we should talk about that.'

'I am a useless woman, I know. I feel ashamed. I have never worked, never had a child . . .'

'And why have you never done these things?'

She looked at him again. 'I think you know why. My mother needed me. She was of that generation of women who expected to be protected. She was a widow, not very competent, used to being spoilt. I loved her. She loved me – not in any very helpful way, I admit. You must remember that we were used to each other. We knew so few people! My mother's illness began when I was about fourteen, and we were both very frightened. But she seemed to recover for a while, I remember, and life was almost normal, normal enough for me to go to school and university, and then have

162

my year abroad. After that, she got worse. The piece of work I had started hung fire: it wasn't important, just something that interested me. Then she got worse again, and it was difficult for her to go out alone. When she did . . . Well, she usually had to be brought home. On the whole people were very kind.'

She closed her lips on the whole confession. She never spoke of the Ainsworth incident, feeling a need to protect her mother even in death. It was a matter of indifference to her that several people, including Halliday, knew about it, but even Halliday was not in possession of all the facts, merely remembering that Mrs Durrant had made an abortive second marriage, which ended, as he thought – as most people thought – in divorce or separation. When he had got to know her she was alone, with her daughter: there had been no trace of a man in the flat. He had sensed a tragedy of some sort, had recognized the bracing quality of the younger woman's affection, and the languor of his patient, had put it down to mourning. Perhaps the husband had died? No one had told him anything, but as he was new to the practice, he did not expect to be given the full story, especially if it were scandalous, though he had no reason to believe that this was the case.

He preferred not to think of the years in which he had known Anna and her mother, and the way in which Anna had removed them both from his care. That had hurt him: he had thought her implacable, and he had always been sensitive to the withdrawal of favour. He was perfectly capable of maintaining his professional detachment, and in any event was fond of Mrs Durrant. He was, as he had since realized, more than fond of Anna, who had banished him. For that reason he desired her forgiveness, as he would have desired his mother's, had he ever hurt her. But he thought that he had never done so. Anna represented a monstrous wrongdoing, perhaps the worst he had ever committed, in the course of a relatively blameless life. Uneasy now, in the middle years of that life, wondering why he could not be pleased, even cynically pleased, at his upward progress, he felt that at some point he had made a fatal decision, had abandoned the simple standards of truth and honesty with which he had grown up, in favour of a satisfaction which he now saw as illusory.

One of the things which separated him from his wife was the fact that she hated her mother, whom she saw as a rival for her adored father's affection. Initially he had thought this situation to be of more than passing clinical interest: he had never before come up against so clear-cut an illustration of what he had privately believed to be a psychiatric myth. It came to repel him. All parties in the case seemed to him crude, without shame. He was married by then, and used to hearing his wife's indignant denunciations of her mother: he suspected that his mother-in-law, a dry uncommunicative sort of woman with whom he had nothing in common, looked on her daughter with some distaste. This in its turn increased his pity for his wife, whom he now saw as a victim of debased familial affections. He was bound to her by rage and compassion, the one emotion usually cancelling out the other. He supposed that he would continue to be involved in this way until one of them died. But he found it tiring, and ultimately disappointing, that his marriage should have come to this, and blamed himself for succumbing so easily to the sexual lure, defiantly enjoying its excitement, while uneasily aware, all the time, that he would have to deal with his wife's conflicts, of which she, in her turn, remained remarkably ignorant.

It was part of his job to keep her ignorant, he supposed, although she was so shrewd in other ways, particularly where her own interests were concerned. But how could he enlighten her without telling her that she was shallow and greedy, accusations which she would indignantly refute? How could he, at this late stage, inform her that he thought her father monstrous, and dreaded the annual holiday, part of which was always spent at the Gibsons' large house on the Dartmouth estuary, where his father-in-law, in peaked cap, sailed his boat, and insisted that Lawrence come along as crew? He hated the water, hated his father-in-law, wanted only to walk for hours, alone, to stop at a pub for lunch – still on his own – and not to go back until nightfall, by which time he would almost be glad to see them. When he had voiced his simple desire to Vickie she had immediately assumed a look of reproach.

'But Daddy would be so hurt,' she had said. 'And you know I don't like your going off on your own like that. It looks so rude. After all, we are guests. We're not at home, Lawrence.'

'We could be,' he had once said. 'We don't have to come here.'

'But I love it here! How can you be so mean? We've always come here in the summer, ever since I was little: this place means everything to Daddy. And anyway, I think of it as my house. You know Daddy's going to leave it to me.'

'What about your mother? Won't she want it?'

She had given him one of her rare appraising looks.

'You don't want me to have it, do you? You don't like my having more money than you.'

For Gibson had settled a considerable amount of money on Vickie when she married.

'No need for you to put your hand in your pocket,' he had said officiously to Halliday. 'She'll have everything she wants.'

He was quite surprised to realize that although his own background was humble the errors of taste were all on the other side.

She was a poor tiresome little girl, and he was bound to her for life. He could think of no reason for divorcing her, and knew that if he ever mentioned it he would merely store up more wrath, more tears, more parental disapproval, although he got a fair measure of all these things when doing almost nothing to inspire them, as if he were always and entirely in the wrong. He supposed he must be, for his wife seemed relatively happy, although he suspected that he had initially appealed to her ambition rather than to her desire: she saw in him a husband for whom her friends might envy her, but she also saw a helplessness, a lack of resolution, which she could mould to her will. As she had done. Her friends duly envied her, and he, within a very short space of time, felt lonely. He had been lonely for years. These days he thought of his mother, and although he was glad she had not lived to be rebuffed by the woman he had made his wife, he longed for her company, and for the joyous love she had had for him. No one would ever love him like that again. All he could hope for now was evasion, for small intervals of time snatched from his busy life in which he could indulge his own thoughts, his own memories. He longed for silence, and thought that if he ever possessed a measure of it again he would willingly forego sex, if that was the price to be paid. Sex with Vickie was violent, uninhibited: she was a conscientious and eager lover, thought out enticing scenarios, to which he always responded. Afterwards he felt something like shame, certainly impatience. This is not grown up, he had thought at one point. Yet what else was on offer? He could not find another woman, for his wife was all-enveloping. In many ways he would have preferred no woman at all. He knew that if he had married Anna he would have gained a discreet familiar, whose presence would have absorbed all hurts. While she sat on the opposite side of his desk, in the chair reserved for patients, telling him about her mother, he longed to tell her about his own. Such effusions, such confidences were now barred to him for life. Of the two of them he considered himself to be the loser. Her own pain he had thought – if she had in fact felt any pain – had been overcome by sheer strength of character. He would have liked to have had that strength of character on his side. Yet he knew that while he despised the games he played with his wife he was now their victim, simply because he did not fear her judgement. She was his partner in vice, as Anna could never be. And there the matter more or less rested.

Anna, on the other side of his desk, thought that he was probably not listening to her, that in any event she was not saying anything that could possibly interest him. The facts of her life, as she saw it, were facts which could be ignored. But it was true that she did not feel as well as she usually did, had not felt well since returning from Paris. She had forced herself to think about the events that had taken place there as steadily and as objectively as she could. One thing was certain: the friendship with Marie-France was eroded. Even if she had taken Dunoyer's attentions too seriously, there was always the hurt that Marie-France would feel if her lover's eye ever so much as entertained the thought of another woman. At her age she had so much to lose! And why should Marie-France not revel in her innocent pride at having captured Dunoyer as a husband? Any woman might be forgiven this moment of vainglory, of victory. She had played her part already, that reduced part which was now required of her: she had already been an admiring audience, had drunk the champagne, and had made her unaccompanied escape into the dark night, an escape witnessed by Dunoyer, who had taken a moment's profit from it, and perhaps enjoyed a moment's speculation at the same time. That was all there was to it, yet instinct told her not to go back. Marie-France would now go over to the other side, and she herself would dwindle in comparison with Marie-France's happy state.

She had a horror of compassion, both her own and that of others. She was determined never to be perceived as a victim. All her life she had outfaced those who offered her their sympathy, for what they supposed was her hard life, bound to her mother as she was, and had simply smiled by way of an answer. Those who had expected more found her cold, unnatural. She had trained herself never to weep, since the few tears she had shed as a child had affected her mother to an inordinate degree and were wont to bring forth tears in return. Since learning that lesson her eyes had been dry. Stoically, like the Spartan boy with the fox beneath his shirt, she had pretended to feel nothing, had turned away slights with the same patient considered smile. Halliday, who was in fact paying attention, could see the stratified layers of self-control, and wondered, with professional interest, what would happen if a fault line ever developed. A breakdown? Unlikely: she was a strong character. But some kind of excess, perhaps. Maybe his role was simply to keep a watching brief. For in many ways he considered her to be at risk.

They watched each other carefully, recognizing disappointment. While Halliday studied her still pale face, the crasser, more jovial face of his father-in-law impinged, crowned with a peaked yachting cap, the stub of an extinct cigar clamped between yellowing teeth. Were it not for his father-in-law, he thought, his marriage might not have taken place. But it had been masterminded, for whatever Vickie wanted her devoted father saw to it that she got, and got in full measure. Anna, looking past him, saw a darkening room in Albert Hall Mansions, heard her mother's voice from the bedroom, 'Are you there, darling? Has he gone?' Neither of them had been strong enough to break away. They saw this, in an instant, as they had never seen it before. Dimly, they had blamed themselves. Those who love us are the most difficult to withstand. This is the first lesson to be learnt, she thought, but now it is too late.

Aloud she said, 'And yet I loved my mother,' and stopped abruptly.

'Yes?'

She said nothing.

'Your mother is dead,' he prompted.

But it was important to her to reach the end of this train of thought.

'It was not that my mother prevented me from marrying,' she said. 'She longed for me to marry. But only after her death. She thought that that might be arranged.'

'There's no pleasing mothers, is there?' he put in quickly. Yet he had always pleased his own.

Just as quickly she shied away from the subject of her

mother. He noted her switch of attention, but it seemed important that he give her what information she might need.

'Your mother had a mitral valve lesion,' he said. 'For her age she did quite well. She was not ill all the time.'

'I thought she had heart failure.'

'Hearts go in and out of failure,' he told her.

But her mother's heart had failed in other ways, Anna thought.

In Rome, on his honeymoon (for which his father-in-law had insisted on paying) he had been particularly impressed by a picture in the Borghese Gallery, Titian's *Sacred and Profane Love*, which shows two beautiful women sitting on the edge of a marble well-head. One is naked, the other clothed. It had puzzled him at the time, since both looked chaste. He had assumed that the naked woman represented profane love, the love that obtains at nightfall, yet she had leaned towards the other in a gesture of friendship. Sacred Love was richly dressed, but seemed indifferent. He had bought a book on Titian, and looked up this particular picture. Much to his surprise he had found that the unclothed figure was deemed to be sacred, while the other, in her brilliant dress, represented the pomps of this world. He had rejected this explanation. What he knew of love at this time had been confused with nudity, with the shedding of garments, and with them of disguises. He had acknowledged the gross disorder into which he fell when his wife removed her clothes, which she did carefully, seductively, with one eye on his reactions. He thought all this a syndrome of profane love, and was forced to accept his own untutored reaction. Anna, sitting there in her careful blue suit, seemed to him as distant, as untouchable, and as untouched, as the beautiful creature in the picture, and he was never to know whether or not his judgement was correct.

And yet she was affecting, even disturbing. Something about that pristine remoteness attracted him, as might a temperate climate, or a serious book. He read so little these days: his work kept him occupied, and his wife was talkative.

He thought, once more, that he might have made another life with her, and suspected that it might be superior to the one he currently led. When a patient telephoned him at home, and his wife answered the call, she fell into a mode of exaggerated sympathy, which caused alarm. She had proffered advice, until he had stopped her: her dignity was manifestly, and ostentatiously, offended. People admired her, he knew, and even envied him, and of course he could never be disloyal. He felt sadness on her behalf, that she could never be other than a lightweight, yet it was her lightness, her frivolity, that had initially broken down his reserve. He bore the responsibility for keeping her in a good mood, something she was not able to do for herself. He tried to suppress his irritation with the fact that despite her frequent protestations of being over-burdened she was in fact idle. 'Why don't you do some voluntary work?' he had asked.

'What, with all I have to do in the house?' she had replied. 'And all the entertaining you like me to do?'

The house was cleaned by a stoical Portuguese woman. As for the entertaining, he knew, as she must surely do, that she insisted on it, as being good for a man in his position.

'But my position doesn't depend on my entertaining people,' he had protested.

She had given him one of her level looks.

'If it weren't for me I doubt if you'd have any friends,' she had said.

This was true. He had become secretive, and disinclined to share his life, or that part of it which she allowed him. But his irritation persisted, and now spilled over on to Anna. His own mother had impressed him with her unstinting labour. Why, then, did these healthy women not work?

'What about that piece of research you were doing?' he now asked.

'A fiction,' she replied, seeing it at last for what it was. 'My mother liked to think of my being absorbed in something that would not take me out of the house, and I suppose I went along with this. Oh, it was an attractive project, and

I was quite interested, but on a purely amateur level. I could carry on with it, and pretend to be a professional, but no one would take me seriously, least of all myself.'

'So how do you spend your time?'

'I doubt if I could tell you.'

'Why is that?'

'I think you might feel sorry for me. But it has only been a year, you know . . . If I said I was "adjusting" would that be more acceptable? Don't worry, if you are worried, that is. I'll get a job.' She smiled. 'There shouldn't be any trouble. After all, I'm good with old people.'

He ignored this.

'You live alone?'

'I live alone.'

'And I suppose you don't bother to cook for yourself?'

She looked at him in surprise.

'I assure you that I eat quite adequately.'

For she was bored with this insistence on her bodily condition, and would have liked him to have asked her questions of a more philosophical nature, although she knew that this was impossible. He had disappointed her, much as he had disappointed her in the past. She had come to him for help, in hope, feeling genuinely unwell, something which rarely happened to her, and he had made pedantic noises about food, about work, whereas she had wanted something impossible – a remedy, the philosopher's stone, some magic word or gesture which would pierce the carapace of good manners with which she had armoured herself against him on all previous occasions. He had, in some way, let her down. She caught his eye then, and saw it steadily fixed on her. She returned his look: his own eye wavered and slipped away.

'I'd like you to come and see me on a regular basis, Anna. I need to monitor your weight.'

She agreed languidly. Now that the interview was over she felt an immense desire to yawn, to lie down, to drift into sleep.

'There's nothing else you're worried about?'

'Nothing at all.'

He recognized the spark of irony that he had noticed once or twice before. He had not been entirely sure that it was there: he had perceived it as a moment of discomfort for himself, and it had forced him into further deception. For deception had been forced on him by Anna in the first place: a collusion, a conspiracy into which he had fallen, half willingly, half unwittingly, and from which he had freed himself only by the violent action prompted by his impatient body. He had escaped from a dream, a spell, which had threatened to put him to sleep. And the wrench was violent. Desire had not been properly engaged, yet it had been necessary for him to escape from that shadowy room in which Anna seemed to have her being. He had been impressed by, and grateful for, her subsequent reserve, and had tried not to notice the irony in the gaze she directed at him like a beam of light into a dark corner. It had established his status as a deserter, after which only superficial conversation was possible. There was between them a failure, and not simply a failure to communicate: there should have been an accusation, a defence, followed by mutual forgiveness. A failure of nerve, perhaps. He was still able, even at this late date, to experience discomfort because of it. Her patience maddened him, made him want to handle her roughly.

'You should get out more,' he said in a suitably jovial tone. 'We can't have you sitting alone every evening.'

But she had heard this sort of remark before, and turned a deaf ear. She supposed that she had taken up too much of his time, that this was his signal for her to go. She had probably bored him, she thought, and had to assume a particularly bland expression in order to meet his eyes. When she did he flushed.

'You must come to dinner with us,' he said. 'I'll get my wife to telephone you.'

'I rarely go out in the evenings,' she replied calmly, pulling on her gloves.

172

'Well, I think you should. Don't worry, I'll take you home afterwards. And my wife would love to meet you again.'

He knew this sounded false, even as he said it. Vickie's friends were of an entirely different type: he found them noisy, materialistic. Many of them dated from her days as an estate agent. The men arrived with loosened ties, bottles of champagne in hand, and cheerfully announced their intention of getting drunk: the girls, in very short skirts, shrieked and protested, but were exceedingly tough. He suspected that they found him provincial, although he had long spoken without the trace of an accent. His appearance was against him: his fair good looks, his height and his leanness conferred on him an assurance which he did not feel. He had a stay-at-home soul, frequently assented to opinions which he did not hold, less out of cowardice than out of a desire to absent himself from the ensuing discussion. He strove to keep a little silence for himself, had an odd vision of himself sitting by the fire, reading, yet the fire was like no fire that he could trace, unless it was the kitchen range at home. He still thought of it as home. The house in Tryon Street had no fireplaces, and the radiators were extremely hot. He went round turning them down. Vickie turned them up again.

He hated Anna to leave him on this false note, knew that he had let her down, that he had compounded, even in so minor a way, his original fault. Seeing her sitting in front of him, attentive to his banal words, he had realized the full weight of his original desertion. He could have saved her, he knew, and then she in her turn could have saved him. And the moment when he could have made his choice had passed, or else he had given it the slip; he had pretended, entirely for his own purposes, that she did not exist, did not pose a problem, did not need to be saved. He was aware, seeing her now, that she still needed to be saved, and that all that he could legitimately offer her was care of the most routine kind, care of her body, that body which he had so singularly failed to claim for himself. He could monitor her food and see to it that she slept, knowing that all this was within the bounds prescribed by his professional conscience, knowing at the same time that it was a sham.

And yet he did not want to see her go. Her composure struck him as frightening, almost grotesque: he feared for her. He had long feared for himself, knew himself to be alienated from his own life, had joked, even to himself, about a mid-life crisis, a male menopause, had even advanced the understanding of such disorders. He knew that men like himself, nurtured by loving and sacrificial mothers, would always want a woman's approval, would seek absolution from a woman for any faults too hastily committed, would want to be forgiven and consoled. He sensed, in Anna's drooping head, that he had failed her, and tried to summon the energy to be exasperated. She noted that he was becoming irritable, unable to banish unwelcome feelings as they flooded in, and regarded his baffled eyes with pity.

She held out her hand.

'Goodbye, Lawrence. Thank you for giving me so much of your time.'

'Goodbye, then, Anna. I shall want to see you in a couple of weeks' time. Oh, and don't forget that you're coming to dinner! I'll get Vickie to give you a ring.'

He is worried that I might commit suicide, she thought, as she walked neatly down Cheltenham Terrace. The odd thing is that if I did he would feel responsible. Therefore I shall never do it. She saw the difficulty he was in, not quite happy with the life he had chosen for himself, lonely in the company of his wife, only at ease with the sick and the weak, offering his own weakness in the form of comfort, a hand held, a reassuring smile, taking strength from such contact as from an immense pool of loving-kindness. Though she knew nothing about him beyond what he had told her of his mother and her sacrifices she had a vision of his early life, of the chapel in the back streets of Leicester, of dull moody Sunday afternoons, of lowering skies, of abandoned newspapers blowing in a gritty wind, of the smell of kitchen soap.

174

She could not blame him, she did not blame him for exchanging this bleak landscape for something more enlivening. She blamed herself for failing to keep him entertained. For he would respond quickly, she saw, to any kind of display. Now she felt sadness for them both. Of the two, her part seemed the easier to bear, with no witnesses, no dependants. She longed to see him happier, and in the middle of the King's Road, on a misty Monday afternoon, knew it for a fact that she could have made him happy, that she knew this, and that he knew it too.

15

At last the whitening sky promised some relief from winter. There was as yet nothing in the way of spring, but every morning it got light earlier, so that Mrs Marsh, preparing Nick's breakfast tray in the kitchen, could see quite clearly, instead of feeling her way around, as she seemed to have done for so many months past. A cruel winter, she thought, as she poured hot water into the teapot to warm it, and not quite over. Yet when she had been shopping, on the previous morning, she had noticed frail blossom on the branches of the two almond trees in a nearby garden; looking up, she had seen thick buds, pregnant and ready to break, on the magnolia, the pride of the little street. But it was the air itself which promised change. It seemed charged with a new expectancy, as if each day it might attempt more in the way of progress. After early mist and frost a pallid sun appeared in the sky, first as a puddle of white light, and later as an almost recognizable yellow disk. There was no heat in the sun; indeed it seemed charged with coldness, as did the air, which, at the end of the afternoon, declined again into mist. Yet for those few hours it was possible to feel a new optimism, to step less heavily than usual across to the fishmonger, to put an extra pint of milk into her basket on wheels, to exchange a few pleasant words with the chemist as she bought more Kleenex, and to reach the flat again, a little out of breath but triumphant, as she had not felt for years, she now realized, since the children were young, before she was widowed. And yet I have not minded living alone, she thought. It is just that this little illness of Nick's has reconnected me with happier times. She smiled almost shyly at the thought that she had once been happy. She was even happy now.

He had been with her for five days, most of them spent in bed. He was a docile patient, although he did not seem particularly ill. She suspected that he was enjoying this period of enforced rest, during which he too could revert to a simpler time in his life, before he was married and divorced and disillusioned, and assiduous and dismissive towards women for whom he did not care. All the complications of his life seemed to have been lifted from him, as he lay in bed in his mother's spare room, with its white walls and its blue carpet, and its white curtains patterned with blue flowers and green leaves. A certain amount of furniture had found its way into this room from other parts of the flat: there was a bulky mains radio, which had been replaced by various transistors, and which still worked, though faintly, and a desk in which his mother kept her insurance policies and other, similar documents. In the wardrobe, he knew, there was a large roll of wallpaper, left over from the time when the flat had last been decorated. A handsome mirror, gilt framed, and decorated with curlicues of golden plaster, now dusty and slightly chipped, hung on the opposite wall, above a small bergère: if he sat upright in bed he could see his face in its dim lunar surface.

He was strangely contented. Every morning he devoted to being ill, and every afternoon to getting better. He listened to *The Archers* and the afternoon play. This was his favourite time. With the advent of the news and more serious programmes he was reminded of the fact that he was fifty-one, a responsible citizen, and a businessman who was due in New York the following week, all of which information struck him as highly unwelcome.

Mrs Marsh, waking from her nap, which she took in her

chair in the sitting-room so as not to disturb him, would hear him moving about in the bathroom. He usually took a bath, while she prepared the tea. No cook, having made few successful cakes in her life, she was somewhat at a loss when it came to tempting his appetite. Fortunately he did not seem interested in food, although he ate his lunch of grilled fish uncomplainingly, largely because it came on one of the few beautiful plates left over from one of the services he remembered from the old house, and because the fish forks, though a little tarnished and in need of silver polish, were heavy and ornate. He had always loved them and now he supposed that they would be his when his mother died. This introduced a morbid train of thought, which he quickly banished with a radio phone-in. He had previously had no idea that people listened to such things. For tea they ate biscuits, guiltily but with pleasure, aware that people of their sort would normally be served a toasted tea-cake or a slice of freshly made jam sponge. Where had she had that sort of tea, Mrs Marsh wondered. Was it with Amy Durrant? She had not thought about her for some time, even less about Anna; indeed she had thought about nothing but Nick for five happy days. Tired she might have been; she could not deny that she was tired, that she found it hard to suppress a groan when she sank into bed at night, but there was no doubt that she felt more hopeful, more optimistic. She did not even mind relinquishing *The Times*, even before she had been through the Deaths and In Memoriam columns: she promised herself that she would look at them in bed, but by that time she had almost lost interest, and simply wanted to close her eyes and sleep, and thus gather the strength to get through the following day. For her days were busy now.

Shopping, which she had always detested, now yielded unexpected pleasures. 'What would you recommend for flu?' she asked Mr Davies, the chemist. 'I've got my son at home in bed.' It gave her pride to say this, knowing that some might have pitied her for being a widow and alone. 'Getting on, is he?' asked her new friend, the fishmonger. 'Mind you don't go catching it now – there's a lot of it about. I've got some lovely plaice this morning. Do you a couple of fillets?' 'Make it four,' she said happily. 'His appetite is a lot better now.' They had lunched on fish and mashed potatoes for the last couple of days; she had few dishes in her repertoire, although she had once appreciated fine food. She decided to roast a chicken for the weekend, if Nick were still with her by that time. She feared not: he had spoken of New York, and would want to go home to pack and prepare his papers. In fact this might be his last day with her, unless she could prevail upon him to stay a little longer. He was quite well enough to go home, although strangely disinclined to leave the spare room. Nick's room, she thought of it now.

In the evenings, when he sat with her, they spoke of his father. She had not realized how devoted Nick was to his father's memory, though with something of her old shrewdness she thought that his brief illness might have made him softer, almost sentimental. He looked like his father, of that there was no doubt, especially now that his face had settled into mature folds. If only he could remain like this, subdued and agreeable, receptive to her reminiscences and observations! He himself seemed to be thinking along the same lines. It was as if, restored to his mother's ministrations, he had laid aside his conqueror's sneer, had relinquished his role as married woman's escort, lover, flatterer, betrayer, had become naïf and hopeful once more. He liked being the object of a woman's attention, when that attention was not carnal: he found it natural.

In addition to his mother's austere care he had profited from the enthusiastic presence of Mrs Duncan, who had been subjugated at an early stage. Sometimes it seemed to him that Mrs Duncan and his mother vied with each other as to who was to take in his mid-morning Bovril or to prepare his lunch-time tray. Mrs Duncan liked to put her head round the door to wish him goodbye as she was leaving, and would even ask Mrs Marsh if there was anything she would like her to bring in on her way to work the following morning.

Nick had effected a timely rapprochement between the two women, who found that they could converse quite happily as long as a man was the prime topic under discussion. Mrs Marsh stopped worrying about Mrs Duncan's finer feelings, and Mrs Duncan raised no objection to working extra hours. The money was useful, and she had her sights set on a new microwave, which she could take down to the house at Easter.

But the day came, all too soon, when Nick stood in the hall, with his overcoat buttoned, and his briefcase once more in his hand, and said goodbye to his mother. She found herself longing for him to stay, although she now realized that she was very tired. It might be pleasant to sit through the morning with the paper, to doze in the afternoon without listening for him, but nothing would ever again compare with the pleasure of looking after him – so brief and unexpected a pleasure, which had restored her to life when she had almost despaired of the long winter and what it was doing to her. She had never been worried about this illness of his, had felt a mother's strength and confidence when his temperature was high, and had been convinced of a good outcome, even in the sharp cold nights, when natural fatigue wore down her own resistance. She had equated his illness with the lightening morning sky, and thus with a time of hope. She thought that he too had enjoyed this brief respite in his busy and predatory life, and it was with regret that she saw his face, its colour once more normal and healthy, resume its harsh expression, as if the boy he had been were once again becoming the man he thought he had to be. He did not need to bend far to kiss her; they were nearly the same height. She thought that she had never seen him look so handsome. He thought that without her almost girlish smile she would have looked quite shockingly old. He was going to New York. She would not see him for a week.

She felt her way back to the sitting-room. The day seemed to have darkened, and once again she sensed the cold air pressing against the windows. Strange, when she had been so convinced that the winter was past. She even thought of switching on the electric fire, something she normally never did until the evening, and not always then. She supposed that she could now tell Mrs Duncan not to come every morning, although it was quite pleasant to have her company. But perhaps her own attractions would naturally diminish now that Nick had gone, and Mrs Duncan would wish to return to her fascinating life, away from the flat which now contained only her bleak and unrewarding self.

She supposed that the barriers would now go up again, and even thought that they must do. She had enjoyed those mornings sitting over the coffee in the kitchen, discussing Nick's likes and dislikes, crumbs of biscuits all around them, but looking back she had felt a little sad and guilty that her own rigid standards had dropped, even by a fraction. She saw herself in caricatural pose, gossiping with Mrs Duncan, who needed no encouragement, and who was willing to discuss her children's ailments by way of fair exchange. Nick's altogether correct symptoms were as nothing, Mrs Duncan pronounced, compared with the time when Keith had had mumps. This was a worry of a quite different order, said Mrs Duncan, lowering her eyelids discreetly. Mrs Marsh would understand what she meant; there was no need to spell it out. 'Quite,' said Mrs Marsh. 'I wonder if you'd be so kind as to bring me a couple of tins of vegetable soup when you come tomorrow? I feel a little tired now. The soup will do for my lunch. I don't particularly want to go out.' There was a quid pro quo about these matters, she reflected. Without Keith's mumps she would not have had the courage to ask for the soup. They both rose reluctantly. Mrs Duncan would have liked to smoke a cigarette, but did not quite have the courage to do so. I must give it up, she thought; it spoils my image. There was an air of regret about the two of them, as if both had belatedly realized that their children had grown up and gone away. When Mrs Duncan said, 'You'll miss him,' Mrs Marsh nodded almost sadly. Then she thought it time to bring this sort of conversation to a close once and for all, for she feared further examination of her feelings, preferring to keep them to herself.

She no longer looked forward to going to the shops, to exchanging a few words with the shopkeepers, whom she suddenly seemed to know quite well. Just as suddenly they joined the cast of characters in her mind, for she doubted that she would have much more to say to them. With Nick gone it seemed as if all the springs of communication had dried up, leaving her to be the same terse old woman she had been before those blessed five days. She sat on in her chair, brooding, while Mrs Duncan turned out the spare room, stripping the bed and opening the windows wide. Somehow she could not settle to *The Times*: she still had yesterday's copy, with the crossword half filled in by Nick. Tomorrow he would be doing the crossword as he crossed the Atlantic, in Concorde. She felt tired now; when Mrs Duncan had gone she would heat up some soup and have it for lunch, with a wholemeal roll. There was no hurry; she was not hungry. She might even lie down properly this afternoon, although it was her day for the hairdresser. She supposed that she would keep her appointment; there was no point in letting one's appearance suffer, even if one had never been a beauty. But she felt rooted to her chair, and when Mrs Duncan announced that she was off now she felt quite startled, as if she had been asleep, or at least had fallen into some kind of doze. 'Goodbye,' she said, recovering herself with difficulty. 'Thank you for everything. See you tomorrow. Goodbye now.'

She crept to the hairdresser's as if it were her last assignation on this earth. She was aware of feeling weak, too weak to sit under the dryer, which always made her feel uncomfortable, too weak to enquire after Tony's fiancée and the shampoo girl's wedding plans. These were going ahead, she knew, and it became her to show an interest. Trailing the limp fastenings of her gown she took her place at the basin, and was aware, as she leaned her head back, of a stiffness in her neck. 'A little tired,' she allowed, as the girl asked her if she were all right. 'I've been looking after my son. He's had the flu.' But the incident now seemed drained of interest, as if it had taken place a long time ago and was now buried in the past. Sitting stiffly before the mirror she tried to concentrate on an article in a magazine the girl had kindly put in front of her. 'How to tell if you've had an orgasm,' she read studiously, without understanding what it was all about. She supposed this information was meant for the very young; such matters were never mentioned in her day. She felt as though she were eavesdropping on a subject she had no business to entertain, but the young were different. Gail, the girl who had washed her hair, was full of life and curiosity. Although the day was cold she wore an abbreviated T-shirt which seemed designed to slip off her shoulders. She always enquired kindly after Mrs Marsh's health, but as if the answers could not possibly concern her. Combing through the wet grey hair, she kept her eyes averted from the pink scalp underneath. The skull beneath the skin, thought Mrs Marsh, who repeated the phrase to herself every time this happened.

Tony came up with his usual swagger; a soft-hearted boy, he had adopted the stance of an athlete or a gangster as being appropriate to his status as chief stylist. 'You look as if you're about to take part in the Tour de France,' she had once said to him, in a moment of exceptional effervescence. He had been delighted, and had had a special regard for her ever since. 'How is Sandra?' she managed to say to him, although her mouth was dry. 'Oh, busy,' he said indulgently. 'Full of plans. You know how they are.' He spoke as if Mrs Marsh had long been out of the running, even out of the human race. She laid down the article on orgasms as the dryer was fitted over her head. 'Tea or coffee?' asked Tony, lowering his face to hers. 'I wonder if I might have a glass of water?' she managed to ask.

'All right, are you?' they said to her, as she slowly shrugged her way into her coat. She could hear the unspoken words as she negotiated the door. 'Poor old thing,' she repeated to herself, as if the words had really been spoken. She reached the flat and sank down in her chair, looking around her with dismay as she realized that she might never move out again. I can't be ill, she thought. I have never been ill in my life, and now I am too old to endure an illness. I might die, and the children would be shocked, even disappointed. The thought of Nick looking in, as he had promised, on his return from New York, and finding her dead, prompted her to telephone the doctor. 'He's rushed off his feet,' said the receptionist. 'There's so much of this flu about. I should go to bed if I were you. I doubt if he'll be round tonight. I'll give him the message. I dare say he'll fit you in tomorrow.' Suddenly there was nothing to do but endure whatever was in store for her. She found she no longer had the strength to make a cup of tea or fill a hot-water bottle. In any event she felt very warm. She managed to remove her clothes and even to hang them up, and to fetch a glass of water, although she rarely did so these days for fear of knocking it over. When had that happened? When her leg was bad? Well, I got over that, she thought, and I shall get over this. But by now she felt very ill indeed.

The night passed vividly, in the form of streaks and flashes, of sudden illuminations. Some time after midnight it occurred to her to wonder whether Bill had ever had an affair with Phyllis. They had liked each other, that much was clear, and Phyllis was having a wretched time with Archie, who was drinking too much. She fell asleep on this thought, woke up again, and realized that Phyllis would most probably have talked him out of it. That was her speciality. But there had been that associate of his, that lady broker, unusual for those days, whom he had asked her to invite to dinner, and with whom he occasionally travelled to meetings. She had not thought to enquire too closely. In any event he had come back to her in the act of dying. She remembered his eyes following her longingly round the room. It was life he longed for, more life, and she had been unable to give it to him.

She longed for life herself, all thoughts of dying vanquished. She only wanted to die in perfect health, with her faculties in good order, not like this, in a bed which was alternately too hot and too cold. Her head ached and her mouth was dry, but she felt too shaky to reach for her glass of water, and quickly became dizzy if she tried to sit up. She must lie as she was until somebody turned up: the doctor must see her at her worst, and then, only then, would she make the effort to get better. She knew that it would be a very great effort this time, and it occurred to her that she might not be up to it. The thought frightened her. The night seemed huge and menacing, a portent of the night to come. She grappled with her fears until they exhausted her. Towards dawn she slept.

She made no attempt to get out of bed in the morning, but waited until she heard Mrs Duncan's key in the lock. Mrs Duncan entered on a blast of scent (Keith kept her well supplied, she had told Mrs Marsh) and immediately assumed a look of horror.

'I don't want to come too near,' she said. 'They'll kill me at home if I catch it.'

It seemed as if Nick's flu had been in a different category, indulged, non-contagious.

'I expect you'd like a cup of tea,' she said, backing away. 'Then I'll do the sitting-room. I don't suppose you'll want anything to eat. I won't stay too long, if you don't mind. Maybe you'll feel better tomorrow. Only I was going to ask you if we could go back to three mornings a week. My husband doesn't want me to overdo it.'

'If you could just wait until the doctor's been,' whispered Mrs Marsh.

'Oh, doctor's coming, is he?'

She immediately looked more competent. Later she brought in a cup of tea and *The Times*, both of which lay untouched, until she took them away again, when the doorbell rang. Mrs Marsh noted that she had taken off her overall in honour of the doctor's visit. There was a sudden aroma of coffee, again in honour of Halliday. He came in smelling of the cold outdoors, but without a coat. Take care, she wanted to say to him, but she was too tired. He smiled at her, and said, 'I'm just going to take your temperature. You can relax. It's only the flu. Three days and you'll be better, I promise!'

How kind he was! He raised her up, listened to her back and to her chest. She looked at him worshipfully, no longer ashamed of her flattened breasts, for he was no longer an attractive man, but every mother's son, and she longed to tell him so. When he assured her that she was a healthy woman, and that she would soon be well, she believed him and longed to thank him. Even Mrs Duncan was mollified, and brought in two cups of coffee on a tray, with the eternal biscuits on which she seemed to thrive. This time, with the doctor in the room, Mrs Marsh made an effort to drink and found that the hot coffee seemed to restore her.

'I'm sure you were good to your mother,' she said to the doctor's kind face.

His smile faded. 'Not good enough', he said. 'I was with her when she died, but only just. Most of the time I was too far away.'

'I'm sure you were a good son,' she said, this time more firmly.

'Do you think so?'

'Oh yes.'

'I still miss her,' he said.

'That proves how close you were.'

She saw his smile, which seemed to linger in the room, even after he had gone. She wanted silence, then, after this significant exchange, and reassured Mrs Duncan, who agreed to come in on the following morning. She thought she might sleep, if only she were left alone, and in fact welcomed the lonely afternoon, for her thoughts no longer frightened her. She prepared for sleep, mindful of the night to come, when more sleep would be needed and might be in short supply. She lay on her bed as if on a great raft, willing to be led out into the sea. She lay becalmed; all fear had left her. She felt the tides drawing her on, and when she woke it was with a feeling of surprise. She heard the clock in the hall strike six. She slept again and woke in the dark, but the dark was dense, and she felt a flicker of fear. But then she heard the clock strike again: five this time. She had slept through the night.

The second day was easier. Reserves of sleep had fortified her to endure the long hours ahead, and there was a slight, a very slight, return of confidence. Mrs Duncan, unsettled by Mrs Marsh's silence and passivity, co-operated to the extent of bringing cups of tea and placing a jug of water on the bed-side table. Most observations, however, were aimed from a safe distance, and Mrs Marsh had to turn a painful head to the doorway of her bedroom, in the shelter of which Mrs Duncan stood in a defensive attitude. No backbone, thought Mrs Marsh briefly, a thought which was reinforced when Mrs Duncan informed her that she would need some time off: her daughter wanted her to go shopping – a treat they both enjoyed – and they planned to go to the West End on the following day, if that was all right with Mrs Marsh.

'Quite all right,' said Mrs Marsh.

Mrs Duncan hesitated. 'Only you shouldn't be on your own. Isn't there someone I could telephone?'

'My daughter is far away,' replied Mrs Marsh, feeling an upsurge of sadness for the daughter who would have to look after her when the time came, if indeed it were not already here. She supposed that Philippa should be told, in case she were to die, but was unwilling to summon her. If I get better it will be time to talk to her then, she thought, for the idea of frightening Philippa into attendance was repugnant to her. She was a good girl, had always been good, her father's favourite, just as Nick had been his mother's. Philippa had been plain but sunny-natured, sometimes puzzled, never resentful. She had married her first boyfriend, had cheerfully gone with him to Norwich, had had two cheerful children, and survived her husband's early death if not cheerfully, then at least sensibly. And now that there was the possibility of someone new in her life her unremarkable face had taken on a certain serenity, a dignity that became her. Shocked as she would certainly be when she heard that her mother had been ill, and virtually alone, she could at least be spared a sickroom at its worst, thought Mrs Marsh. She was aware of the tired smell of bedclothes, of her own unwashed face. Thank goodness I had my hair done, she thought.

'Well, I've done it,' announced Mrs Duncan defiantly, from the doorway.

'Done what?'

'Made arrangements for someone to be with you. You can't be left alone like this.' She could not quite admit that she was doing the leaving. 'I telephoned Anna Durrant. Well, she's got nothing to do all day, and she could get you a bit of shopping.'

'You shouldn't have done that,' said Mrs Marsh, who was sincerely annoyed.

'I could never forgive myself if anything happened to you.' There was a slight silence. 'And I do want to see my Louise,' she said in an altered tone.

She was on the verge of tears, torn between her conscience and her desire. How she longs to be free, thought Mrs Marsh. She is as impatient as a girl, her good nature fretted by anticipation.

'You go,' she said, feeling weak at the thought of being alone again. 'If you could just take the key round to Anna . . .'

Mrs Duncan assented with alacrity. When the door finally closed behind her the silence grew enormous. Only the clock in the hall gave forth a sound, and once it had struck all sense of time was lost. She was almost impatient for the sound of the key in the door. It hardly mattered whose key it was, so long as somebody came. It was Anna who came, on almost silent feet; it was Anna's face bending over hers, her expression neutral, studious. She disappeared silently, and reappeared with a hot-water bottle.

'Hold this,' she said. 'I'm going to get you into the chair while I change your bed.'

Mrs Marsh followed the beautiful swirl of the unfolded sheet with grateful eyes. Such whiteness! Such pillows! She felt that she would never leave such a bed again, but Anna had other plans. An eiderdown was tucked over her in the chair, and a cup of bouillon placed beside her.

'How long have you been like this?' said the distant voice.

'I can't remember. Two or three days, perhaps.'

'You had better eat something. I'll be back in about twenty minutes. I'm just going out shopping.'

As a nurse she seemed austere, unloving, which was surprising in view of her closeness to her mother in those last years, thought Mrs Marsh. But she had a curious authority: she knew about illness and did not sentimentalize it. She had said little, had seemed terse, but had effectively taken charge. With this change in her fortunes Mrs Marsh began to anticipate recovery.

Lunch came on a tray: a little halibut, taken off the bone, turned in butter, sprinkled with grated cheese, and grilled, followed by a baked apple. After this she crept along to the bathroom, washed her face, and felt better. She was not, apparently, to be allowed to return to bed, but was given another hot-water bottle and supplied with *The Times*. She is quite cruel, really, thought Mrs Marsh, saddened by her own submission. But she felt better, stronger, consented to change her nightgown, and got thankfully into bed, drooping with tiredness at six o'clock. When Anna left Mrs Marsh began to revise her plans for letting Philippa know about her illness. Compared with Philippa (whose happiness must be sacrificed, alas) Anna was without feeling, moving as efficiently and as wordlessly as any hospital nurse. And yet she was grateful for that very wordlessness, so different from Anna's earlier and almost embarrassing affection. Mrs Marsh feared that if Anna were to show the same affection in these changed circumstances the embarrassment would be difficult to bear. She meant her own embarrassment, for she felt threatened by gratitude and had never found it easy to show her feelings.

Two days later she was seated in the sitting-room in her dressing-gown, *The Times* open at the obituaries page but as yet unread. Anna was in the bedroom, remaking her bed. I have recovered, thought Mrs Marsh. It was not easy, but I did it. Tomorrow Philippa would be here, and then she would go back with her to Norwich for a week or two. Anna could somehow return the key to Mrs Duncan. The details of how this was to be done were unclear, but she decided not to worry about them. When she heard Nick's key in the lock she could hardly suppress a murmur of joy, for she had seriously thought that she might never see him again.

'Well, Mother, what's all this?' he said, bending down to kiss her.

'Only the flu,' she said, deliberately offhand. 'I have been well looked after. The doctor came,' she added.

Anna came in, pale, in her red suit.

'Oh, good evening,' he said, surprised.

'Good evening. Your mother has been quite unwell, but I think she is better now. Your sister will be here tomorrow.'

He found her tone repressive, was puzzled and a little annoyed by her presence.

'Anna has been very kind,' said Mrs Marsh. 'I won't keep you, Anna. Nick will stay with me for a bit. And Philippa will be here tomorrow.'

'If you're sure,' said Anna.

'Very kind of you to look after Mother,' said Nick. There was a brief silence, in which, thought Mrs Marsh, Anna would surely protest her willingness. But it was Nick who said, rather automatically, she had to admit, 'Perhaps you'd like to have dinner one evening?'

Anna smiled, and laid her head close to that of Mrs Marsh.

'Goodbye, Aunt Vera,' she said. 'Call me if you need me.'

She made as if to kiss her, but Mrs Marsh felt tears of weakness and gratitude threatening and turned her head abruptly away, pretending to search for a handkerchief in the handbag on the floor by the side of her chair.

'There was no need to ask her out,' she said to Nick, after the door had closed.

'You've changed your tack, Mother. Last time round you wanted me to marry her.'

'She seems different now, quite hard.'

'Don't worry. I doubt if I'll get in touch. I doubt if she'd want me to.'

'You know how to ensure a refusal, don't you?' said his mother, with a touch of her old asperity.

But Nick, who had met a certain Mrs Tierney, a divorcée, in New York, and had been greatly taken with her, thought that all that might soon change, but that there was no need to worry his mother in her weakened state with speculations and assurances which he intended in any event to keep to himself, at least for the time being.

16

The call came all too soon.

'Anna? How are you?' Again the swoop of commiseration. 'It's Vickie here. Vickie Halliday. Lawrence's wife. He's mentioned you several times.'

'Yes, he is my doctor.'

'Well, of course he is! Now the thing is, we want you to come to dinner. Nothing formal, just the three of us. We want to get to know you better.'

'Actually, I'm not going out much in the evenings just at present . . . Later, perhaps . . .'

'But you must! We can't have that, Anna! You mustn't give in, you know, you must make an effort. There's no need to sit in a corner just because you're on your own.'

'I don't think . . .'

'Is there any reason why you can't come?' said the voice, more sharply this time. 'Or won't come? Is that it?'

There is every reason, she thought. Because you set my teeth on edge. Because you offend me without even being aware that you are doing so. Because you are trying to be kind to me out of the immense reserves of what I am supposed to think of as your charity. Because, for some reason, you dislike me, regard me with suspicion. Because you are displeased that I pre-dated you in Lawrence's life. Because you want to remind me that he married you and not me. Because there will be a show of domesticity which

I shall find hard to bear but which will be put on expressly for my benefit. Because we should get along much better, if we have to get along at all, if we view each other from a distance.

To say all this was impossible on many counts. It had been decreed by Vickie that a sort of friendship was to be enacted, although it was clear that she already felt a sharp animosity with regard to her husband for requiring this service from her. For Vickie, marriage had been easily accomplished, so easily that she regarded the unmarried with contempt. Graceful and insinuating, she had been her father's pet, and had simply carried her assumption of favours granted over into her relations with other men, except that with other men she could use her sexuality to good effect. She had not, perhaps, looked for intimacy, beyond the intimacies of sex: to be known, to be explored, to be understood, to be instructed had never been her ambition or her desire. Her character, she thought, was fully formed. She considered herself to be more mature than her husband, who had nevertheless passed several critical tests: he was very attractive, he was a professional man, he had a responsible nature, which meant that he would look after her, and he was very slightly in awe of her temper and her tears, both of which she used unselfconsciously and to good effect. Her idea of marriage was to pass from the care of her father to the care of her husband; she expected the same degree of indulgence and of cherishing, and could continue, in some ways, to be a child, with the child's right to care and constant attention.

With this childishness went the intermittent maturity that had caused her to single out Lawrence in the first place. 'He will do,' had been her first thought, for she was not getting any younger and she had been to too many weddings. She knew that she had certain advantages: her father's money, her pretty body, which she seemed anxious to indulge. She saw his eyes linger on her and sharpen slightly; she saw him turn reluctantly back to the girl whom he had brought to the party at which they had met. When he looked at her again he flushed, and she knew that he would offer no resistance. After that it had been easy to detach him from his girl and to carry him off. Confidence had made her indifferent to the clichés of courtship, and she invited him into her flat for coffee after he had taken her home. The rest was a foregone conclusion. Steered towards her family, made privy to the jokes which passed between Vickie and her father, there was no possibility that he would be allowed to remain as her lover unless something more serious were in the offing. The marriage, it seemed, was a triumph for both of them, although they experienced a certain amount of difficulty in steering it past the wedding and the honeymoon.

Since that time Lawrence had diminished slightly in her eyes, although he had retained his looks, and his professional standing had increased. I do what I can to help him, she told her friends, and from time to time Lawrence himself. She would even help him to the extent of inviting his very few friends to dinner, although they were nothing like as amusing as her own. In so doing she was aware of conferring her favour, even, for the space of an evening, her patronage. She usually complained of tiredness once they had gone. In this way Lawrence saw his own circle reduced, and was forced to rely on his wife's friends, whom he did not much like. His passive disposition helped him there.

The energy with which he had suggested that she invite Anna had momentarily annoyed her; she did not see why this woman, whom she had met only briefly, had to enter her house. Questioning had brought to light something of Anna's story. 'I have known her for some time,' he had said, which alerted her to a possibility of danger. But what danger could there be? Anna Durrant was a quiet woman in middle age, with nothing much to show for it, no husband, no lover, and no possibility of either, if Vickie were any judge. Yet there was something about her very quietness which gave her pause. Her own husband was remote in the same way when it suited him. She suspected an affinity which put her on her guard. Her instincts were acute, and although she despised what she thought of as Lawrence's weakness she knew that he might, if the circumstances were different, be drawn towards that impression of silence and strength which Anna had conveyed at their last meeting. She knew that there was no better way to neutralize Anna than to be friendly with her, as only she knew how to be friendly towards those who were vaguely unfortunate. For Anna was surely unfortunate. Nevertheless she would be on her guard.

Anna, at the end of the telephone, felt driven by a hard will to consent to what was being proposed. Besides, as was being pointed out to her, she had few other calls on her time. But that is rather the point, she wanted to say, and it has been overlooked. When people remember me I am supposed to be grateful. It is assumed that I am so deservedly humble that I shall be overcome when any attention comes my way. That is an error. What she wanted to tell Vickie Halliday was that it would be better all round if this dinner did not take place. Lawrence would not have a false feeling of security from having brought his affections out into the open (and under the scrutiny of his wife), Vickie could continue to ignore her completely, and she, Anna, could avoid the glimpses of domesticity which they both, in their various ways, and for diverging reasons, proposed to offer her.

She was aware, belatedly, of change, of protest, as yet undefined. She remembered her fantasy of escaping to another place, another climate, and wondered if she would ever have the courage to enact it. Certainly she did not underestimate the amount of courage that would be needed. What kept her in her place was a habit of affection, rather than affection itself: she was puzzled when it was refused or denied and tended to persist in its quest, not being quite adept at reading the signals. She did not see why she should relinquish her own memory of Lawrence's past attentions; what she did see was that his wife did not intend to allow her to retain it. She disliked his complicity in this false friendship, and remembered that in the past she had regretted his all too pliant nature. I would have been the strong one, she thought; maybe I still am. She detected a certain wariness in the Hallidays, a wariness which had prompted this unwelcome invitation. She was to be neutralized, made harmless, so that she could be discarded once again. Something about her threatened them, but drove them on in a clumsy attempt to disarm her.

She felt a distaste for their crudeness, felt pity, even, that they were so determined. Poor Lawrence, who only wanted love and approval, who could not bear discord, who wanted all his friends to be friends, who was grateful for even a pretence of affection – nothing could now be revealed to him of her reservations, of her own foreknowledge that this encounter, in these circumstances, would be a mistake, after which perhaps they could never meet again. Nor did she want to see him at home, the home he had chosen, with the wife whom he had chosen. Although her own feelings had, she thought, been dealt with at the time, had been coloured by her mother's plight, and the iron discipline to which she had subjected herself, she was newly aware of a commingling of love and injustice such as she had not fully experienced before. If only he had waited, she thought, and if only I had not. And now it was all over, irrevocable, dead and buried, apart from this new awareness of hers, which led her to reject the plans made for her by others. For that had been the pattern so far. She thought that with a little encouragement she might eventually be free of the past, but that she was not yet angry enough to make the break herself. He could have helped me, she thought. Because he is safe he thinks he is helping me now. It is what is called extending the hand of friendship. But it was love that was in question, and neither of us can quite forget that. His sharp-witted wife is already on the alert, quite rightly, and I am to be comprehensively put in my place.

She was not emancipated enough to frame a refusal which would somehow obey the social rules. How did one refuse an invitation that was angrily pressed on one, when it was pointed out that it was for one's own good, and that in any case one had nothing better to do? Once again she was being reduced to good behaviour, and the falsity of it made her feel quite faint. All she desired now was to be known, if only by one person. Given the choice she would still wish that person to be Halliday, while realizing that this was impossible. She did not contemplate underhand behaviour, for she was a novice in this matter. She wished for justice, that grand amorphous wish, and that she might have some part of it for herself. Again she felt pity for the Hallidays, in whom she aroused such clumsy feelings. At the same time she felt a certain sorrow that she was to be asked to pass yet another test.

Aloud she said, 'Yes, of course, I'd love to come. Thursday would be fine.'

After replacing the receiver she went and stood at the window to see if she could detect any signs of future warmth, but the grass below was sour and livid after a recent light snowfall, which had astonished everyone, coming so late in the year. Trees were in fragile leaf but it was still bitterly cold. She thought, as she always did in moments of exceptional discouragement, of a poem by Valéry, in which the poet, under a burning sky, detects in himself the signs of a necessary change. '*Beau ciel, vrai ciel, regarde-moi qui change . . .*' How did it go on? '*Après tant d'orgueil, après tant d'étrange oisiveté . . .*' She had always supposed that the line referred to the poet's inability to write, to a dry period in his creative life. Now she saw that anyone could undergo this dryness, and could also recover from it. The setting, she seemed to remember, was on the south coast of France, below Montpellier; the atmosphere was one of ardour, the ardour of the great sun awakening a corresponding intensity in the poet. Maybe it was an allegory of summer, not of England's pallid summers but the summer of a shore that looked towards Africa. She envied the poet's sense of wonder at his own metamorphosis, yet knew that she would feel the same if ever fate decreed a different life for her. At the same time she knew that she had both won and lost the battle some time ago, that death would hold no terrors for her now simply by virtue of the fact that she had attained and practised stoicism for some years past. There was too much distance between what she desired (as did the poet) and what was offered.

She went to her wardrobe and took out the brown corded silk suit. She regarded it critically. Disaster seemed to strike every time she wore it; on the other hand she was not expecting to be pleasantly surprised. It would have to do. Afterwards, she knew, she would discard it, wear prettier, less formal clothes. There was no need to dress like a matron. Correct wear had been her mother's idea. Amy Durrant herself had looked her best in brilliant tweeds, with excessively feminine blouses. For a long time they had dressed alike. But now one could wear soft flowered skirts, with brief little jackets, and look years younger. It was a pity that she had no such clothes with which to confront the Hallidays. Idly, she sketched the sort of clothes she would like to have worn. The sketches were satisfactory; the time flew. Vague plans took shape in her mind. For the moment the brown suit would have to do. She looked forward to presenting it to Mrs Duncan in the very near future. She thought it might become her very well.

The weather had reverted to winter stringency. April, although now nearly over, was once again proving the cruellest month. With the fading of the light came frost, and with the frost silence, as if everyone had hurried home. On the Thursday evening, which came all too soon, Anna took from the wardrobe her mother's fur coat, which she had never worn. It was an ample luxurious coat, which her mother had bought in the euphoric aftermath of her meeting with Ainsworth. Had she fallen in love with him already? Certainly her health had improved almost overnight, so that Anna had had a glimpse of what her own life might have been had her mother been confident and happy. She had repressed the thought, for she was accustomed to see her mother falter several times a day, when in need of rest, and there was no physical reason why this pattern should change. Indeed the increased excitement had seemed to make her more vulnerable, so that Anna had to be on hand to watch over her; she had feared a total collapse, even when Ainsworth had taken up residence. In the throes of passion her mother's life seemed to be at risk, as if her very ardour might kill her. And afterwards her collapse was all too genuine. The coat had remained unworn, for Amy Durrant had rarely left the house since Ainsworth's disappearance. Yet she had kept it in her wardrobe as an emblem of happier times. She had not thought to pass it on to Anna, as if Ainsworth might by some miracle be restored to her and she could wear it once again. Anna had inherited it by default, had regarded it with dislike, and had never worn it. On the Thursday evening she put it on and regarded herself with curiosity in the glass. She saw a slight anachronistic figure, but one which looked unmistakably adult. As she was accustomed to thinking of herself as a child this came as something of a surprise.

'Oh, fur!' said Vickie Halliday, in the tiny hallway of the house in Tryon Street. 'I'm afraid we don't approve of fur in this house. Every time I see it I think of the poor animals. Would you like to put it on the chair? You may think me silly, but I don't like to touch it. I'd rather touch the animal instead.'

'You could hardly touch this animal,' said Anna. 'I believe it is fox, or something equally wild. I saw one once, in Hyde Park. It looked very lean and hungry. Good evening, Lawrence.'

Halliday appeared behind his wife, smiling amiably and abstractedly. All the power seemed to have been withdrawn from him. Unless he was called to a patient the evenings were something of a trial to him: he withdrew into himself, thereby making himself unpopular. He had regretted this invitation as soon as it had been offered. Unfortunately, he had insisted on it. He had had some vague idea that it would get him out of his difficulties. On reflection he had been less sure. The house was invaded by complicated smells. Left to himself, as he never was these days, he would have made himself a bacon sandwich or fried a couple of eggs and watched something simple-minded on television. He was aware that there was too little in his life that was serious, that he rarely read anything of substance these days, but supposed that most married men were at the same disadvantage. He had been persuaded into a bright blue shirt that Vickie had bought for him and in which he felt like an ersatz estate agent. Vickie wore her short red dress, with the exaggerated shoulders, on which Anna had remarked at Mrs Marsh's party. Although the evening was cold she seemed to smoulder with heat.

Seated in their small front room, too small to be called a sitting-room, Anna was surprised at the discomfort of her surroundings and also by their chic, which did not marry with what she knew of Lawrence. The striped wallpaper and the heavily ruched curtains seemed to close in on her: the lights were much too bright. She was given a glass of sherry and was asked how she was.

'I'm fine, I think,' she said.

'Only think?' said Vickie. 'Oh, that's too bad. We must do something about that.'

'No really, I'm fine.'

'We shall have to keep an eye on you, then,' said Vickie, whose attention seemed intermittent. 'Lawrence, darling, give Anna some nuts. Make yourself useful. Oh, men! At least that's one worry you've been spared.'

Surely she could not be so crude, thought Anna, who felt the onset of something like dismay. To be so transparent! She herself had always been impassive, even in the teeth of major provocations. She regarded Vickie Halliday with well-disguised curiosity, regretting the fact that she could no longer describe her to Marie-France in a finely composed letter. She still wrote – they both did – but the confidences were no longer the same. But the letter she might have written would have seemed like revenge, and she dismissed the possibility. As she saw it, and all too clearly, the onus of the evening was on her, and she determined to carry it through with all the goodwill she could muster.

'We thought we'd have you all to ourselves,' said Vickie, who had registered the remark about the fox. 'So that we can find out something about you.'

'Well . . .'

'Darling, could you turn off the oven? We'll have to eat fairly soon,' she said, turning back to Anna. 'I've made something rather special and I don't want it to spoil. Now, where were we?'

'I believe you're an excellent cook,' said Anna, who supposed this to be in order. Indeed, she remembered Vickie inviting Nick Marsh to sample her food.

'Yes, I am. I hope you're going to do justice to my new recipe. It's always very exciting for me to give my guests something out of the ordinary. So you're quite happy, are you? Well, that's good.'

She got up and turned up the radiators.

'Darling, must you? It's not healthy.'

'Oh, nonsense, we'll freeze in here.'

'If you wore more sensible clothes, a sweater or something.'

'Dar*ling*! You're boring Anna. Take no notice,' she said to Anna. 'He's a terrible worrier. But he's a dear, really. I've no complaints. Shall we go through?'

The dining-room was in fact the other half of the room, made smaller by a round table, a sideboard, and more excessively ruched curtains. Lawrence, who had not said a word, poured wine.

'Is that one of Daddy's?' said Vickie. 'If so it'll be very good. Daddy has an excellent cellar. He's trying to train Lawrence's palate, without much success, I'm afraid. I think he'd prefer beer.' She laughed.

'I never drink beer these days,' said Lawrence sombrely.

'Well, I should hope not! What would the patients say? Anna, tell me what you think of my terrine.'

Too much gelatine, thought Anna, as she negotiated the slippery slice. It was unpleasantly chilly; she felt as if she were eating ice cream. 'Delicious,' she said.

'But you haven't told me anything about yourself,' protested Vickie. 'I don't feel as if I know you yet.'

'There's so little to tell, really. I'd rather hear about you.'

'I don't know where to start. There's the house, of course, and Lawrence's work – that keeps me pretty busy. And I'm interested in various charities. Animal charities.'

'Oh, what a good idea.'

Vickie's expression became tragic. 'Such terrible things go on, Anna. The poor calves! And the lambs, going over to France in those lorries!'

'Darling . . . '

'I can't bear to think of them. It makes me feel quite ill.'

Anna watched in fascination as two perfectly formed tears fell down Vickie's cheeks.

'Darling, do we have to talk about animals at dinner?'

'I can't help it if I'm sensitive,' she said, touching her napkin to the corners of her eyes. 'I've always been sensitive to wrongdoing. And it's wrong, Anna, to send those poor animals to France like that.'

'I'm sure it is.'

Lawrence quietly got up and turned the radiators back to their original low setting.

'So you're not getting any meat this evening. We're cutting out meat. I've made a fish stew,' she announced. 'And I'm counting on you to do justice to it.'

Gusts of fishy heat rose from the soup bowl which was lowered before her. The tiny jaws of mussels gaped from its almost crimson depths. Anna looked down in consternation. Courage was called for beyond the demands of politeness. Lawrence tucked a napkin into the neck of his cerulean shirt and set to with a pantomime of enthusiasm. The chunks of white fish which occasionally bobbed to the surface were not quite cooked through.

'Some more?' urged Vickie. 'It's all got to be finished.'

'No, really . . . '

'Don't you like it?' she said, surprised.

'I very rarely eat much in the evenings,' said Anna, who usually had a banana and a glass of milk.

'That's why you're so skinny. You'll never be asked out if you don't eat, you know. You want to get married, don't you? Men hate finicky eaters.'

Lawrence, in despair, got up and returned with another bottle of wine. He tilted the bottle at Anna enquiringly. Vickie frowned. He filled their glasses and sat down, defeated.

'Cheese and fruit,' announced Vickie. She seemed to have lost interest in the evening, but made an obvious extra effort. 'I can introduce you to some very nice people,' she said. 'We can't have you sitting on your own every evening.'

'But really, I rather like sitting on my own. I'm not much good in company. I suppose I like a quiet life.'

'Isn't that a rather selfish attitude?' asked Vickie, with a fine smile.

'I suppose I am rather selfish. But as long as it doesn't hurt anyone . . . And I do go out, you know. I go to the latest exhibitions. I go to concerts. As I dare say you do. Tell me, what have you seen recently?'

'Well, we don't get much time. We do a lot of entertaining. I don't suppose you do much of that?'

'You must let me take you out to dinner. I must return your kind invitation.'

This was taken amiss. 'Darling, make some coffee,' said Vickie, in a tone not previously heard, a tone used to giving orders. 'You'd like some coffee?'

'Thank you.'

It was a relief when Lawrence left the room. Anna could not bear his discomfiture. Vickie leaned towards her.

'You know, I hate to see you so unhappy.'

'But I'm not unhappy.'

'But you're alone! No one should be alone. What would happen if you were ill?'

'I suppose I should send for Lawrence.'

It was the wrong thing to say, although it was innocently meant. Vickie's gaze hardened.

'My poor husband is at everybody's beck and call. I try to shield him from the nuisances.'

They drank their coffee, which was black and bitter. There seemed no way in which the evening could be prolonged. In any event all recognized it as a mistake. Vickie viewed her guest with dislike; Lawrence avoided her eyes. When the telephone rang they all jumped.

'I'll come straight away,' they heard Lawrence say. He came back into the room looking relieved.

'I'm on call,' he explained. 'Beaufort Street. I'll drop you off, Anna, if you don't mind a short detour. I shouldn't be long.'

'We'll all go,' said Vickie merrily.

'Darling, there's no need . . .'

'I insist.'

There was no mistaking her insistence.

Anna, in her fur coat, overflowed the front seat of the car. Vickie, in the back, was strangely silent. In the face of this silence there seemed little more to say.

'Thank you so much for this evening,' said Anna, as the car drew up in Cranley Gardens. 'You must be my guests next time.' She doubted if she would ever see them again, although the invitation would be offered in due course. No doubt Vickie would know the right form of words with which to refuse.

Lawrence came round and opened the door.

'Shan't be a moment, darling. I'll just see that Anna gets in safely.'

'Don't leave me alone in the car,' said Vickie obdurately. 'You know how nervous I am.'

'It's only for a moment. Nothing will happen to you.'

'I don't want to be left alone,' she repeated.

Again, there was no mistaking her insistence.

'Please don't bother,' said Anna quietly. 'Goodnight, Lawrence. Goodnight, Vickie.'

In the blessed silence of her flat she stood for a moment at the window, still in the heavy fur coat. Weak, she thought, weak. Down below, the car had not moved off. She imagined an altercation taking place. Another man would have ordered things differently, but she would not have wanted another man. Without his wife he had seemed stronger, and she had felt that she had got to know him all over again. And he was unhappy, that was all too clear. What she had once suspected was now confirmed.

Strangely, she could not blame Vickie, despite her stunning rudeness. She was defending herself the way she knew best, possibly the only way she had ever learned, with hostility. Anna thought this pitiable from every point of view, not least Vickie's. And she herself was not exemplary. She should have refused this invitation, as any sensible woman would have done, should have said that she was going away, should in fact have gone away. She saw that now. But to be forced out into the cold, in the cruel days of this late spring, was somehow not to be borne. Puzzled, she wondered how and where she was to go. The difference between fantasy and reality had never seemed so difficult to bridge.

She took off the coat and hung it up, noting absent-mindedly that it suited her quite well. She took off the brown suit and made it into a parcel which she would leave for Mrs Duncan, with a note, on the following Wednesday. She ran a bath, although she had already taken one earlier in the evening. It seemed important to obliterate every trace of recent events. It did not yet occur to her to feel anger. Her most instinctive reaction was one of amazement that two people should willingly form an alliance based on such negative feelings as fear and pity. Lawrence felt pity for his wife who was still the protected child she had always been in her parents' house, or rather her father's house, since she had alluded to Daddy more than once in the course of the evening. It was even significant that a woman on the verge of middle age should refer to her father in these terms. Her sharpness, her superficial sophistication, even her terrible cooking, marked her out as one who seemed old in the ways of the world but unprotected against herself, and genuinely unable to read her own unfinished character. She was attractive, Anna freely admitted, but she was attractive principally because she was greedy, and because her greediness was intimately bound up with, even redolent of, sexual appetite. For such a woman the need for a man was obvious, even if the man's role was thereby reduced.

Anna felt immediate embarrassment on Lawrence's behalf, although she had been able to overlook his social unease. He had had a sheepish look, for the resources of his own character were unequal to those of his wife. She had even surprised him looking wistful, as if everything he cared for had been taken away from him, leaving him with poor substitutes which saddened him. No wonder he felt so deeply for his patients, those marooned by sickness or disability in their own isolation. No wonder he was such a good doctor. But he would not go far, for sharper minds than Vickie's would assess his suitability, would observe his wife. There would be dinner parties of greater consequence at the homes of colleagues, where it would be decided that Halliday, in the long run, would not make senior material.

All this was very sad, particularly, Anna thought, because she had offered so little in the way of provocation. Yet she had been treated as a rival. It seemed that she had achieved posthumous status as Lawrence's girlfriend, yet when she looked back she realized how little had passed between them. It was nevertheless possible, on the evidence of this evening, that Lawrence had felt more deeply for her than she had suspected, that he now regarded their former friendship as one strikingly failed test in what must by now be registered as a disappointing life. With the knowledge that she could have protected him against such disappointments she must now content herself, for it seemed now that she was rather

206

strong herself. This surprised her, for she was not adept at discerning her own advantages, and was accustomed to a rigorous scrutiny of her defects. Yet the sadness induced by the evening and by the spectacle of such emotional disarray was giving way to an odd feeling of comfort, as if she had survived, intact, an ambush for which she had not been prepared.

She drank her tisane. She would not need a pill tonight, perhaps would need fewer of them in the future. Some kind of plateau had been reached. With a feeling of gratitude she arranged herself in the bed and prepared for sleep. Staring into the dimness of the room, momentarily lit by passing late cars, she thought again of the poem which had beguiled her earlier in the day. 'Après tant d'orgueil, après tant d'étrange oisiveté . . . ' How clever to put pride and apathy in the same category of misapprehension. How did it go on? The poet was after all speaking of change, of metamorphosis. 'Après tant d'orgueil, après tant d'étrange oisiveté, mais pleine de pouvoir . . . ' That was it, the renewed feeling of power, power in the sense of strength, the strength born secretly, mysteriously, out of oisiveté, idleness or inaction. It was the intimation of this strength which presaged change. This message, a voice for her ears only, seemed a surprising coda to the evening she had just endured, and she resolved to subject it to further consideration.

17

April became May, and at last the warmth returned. People
lifted their heads with amazed gratitude to a blue sky and a
gentle softening breeze. After such a harsh winter the lilac
and the hawthorn were late but did not appear to have suffered from the punishing recent frosts. The world became
green again and tempers improved. A reprieved population
smiled as it went about its daily business, and hopes rose
for a long and exceptional summer. It was reckoned to have
started early; the many months of cold grey weather were
forgotten. Talk turned to holidays, a sure sign that a siege
had been successfully withstood and that hope had returned.
Among the old people there was a latent fear of the winter to
come and a determination to enjoy one last summer, if that
was what it turned out to be. Heavy clothes were thankfully
stored in the cupboards of spare bedrooms. Sticks tapped on
pavements as elderly residents took once more to the streets.
In the shops news was exchanged about relatives, not seen for
some time but now visited at weekends. Children, walking
in single file to the swimming baths, longed for release. The
young took off on their annual migration, here one moment,
gone the next. Restaurants put a cautious table or two on
the pavement; pubs overflowed. At dusk joggers pounded
through the newly friendly urban jungle. The leisure pages
in the newspapers went into full production. Weather men
on the radio permitted themselves a cautious optimism,

although warning of mist after dark. This was largely ignored: after such shining days the nights were easy to discount.

Halliday's work decreased: whole evenings went by without a call. He took up running, for various reasons, not all of them to do with his health. It was certainly a relief to be out after a day in the surgery, but it was even more of a relief to be out of his own house and away from his wife. In order to circumvent her cooking he had decreed a regimen of low-fat foods: this, however, was only partially successful. Running, for upwards of two hours every evening, he was able to ignore his life and its disappointments. Sprinting down Sloane Street on his way to the park he attracted admiring glances which he was able to ignore: he had never been vain. He thought, occasionally, of Anna Durrant, whom he would telephone after a decent interval. 'Sorry you had such a boring evening,' he would say with a smile, the smile which had always endeared him to women. A decent interval was necessary before they could face each other again. He had no doubt that she would be compassionate and understanding, as she had always been. The beauty of Anna was that she never required explanations. As he entered the park he almost persuaded himself that they could return to their earlier veiled intimacy. He would give it a month, he decided, just in case she was a little annoyed, and then he would contact her. Either that, and it was perhaps a little unorthodox for a doctor to contact a patient, or she would turn up of her own accord. That was the most likely.

This scenario fitted in very well with his own plans. He was taking a month's holiday from mid-June to mid-July, not, for once, in accordance with his father-in-law's wishes, although these had been made known, but because his previous locum, a man he trusted, was free at that time, and because a woman was joining the practice later in the summer. The date had been fixed by her, and he had thought it unusual until she explained that she had spent the previous winter travelling in Africa, and that she might want to take her own holiday the following January in order to return there. Her name was Sarah King and she was pretty, a slight cockney accent adding to her charm. She would be pleasant to have about the place, with her short hair and her long eyelashes and her extremely forthright disposition. When he wondered about the advisability of her travelling alone in Africa she had told him shortly that she always went with her friend. There was no clue as to whether this friend was a man or a woman.

She had been to dinner in Tryon Street, and had eaten her way through the menu, although without enthusiasm. Vickie, who had not liked her, had asked all her usual questions, to which Dr King, without any apparent change of expression, had replied factually but with decisive brevity. 'Oh, dear, are you a feminist?' Vickie had enquired. 'Yes,' was the answer. 'Does that mean you don't want to get married? I always think that's such a shame.' Sarah King had looked at her inscrutably. 'Yes,' she had said. 'I can see that you would.' She appeared to be longing for a microscope with which to examine this dangerously ill-adapted species. 'We'll see you home,' Vickie had said. 'I don't like to think of any woman out on her own at night, however emancipated.' Dr King – and she had not invited them to call her Sarah – told her not to bother: she had come on her bike. In Halliday's eyes she had judged the situation perfectly. He looked forward to working with her.

Before she took up her duties, however, there was the holiday to be endured, and it would be the same as always, he supposed. His father-in-law remained monstrously vigorous and dictatorial, and Halliday was at last able to confide to himself that the man was odious, not only odious but perhaps responsible for all his troubles. He would be subjected to days spent on the boat, with the smell of Gibson's dead cigar assaulting his nostrils, and return, sunburnt and queasy, to the house, to be asked, 'And what have you two been up to?' He did not know what offended him more, the days spent far from the land he longed to explore, or the peculiar staleness of the evenings, when his father-in-law watched television, legs outstretched, and a further cigar clamped between his teeth. Out of politeness they were forced to join him. At least, it was politeness on Halliday's part: Vickie was, in this, as in all else, an uncritical adherent of her father's wishes. Occasionally he would wander through the house in search of his mother-in-law. He did not much want to talk to her, but she was minimally more sympathetic than her husband. At least if she was outside, watering the garden, he could enjoy the air and the night sky. 'Aren't you coming in?' Gibson would shout from the study, to which they would be forced to direct their reluctant steps. 'I'm going up now, Henry,' his mother-in-law would remark from the door in her peculiarly uninflected voice. And then he would be stranded again. It always felt as though she had abandoned him: her husband and daughter she appeared to have abandoned long ago, seeing them so well satisfied with each other. She had been beautiful, a vague flower of the upper classes. Now, he noticed, she was becoming increasingly deaf.

This year he would run, he promised himself. He would tell Gibson that he was in training, or some such nonsense. He would get into his shorts and his T-shirt and pound away until he was out of sight. Once past the village he would put on the light anorak which he carried in his rucksack and be a tourist, humble and innocent, like the city boy he had once been and still was at heart. Although he loved the air and the open space he did not really enjoy the countryside; it lacked conviviality, he thought, and conviviality was what he sought. He liked to drink a cup of coffee in the town, linger in newsagents, examine racks of postcards. At last he could satisfy his longing to have a newspaper to himself. Lunch would be taken in a pub, shepherd's pie and a glass of bitter. Nobody spoke to him, or consulted him about their backs or their ulcers, as they would have done had he not been so carefully anonymous. In such circumstances he was almost happy.

The afternoons would be more of a problem. He could hardly pretend to run all day, and his conscience would begin to nag him. He would make his way back, with as good a grace as he could muster, knowing that Vickie would ask him crossly where he had been, and tax him with rudeness. He did not mind being thought rude, since his father-in-law had been rude for as long as he could remember. He would drink cup after cup of his mother-in-law's pale frail milkless tea, wishing that it were PG Tips, with plenty of sugar. Then a bath, though for some reason it was thought unfriendly if he locked the bathroom door. This meant that he had to announce his decision in a loud firm voice, although he was terrified that no one was paying any attention. His nightmare was that his father-in-law might come in and use the lavatory. This had happened on more than one occasion, and he had felt himself shrivel under the water. Henry Gibson had raked him with his eyes and noticed this. 'Hope you're managing to keep yourself in good order,' he had said. His implication was clear. His daughter's sexuality was as precious to him as his own, which he satisfied elsewhere, with a compliant partner, at an address in Westbourne Grove. He had even let this be known, and had once told Halliday that his wife was good for nothing these days. If he had hoped for a manly exchange he had been disappointed. This disappointment had not been entirely forgotten or forgiven.

His last visit, before leaving London, was to Mrs Marsh, who was feeling under the weather. The sudden warmth had affected her leg slightly, but mainly she complained of fatigue and of difficulty in getting about. 'I don't feel steady,' she said. He examined her and found nothing wrong with her, apart from the inevitable damage done by old age. He considered the matter. She was a healthy woman, but he sensed the first misgivings that might turn her into a recluse, if she were not watched. He looked round the room and found it to be clean but gloomy. 'You've been cooped up for far too long,' he said, in a voice which combined tenderness with authority. 'It's time we got you out and about. Have you thought of going away?'

Mrs Marsh smiled, as she could not help smiling when he took a firm line with her.

'My travelling days are over,' she said. 'When my husband was alive we went about a great deal. When he died there didn't seem to be the same enjoyment.'

She remembered a visit to Venice with Phyllis Martin which she preferred not to think about. Phyllis had changed her clothes three times a day, while Mrs Marsh waited for her in the bar. Both had been disappointed in each other's company but were too valiant to complain. Besides, their sort of people never complained. Nevertheless, they had never repeated the experiment. They had gone to the Cipriani: such a waste of money, she thought.

But it would be good to get out of this flat, away from the limited friendships she had made, away from her weekly appointment at the hairdresser's, and the conventional remarks she was forced to exchange with the shopkeepers. 'Your son better?' the fishmonger still asked her, although it was weeks since Nick had stayed with her. Besides, he was in New York, and that did not bear too much thinking about either. She thought she knew the reason for these frequent and extended weekends, and could not pretend to be in favour of them. A daughter-in-law was one thing, but a daughter-in-law who had her own model agency in New York and intended to keep things that way was quite another. Mrs Marsh did not know what a model agency was, but it sounded disreputable. She knew that Nick could get a transfer to the American branch, and almost hoped that his old habits of caution and evasiveness would reassert themselves. She decided that it was worry about Nick and his future that was making her feel unwell.

'What about your daughter?' she heard Halliday say. 'Couldn't you go and stay with her for a bit?'

Well, she could, of course, if Philippa would have her, but there was no reason why Philippa should not have her.

She appeared to live contentedly in her little house, and if she wanted company could find it in that art appreciation class she went to once a week. It might be restful, in these fine days, to sit in Philippa's garden, to have a cup of morning tea brought to her, to get in the car and drive, with Philippa, and the children, if they could spare the time, to Blakeney for the weekend. Or weekends. There was no need for her to hurry back to London. Mrs Duncan was about to leave, and there would be all the bother of finding someone new; hopeless, she thought, before the holiday season. Mrs Duncan had offered to find her a replacement, but she might forget. She made a mental note to remind her. And she must give her a leaving present. Money would be best: she could hand it over and go to Norwich, thus being spared the final farewells. In any event Mrs Duncan's mind was no longer on her work. As recently as the previous week she had shown up in a very smart brown silk suit, which Mrs Marsh thought seemed vaguely familiar, though hardly practical. She decided to give her a substantial present, thus ensuring her goodwill in the matter of organizing her successor. 'A friend of mine might help you out,' she had said. 'Her husband keeps her very short. Only she won't be free before September.' Mrs Marsh placed no faith in this promise, but took the woman's telephone number. She was rather relieved at the prospect of being out of Mrs Duncan's way, while she completed her duties. Norwich would thus fit in very well.

'I might go to my daughter for a bit,' she conceded.

'Good idea,' said Halliday. And so it was decided.

She travelled down in her car at a stately pace, arriving, conveniently, she thought, in time for tea. Philippa had no help in the house, but then, thought Mrs Marsh, I do not make much in the way of work. She was not inclined to help, indeed looked forward almost childishly to something of a holiday, since it had been decreed by Halliday that she needed one. She did not see that she would be imposing in any way, for Philippa had expressed readiness to welcome

214

her, and in fact had never been known to express anything else. A good daughter, Mrs Marsh had decided, and a contented sort of person. She was only fleetingly aware that she considered her daughter to be very slightly boring. She had not, in Mrs Marsh's opinion, done well for herself. Her early marriage had not exactly displeased her parents but had not thrilled them either. They had thought that she was aiming too low: Mark worked in a bank, and despite their obvious fondness for one another, Philippa's parents had thought she might have waited until someone more suitable had come along. After all, Bill Marsh was a real banker; he could not help regarding the marriage as something of a *mésalliance*, although Mark was not a humble cashier but a securities officer. But Philippa was his favourite child, and he forced himself to be amiable to Mark Barnard, whose parents, fortunately, lived a long way from London. They had come up from Devon for the wedding, and had appeared ill at ease. Mr and Mrs Marsh saw no reason to keep in touch, although Philippa, dear girl that she was, insisted on visiting them from time to time. And they had got used to Mark, a kindly though rather girlish-looking young man, who seemed devoted to their daughter. They were an odd couple: Philippa so sturdy, with her burning bush of hair and her high colour, and Mark, so slight and so hesitant. They were obviously happy, which was really, they agreed, all that mattered.

When Mark took up his position in the bank in Norwich Bill had bought them a house, and it was towards this house, where Philippa had remained after Mark's early death, that Mrs Marsh now directed her thoughts. She had expected Philippa to sell up and move back to London, but Philippa had protested that she could not leave her garden. This garden Mrs Marsh now proposed to enjoy. It was pleasant to leave London behind, and she was ready to concede that Philippa had made a wise decision. But she had always been a sensible girl, and with her help Mark had worked steadily up the ladder and had eventually become manager of his branch. That was when they had bought the cottage at Blakeney, where all holidays were spent when the children were little. Mrs Marsh thought this very dull of them, and marvelled at how provincial Philippa had become after her expensive education, and her three months each in Paris and Florence, but she was told that Mark was a keen bird watcher, and that the children never wanted to go anywhere but Blakeney. The place had charm, and Mark had looked a little more impressive in a waxed jacket, with binoculars round his neck. And then to die so young! An attack of flu, which turned into a particularly virulent form of pneumonia: he was dead at forty-two. Philippa had been stoical, had shed few tears. Only her bright habitually puzzled air had deserted her, to be replaced by a sombre withdrawn expression, which only tightened into a smile when she thought she was being watched.

She had remained unspoilt, Mrs Marsh believed. The children had grown up without problems, and were now gainfully employed, though not married. Philippa herself had never married again. That had been a cause for some concern, although she never complained, and never exhibited the restlessness which might have beset a woman who had been unpartnered for too long. But then she had had that excellent education, and her breeding was suitably inconspicuous, and all the more attractive in that she was so unselfconscious. Mrs Marsh supposed that she had friends, kept in touch with current events, made quite a decent life for herself. She had even wondered whether there might be a second marriage, some time in the future. Philippa had changed slightly, or perhaps she was simply getting older: it had occurred to her mother that Philippa might have a suitor. There had been one or two evenings at Covent Garden which had not been satisfactorily explained, or rather for which explanations had not been forthcoming. Mrs Marsh thought in terms of someone elderly, retired, who would care for Philippa, and who would, perhaps, be more suitable than poor Mark. She would make a point of getting on good terms with him, for she had no doubt that Philippa would take advantage of her visit to produce the suitor, as she thought of him, for her mother's approval. There was no hurry, of course. The beauty of a mature courtship was that it could be pursued at leisure.

Mrs Marsh half hoped that this nebulous courtship might go on in a pleasantly unresolved fashion for some years. Although she sincerely wished for her daughter's happiness she was not anxious to see too many changes in her lifetime. Besides, she thought, it should be the grand-children who got married first. Once they were both settled Philippa could do as she pleased. Mrs Marsh knew that Philippa could be relied upon to do the correct thing, and did not think she was being selfish in wanting to keep her daughter as she had always been: cheerful and obedient and unselfish. I never told her that I loved her, she thought, but then there was no need. She had always assumed that love was all around her: that was her greatest gift. That was her gift to her father, her husband; neither had ever had cause to doubt her. Growing older she had gained a dignity which had hitherto escaped her. Mrs Marsh saw her now, at the window, watching out for the car, and marvelled at the seriousness of her expression. A trick of the brilliant light, perhaps, had made her look almost stern, even careworn. My child, thought Mrs Marsh, and hobbled up the path. She had brought her stick with her; she was taking no chances.

'Well, Mother,' said Philippa, leaning forward to kiss her. 'Good journey?'

'Excellent, thank you.' Mrs Marsh looked round the pretty room with satisfaction. Philippa's taste was entirely conventional: faded chintz and Staffordshire figures, water-colours which she had picked up locally, and a small but rather fine brass fender. Everything gleamed.

'Would you like to wash? Or shall we have tea straight away? The kettle's boiling.'

'Oh, tea,' said Mrs Marsh, settling herself in the large wing chair which had been Mark's. This was better than the flat in London, she thought. These radiant days should be spent in gardens, or near the sea. She thought with pity of her circumscribed days; she was not anxious to go back to them.

'Can you put up with me for a bit?' she asked. 'I've had rather a bad winter, on the whole. It was the doctor who suggested that I come down here. If it's not inconvenient,' she added.

'Of course, stay as long as you like,' said Philippa, busying herself with the hot water jug. Mrs Marsh thought her tone preoccupied, and was very slightly offended. Her enthusiastic rediscovery of her daughter's virtues appeared to have been mistimed. But then she thought that she was being unjust. Philippa had always been so humble! Who was she to blame her if she had at last grown up? She thought that she saw her daughter's glance steal towards the telephone, but it did not ring. Perhaps she had told the suitor that her mother was coming to stay. Well, I shall be very pleased to meet him, she thought, finishing her tea. I hope I know how to be civil. No one has ever had cause to complain on that score.

Scrutinizing Philippa over dinner, she thought that she had lost weight, quite a lot of weight. That was what made her look so serious. At last she looked like a woman, whereas before she had always looked like a girl. She had had her bush of hair tamed, and even wore make-up, which she had always previously disdained. She was now an attractive woman. She had always been a good cook, an excellent housekeeper. And she had her own money. All in all a first-class wife for any man.

'If you want to go up to London,' she told her, 'I'm perfectly all right here on my own.'

'Don't worry, Mother. I don't want to go to London. You do remember that I'm going to Paris in the autumn, don't you? With my art group. I told you about it.'

'Good Heavens, I shall be gone by then. I only meant to stay a week or two, perhaps come back in the summer. Would that be all right, dear?'

'Of course, Mother.' Philippa's tone was neutral. 'Stay as long as you like.'

Mrs Marsh, waking the following morning beneath the plump flowered eiderdown, was as happy as a girl. Philippa had put a tray in her room, and an electric kettle. Mrs Marsh, like many old people, woke early, and frequently made a cup of tea at half-past five. It was good to get out of the brown gloom of her flat. Here she had a garden outside her window, and later she would sit on the little terrace and read *The Times*. She might go shopping with Philippa; she would certainly take a nap in the afternoon. There was no need to hurry back to London. She must have dozed off after formulating this plan, for the next thing she knew was that Philippa had summoned her to breakfast.

The days that followed were infinitely pleasant. She sat on the terrace, conscientiously reading her way through Philippa's small library, and was summoned in to lunch, to tea. After a while she took no notice of Philippa, who was often absent. Of the suitor there was no sign. Twice, when she could no longer avoid doing so, she drove back to London, glanced through her letters, paid any bills, stayed the night, and drove back to Norwich. On these occasions Philippa was able to entertain her lover, Paul Whitaker, and to reassure him that her mother would eventually be gone for good. She hated the deception, but Paul, in his jeans and his open-necked shirt, was not the sort of man to please her mother. He was too young, for one thing. Her mother would be prepared to accept a man of sixty, but not one of fifty, wearing a wedding-ring. He would simply be declared out of order, as Philippa sometimes thought he should be. The whole thing made her sick with worry. Adultery was a grave and terrible matter to her. It enthralled her, excited her, but she sometimes thought she had not really taken to it.

As the radiant summer turned into autumn Mrs Marsh decided regretfully that the time had come for her to leave. There was the new cleaning woman to be interviewed; there were matters to be settled before the days grew shorter, when the long winter siege would begin. Already the evenings were dark, and the nights colder. She found it difficult to believe that she had been away for so long.

'Goodbye, my dear. Thank you for everything.'

'You'll telephone me at the usual time?'

'Of course.'

But when Mrs Marsh telephoned it was to say that the police had been round. Apparently Anna Durrant had disappeared. Halliday had got in touch with them.

'What an extraordinary thing.'

'Of course, it's all nonsense. She's probably on holiday somewhere. To tell you the truth I hadn't given her a thought. I suppose I should have kept in touch. Oh well, I'm sure she'll turn up. Everything all right at your end? Good. Well, enjoy Paris.'

As Paul Whitaker was leading his art appreciation group round the Louvre Philippa discovered that she was not paying attention, which seemed to her disloyal. She really only wanted to be alone in a hotel room, knowing that Paul would find her. But she was afraid that this would be difficult: the hotel had been booked by the group some time ago, and although she had managed to get a room to herself, whereas others were having to share, she doubted whether Paul would take risks, the risk of being seen, the risk of being talked about: the risk of the talk reaching his wife, whom Philippa knew. She made a sign to Paul, who had been discoursing on Mantegna, and who now fell back.

'I'm going,' she said. 'I've had enough. The Flore in half an hour. All right?'

It was a relief to leave the great oppressive building, to walk over the Pont des Arts and up the rue Bonaparte, a relief to sit down in the blessed blue dusk and order a cup of coffee.

'Hallo, Philippa,' said a voice.

She glanced round in surprise, to see a woman in a beautifully cut tan suit, who apparently knew her, at an adjoining table.

'May I join you? You don't remember me, I see. It's Anna, Anna Durrant.'

'Anna,' said Philippa slowly. 'Does anyone know you're here? Only I believe you've been missed.'

'Oh, I'm sure that's an exaggeration,' said Anna, sitting down.

'It's true. Someone got in touch with the police, when you hadn't been seen for a while. I think Mother said it was Halliday.'

Anna laughed.

'Why are you laughing?' asked Philippa.

'But I've been here all the time,' said Anna. 'And I do find it rather odd that people should notice my absence. I made so little impression when I was actually present. Tell them where I am, by all means. Though it's hardly relevant now.'

'Have you run away? Were you unhappy? Did something upset you?'

'Do you know, Philippa, no one has ever asked me those questions before. I was thought to be too obscure to need them.'

'I'm sure Mother was very fond of you.'

'No, not really. I was useful to her, and of course I will be again, if she needs me. But let's be accurate. Inaccuracy is a form of misrepresentation, and I've done with that.'

'We thought you were quite happy.'

'Oh, did you? You see, I had become what people wanted me to be, without their ever asking me what I myself would have wanted. I decided not to be that person any more.'

'What a fraud you are, Anna,' said Philippa uneasily.

'But there are many kinds of fraud, not all of them criminal. I rather think I have stopped being one, a fraud, I mean. Fraud was what was perpetrated on me by the expectations of others. They fashioned me in their own image, according to their needs. Fraud, in that sense, is alarmingly prevalent. And not only between the sexes. In the end I decided to escape.'

'What have you been doing? Since you escaped?'

'I've been here. I've been living in my friend Marie-France's flat while she and her father spend the summer at their house in Meaux. They're in Montpellier at the moment. When they come back I'll find a place of my own. I rather like the feeling of being temporary. I might live in an hotel until I find what I want.'

'Won't you come home?'

'Home?' She laughed again. 'You mean, go back to London? Yes, of course, eventually. After Christmas, perhaps. At Christmas I shall go south.'

'How will you live?' asked Philippa gently.

'I'm going into business. I'm going to design clothes. Women of my age will always want decent clothes. Not everyone wants to be in the fashion, particularly if it looks absurd. That's what I've been doing, designing clothes for Marie-France. She's getting married; her father has given in. They'll have to live with him, of course. The power of the parent – don't you feel it?'

'Yes,' sighed Philippa, who had her mother in mind.

'Don't be too obedient,' said Anna. 'Don't be like me. I believed my mother, who told me I'd be happy in due course, that the best things in life are worth waiting for. And I waited. That was the fraud, the confidence trick; that was the original fraud. All the others followed from there. I blame no one, only myself. I shouldn't have been so credulous, nourishing my hopes in secret. I went along with it, I suppose. I thought it was the well-behaved thing to do. And one deception prepared me for all the others.' She paused. 'You say it was Halliday who contacted the police?'

'Yes. So Mother said.'

They were both silent.

'I hope you'll be happy, Philippa. But be happy now; the future is unreliable. There's a man, isn't there?'

Philippa nodded, feeling the sudden tears sting her eyes.

'Is he married?'

'Yes. I thought I was happy,' she burst out. 'He made me feel happy. But really I can only go on being happy if I'm married. I've only ever been married in my life.'

'He should see that, if he's fond of you. If not, he doesn't know you at all. Or won't see. In which case it's another kind of fraud.'

Philippa looked at her, perplexed.

'You're not as I remember you.'

'How was that?'

'You were, well, so self-sufficient.'

'I am now. I've grown up at last. Do you know how long it takes some of us? And now I'm free. Free of the old self. Free of expectations.'

'Free of hope?'

'Oh, no, never free of hope. Hope is an old habit, not easily dislodged. No, free of expectations. I reserve my hope for a good outcome, a good cause. That is important, I think. A good cause.'

The shadow of a man loomed up beside them.

'Paul,' said Philippa. 'This is Anna Durrant. Anna, Paul Whitaker.'

'Hallo,' said Anna. 'Why don't you take my seat? I'm just going. Goodbye, Philippa.'

Philippa looked at her, as if to pierce the secret of the new life which Anna had proclaimed. The expression was different, she decided. Previously it had been patient, attentive; now it was amused, ardent, even. The face was brighter, the cheeks more coloured. Animated now, as she had never been before, there was an air of alertness, of readiness about her. She looked as if she had woken from the long sleep which precedes convalescence. Even her figure, which was still slight, appeared more substantial.

Anna held out her hand. 'Goodbye. Good luck.' She hesitated. 'You're sure it was Halliday who noticed that I'd gone?'

'Quite sure.'

They watched her slender back retreating. The traffic was dense, the rush hour at its height.

'Who was that?'

'Oh, just a friend. Someone I used to know.'

She saw Anna plunging into the stream of cars, holding up her hand to ward them off. The drivers, she noticed, seemed to take this in good part.

'Someone I hardly knew at all,' she amended. She turned to him, troubled. 'You don't mind if I go home tomorrow, do you? Only I don't think I can go on with this.'

'But Philippa, why? We've had some good times, haven't we?'

His expression was concerned, rueful, but, she thought, polite.

'Oh, yes. But it's not a good cause, Paul. I don't mind taking second place, but it must be in a good cause. I've known you a long time. And I've waited. You know where I am. You always knew where I was. Maybe you'll come and find me one day. But until then it's goodbye, I think.'

Like Anna, she hesitated, unwilling to take her leave. Then she turned resolutely, and followed the path which Anna had taken, out into the bright, dark, dangerous and infinitely welcoming street.